THIS DISTANCE WE CALL LOVE

THIS DISTANCE WE CALL LOVE

stories

CAROL DINES

Print ISBN: 978-1-949039-22-1
E-book ISBN: 978-1-949039-24-5

Orison Books
PO Box 8385
Asheville, NC 28814
www.orisonbooks.com

Distributed to the trade by Itasca Books
1-800-901-3480 / orders@itascabooks.com

Cover photo courtesy of Shutterstock.

Manufactured in the U.S.A.

CONTENTS

For my daughter, Hanna

ALMOST

Pillsbury Avenue, addiction row—a whole street of mansions close to downtown, long abandoned as tax write-offs and turned into treatment centers, methadone clinics, and halfway houses. I parked behind her building, 1950s four-story stucco with steel-framed windows and rusted white overhang above the front door. Across the street a tortilla factory, Mexicans hurrying from the bus stop with steel lunchboxes.

The place smelled different every time I visited—curry, tomato soup, chicken, cigarettes. The second floor always smelled like pot. Next to the basement staircase, two bait-traps and a coffee can brimming with stubbed-out cigarette butts. Up four flights of stairs, I felt a momentary relief when I heard the television going inside her neighbor's apartment and saw a child's drawing on the door, reminding me real people lived here, and she was not entirely alone. Month-to-month rent, new tenants first of every month, belongings in blankets and boxes. I never met the same person in the hallway, mostly young women and children, and once a boyfriend carrying a television up the stairs, yelling, "Move your fat butts." My sister kept a peace sign on the door, as if that would keep burglars out. She'd been burgled twice. The first time they took her television, and the second time they didn't find anything they could sell and wrote *bitch* in toothpaste on her shower, then peed on the dog's bed.

"Probably just kids," she said.

"Some kids have no conscience." I taught high school English, so I knew how cruel kids could be. "You might want to change your locks."

"Least they can spell." Helene shrugged.

Any compassion I might have felt had already been spent on her. From my perspective, people needed boundaries, a little greed—enough to make them self-sufficient, enough to survive.

"Where's Almost?" I asked of the dead dog. She gave her rescue dogs names like Barely, Almost, Sometimes, Last Chance. My sister was a hospice for dying dogs. Some woman named Claire ran a dog rescue and called when she had one that was old and sweet and sick, days numbered. Claire paid for medicines and vet visits, and my sister pulled the dog in an old wagon through the city streets to a vet clinic on Hennepin. She kept the wagon chained to a pipe in the basement, sign on the flatbed: *Please do not steal. This wagon transports sick dogs.*

Six years and no one had taken it.

Outside, a sign read: *Apartments Available. No Pets Allowed.*

She snuck her rescue dogs into her apartment by carrying them up the fire-escape. Ray, the landlord, always found out. He mopped hallways Saturday afternoons, radio blaring baseball games, and when he swished the mop against the door, the dogs barked. Each time, Ray yelled, "You got a dog in there? Open up. You're out! Hear me? Out!" Each time my sister convinced Ray that she would find a home right away for the dog. Six years she'd been there. He always gave her another month. I began to wonder one morning when I brought groceries and he was washing his motorcycle in the parking lot, black hair covering his arms and neck. My sister came outside with me and he smiled big teeth. "No dogs, right?"

She laughed, shaking her head, "What dogs?"

I had this awful suspicion she slept with him to get her lease extended, but some things were too horrifying to think about, like how loneliness was far more motivating than self-respect.

After Almost died, she sent me emails from the public library downtown.

> *Selby, Almost died under the bed, and I can't lift him. My apartment smells like dead dog, and I'm afraid the neighbors will notice and get me evicted. Please come!!!!!!!!!!"*
>
> *Selby, I am home now. Please come!!!!!!!!!!*

She was wearing a white cotton shirt, blue jeans, silk scarf around her neck. She made a point of not looking poor. Helen was not pretty, but she had elegance because she had studied rich people and tried to emulate them. Her features were pointy, but she had good skin and lovely green eyes. Her posture was tall, stately, her brown hair cut in a smooth bowl (she cut it herself after rinsing in a vinegar-lemon solution, olive oil spritz to condition). She shopped at the St. Mark's Episcopal rummage sale where Minneapolis's wealthy donated their Chanel jackets, Gucci boots, and Hermes scarves.

"Thanks." She took the grocery bag full of frozen lasagna, enchiladas, and broccoli soufflé.

"You should put those in the freezer." I nodded at the frozen foods.

“No wine?” She left the packages on the table and led me into her small bedroom, queen bed and dresser set under the barred window overlooking the fire-escape.

I covered my nose with my sleeve. “How long has he been here?”

“Since yesterday morning.” She looked past me, out the window. “I was at the library and didn’t actually realize until he didn’t come out to eat his dinner.”

My sister spent whole days at the library. She said she was looking for jobs but never found one. She studied art books, used the computers, stood at the bus stop talking to strangers and sometimes, hoping for a tip, offered to carry grocery bags. I reached under the bed for the dog—midsized mutt, bristly fur, lab or pit judging by the solid weight.

“Almost,” she whispered, “I hope you’re chasing squirrels in dog heaven.” She wrapped him in an old blanket. I took the front and she took the back and we lifted.

“It’s just his body now.” She shoved feet into slippers, nodding at me to back toward the door. “Dead bodies are heavier.”

“Where are we taking him?”

“Your car. The Humane Society will dispose of him, free.”

After we put Almost in the trunk, she leaned her head against my shoulder. She was taller, so she had to bend her knees and slump. Her head felt heavy and smelled like olive oil. I hugged her. “Almost was so lucky to have you. To end his life with you.”

“I’m the lucky one.” She wiped her cheek. “They’re supposed to take a clay impression of the dog’s paw. Make sure they do that,

Selb. I'm making a necklace of paw-prints."

"Kind of macabre—"

"Every being deserves to be loved and remembered."

Call me judgmental, but her idea of love wasn't healthy or rooted in the real world. Part of me hated her for loving these dying dogs, because this was how she justified her existence, this was what she'd done with all her potential.

Helen was fifty-one, and I was forty-five. I used to be the middle sister before Emily, our younger sister, fired us, fired our whole family. She wrote a letter just before she graduated from Barnard. Apparently, she'd met a Canadian neuroscientist and was moving to Toronto. She explained she had decided not to invite us to her wedding:

> *I am sorry to say I have no positive memories of my childhood, and I no longer feel I need to carry this pain with me into the future. I think it is easiest for all of us if we lead our separate lives.*

Mother and Helen both cried and wrote letters back, apologizing for whatever they'd done to make her feel this way. Mother sent a generous wedding check, asking her to reconsider, telling her she would always be her daughter and would always have a home in Minnesota. I was jealous. I wished I'd been the one severing ties, freeing myself, because Emily saw it, saw the future exactly as it transpired, this constant untangling of feelings, needs, lives.

*

Two weeks later, Helen held up the clay paw-print. "Wouldn't his paw be bigger than this one? I think they mixed it up."

"That's what they gave me." I looked around the apartment, everything inherited. The CD player was our old one. So was the toaster. One wall of bookshelves came from my father's study, filled with his leather-bound first editions of Robert Louis Stevenson and Charles Dickens. Lay-Z-Boy chair, brass lamp, two small oriental rugs laid over the speckled carpet. The rugs and Lay-Z-Boy had been in Mother's assisted living apartment, and whenever the radiators sputtered heat, gave off the faint whiff of hairspray and chicken broth. "Smells like Mom, doesn't it?" Helen laughed.

On her shelf sat three glazed pots. We each got three. Our mother was a ceramicist, solid shapes with spaces carved into the center—crevices, cracks, gaps, and holes, making them look out of balance, as if they were bound to collapse at any moment, but didn't. This was her genius, her message, although she hated the idea of art-as-message.

"Don't reduce it," she told our father when he gave her his interpretation. Inside, that was the point: to look inside, gold and green and blue glazes, reminding you of rivers, waves, grasses that seemed to never stop moving.

"What I try to capture is the tension between static and dynamic, freedom and responsibility, flight and stuck-ness," she said at one of her award dinners, repeating the word *stuckness,* and nodding. As a projector flashed her pots on the screen, I thought about the light trapped inside. I actually felt I knew her that night, maybe the only time.

She taught at the University of Minnesota. She didn't produce very much, maybe three or four pots a year, and she was tormented by her own slowness. She blamed it on the space, light, noise; mostly she blamed it on us. Her workshop was in the basement: blue linoleum floor, pottery wheel, marble slab laid across two saw-horses, plastic bag of clay underneath, walls covered with designs flapping above heat vents. "How can I work when you're screaming at one another upstairs," she would yell. "I can't think."

Twice, she left us with our father, who was supposed to be selling long-term health insurance from his office on the third floor. He made phone calls, but according to Mother, never sold a policy in his life. Instead he read books about animal behavior, wolf packs, whale pods, elephant parades, telling us we had a lot to learn from other species. Our mother teased him when he came downstairs to make tea in the kitchen. *Mr. Silver Spoon*, she'd say, which we understood meant he didn't have to work. Both times she left, she told us she was sorry, but she would die if she didn't do her art. She came back after a few days, begging our forgiveness.

"You know how much I love you."

She never made peace with the tension between love and work. She quit making pots after our father died. She lost her memory in her early sixties. She called everyone Emily, even though Emily had been gone for two decades. I would enter her assisted-living apartment and she would look up and smile. "Emily, how are the kids?" Did she mean my kids, my kids who actually visited her once a month?

My sister's paintings were of animals—fish, birds, elephants—delicate watercolors and ink drawings pinned to walls. Beautiful renderings, revelations of muscles, joints, and wing-span. My favorites were insects: green caterpillars, Jesus flies with crosses on their bellies, dragonflies with magnificent translucent wings that made me want to cry. She was a true artist; she saw things I couldn't.

"It's clearly a fake," she said of the paw-print, folding the empty grocery bag. "I can't believe you didn't bring wine or beer. All I can offer you is tea."

"No thanks." I handed her a stack of *New Yorker*s and *The New York Review of Books,* but she handed them back. "I don't read anymore."

"Why not?"

"Words blur. Hurts my eyes."

"Did you see a doctor?"

"I suppose I should." She had mastered the slight nuances of normalcy, never revealing the depth of her desperation. "When are you free for dinner?"

"Semester is almost over, and once I've turned in grades, I'll call you." My voice was stiff, resistant. I spaced out our visits, knowing it took me days, sometimes weeks to recover.

She'd forgotten, but I hadn't. During our last dinner, she drank too much and talked with her eyes closed for two hours, complaining the whole time. "I can't bring myself to call my agent. Would you do it for me?" she asked, squinting at my cell phone lying on the table. “Pretend you’re me?”

“Won’t she know?”

My sister shook her head. “I email her my work but she doesn’t reply. Please? Call and say it’s me.”

So, I dialed and her agent answered and after I introduced myself as Helen, she said, “You don’t sound like Helen. Who are you? Where the hell is Helen?”

“She’s here. I’m her sister. She’s sick and wanted me to call. A throat condition.”

I handed the phone to my sister who put on a great act. She made her voice hoarse, but she had a certain way of enunciating every syllable, a phony rich person’s voice, my husband called it, and her agent told her, “We’ve run out of options, Helen.”

“I had a cover on the goddamn *New Yorker*,” she shouted into the phone. “Williams Sonoma begged me to illustrate for them. You didn’t do your fucking job!”

The agent hung up.

I tried to be positive, my role as younger sister. “Little tiny paintings look great on iphones, and that’s where art is going . . . flash fiction, tiny paintings, short videos uploaded on YouTube.”

“I hate technology. I hate anyone under thirty-five. Their brains are undeveloped.” Her eyes remained closed as she spoke. “Twitter. Facebook. I hope climate change wipes out the whole human race and the earth can get a fresh start. Animals deserve that. They deserve to be rid of us.”

I listened, remembering that after my father died, my mother did the same thing—she complained he’d never really taken care of her, of us, that we were all doomed.

"Now, I can't even get anyone to *look* at my work."

"I'll look at it," I offered.

The waiter had already removed our plates, and she lay her forehead on the table, rolling it side to side. "There isn't anything to see. I can't afford supplies."

"Have you seen Heather?"

She kept rolling. "Heather who?"

Heather was her former sponsor.

"Charles?" I asked about her high school friend, an art teacher, who for years had tried to help her get her life on track.

"He told me I have a death wish, and I told him to fuck off."

I thought I should get her home before she got even more depressed, but she suddenly perked up when the waiter announced tonight's dessert special was tiramisu. She lifted her head, "Share?"

The wine bottle was almost empty, but she shook the last drops into her glass. "You know what I hate most? When people ask if I'm still doing my art, like it's a hobby. In the old days, artists had patrons, people who believed in them and invested in talent. Now everyone is an artist. If everyone's an artist, no one's an artist."

I dreaded the silence that followed her tirades. I had a name for the silence; I called it *The Inner Crumble*. My therapist told me to think of Teflon. "Just let your sister slide off," she told me. But Helen's life wasn't solid enough to slide off. She was a fog that moved through skin, penetrated surfaces. I came home gutted. Gutted by who she was, who I was, the vast chasm between our lives. I would lie in bed next to my husband, thinking of my daughter and son tucked in bed, and wouldn't be able to contain the sadness that came from her squandered life. I wondered why—

genes or experience or luck, or was it that she came first and was the shield for my sister and me. Did she save us? Asking myself for the millionth time—what does one human being owe another in this world?

She ate the entire tiramisu, scraping the plate clean with the side of her fork. "Doesn't Gordon's office use advertising? Couldn't he find me a job?"

My husband worked as an engineer for a medical device company. "They don't do their own distribution." I dug into my purse for the credit card.

"Before we leave, could I use your phone? I need to send a couple of emails."

She always asked to use my phone. Once, she asked for my winter coat. "You know, for when I get a job?"

When I got home, Gordie was waiting. "What the hell can I do for her?" He held up his phone. Apparently, the emails were to him and he thought I'd put her up to it. "I can't stand her. I can't stand to see what she does to you." He turned down the basketball game. "How did she get my email?"

I was a little startled at her cunning, her mix of animal compassion and human exploitation. Especially since Gordie could barely bring himself to be civil to her on the phone. But then again, she had always looked to men for help.

I turned away, trying to hide my tears because they just made him angry at me for putting myself in the same position all over again.

His voice flared as he set his phone on the table. "She's a parasite . . . sucks you dry. And you let her."

CAROL DINES

*

What always broke my heart were the photos on her refrigerator—us as children, sailing, riding horses, waving from a French chalet. Embroidered dresses or cowboy hats or tennis dresses. She was taller, prettier, resembling our father, who was very handsome. Six years younger, I had my mother's round cheeks, freckled nose, frizzy red hair kept braided until I was old enough to take out the snarls myself. In all the photos, Helen is holding me in her lap or standing behind me with her hands on my shoulders. She is smiling into the camera, wanting to be noticed. I am watching her, already worried.

That worry had never left me. "Just wanted to tell you we're going to Mexico at Christmas." I'd dreaded telling her and to compensate, handed her a bag of specialty cheeses, crackers, olives, nuts, bottle of wine.

She opened the bag of Marcona almonds and ate one. "I wouldn't be able to go anyway. I have a new dog coming tomorrow." She nodded at one of the photos on the refrigerator. "Don't forget your sunscreen. Remember when you almost died of sunburn?"

In the photo I am unrecognizable, my face so burned and swollen my eyes look like staples, two straggly red braids hanging in the air like roots pulled from dirt. She liked to talk about the past, especially those moments she'd taken care of me. A canoe trip in Canada intended to give our mother time to work on an exhibit set to open in a month. White Lake, Crane Lake, no roads, just islands and waterfalls, a map and compass to chart our trip. "Without this," my father said, rattling the map, "We're lost."

ALMOST

Our father was in his early forties then, muscled and tan, blond curls tucked behind ears. He didn't shave on our canoe trip, and my sister hated the bristles, shaking her head at him, "More convict, less father."

He laughed. He made us sit away from the smoke, told us the story about the night he'd spent in jail for protesting a taconite mine in northern Minnesota. After we cooked Bisquick-wrapped hotdogs on sticks, he sang to us, "Where Have All the Flowers Gone," strumming a ukulele he found at a garage sale. My sister harmonized naturally, but I couldn't carry a tune. When I tried to join in, we had to start the song over, so I stayed quiet. Overhead, the stars felt close and the moon came up through the treetops. I kept looking up, away from the darkness full of sounds.

"Just stay together." Mother had warned us not to wander off on our own. "Even when you have to go to the bathroom at night. Wake each other up."

The second morning, my arms and face were raw with sunburn. "Didn't you bring sunscreen?" Helen asked Dad.

He searched his bag and found only a bottle of Coppertone suntan lotion.

"If she gets melanoma in twenty years, it's your fault." Helen had done a science report on skin cancer. She mixed Bisquick with water and plastered it on my face and arms. It kept me from burning, but the batter drew mosquitos. I slapped instead of paddling, slowing us down, and we needed to reach Wolf Island by dark.

"Swim," my father commanded. "Wash that stuff off." Mosquitos were biting him too, right through his shirt and hat.

"No more Bisquick."

My sister broke off branches with wide leaves and made me hold them like an umbrella in the middle of the canoe. "You can rest your arms when clouds come over." She glanced back at Dad, "Don't worry, I'll paddle for both of us."

My sister's blisters became infected. Dad hadn't brought ointment or band-aides. We ended up turning around the third day, arriving home two days early, white puss oozing from my sister's blisters, my eyes swelled so much I couldn't open them. When Mother heard us calling, "We're home!" she came upstairs, shirt buttoned unevenly, hair mussed.

"I'm dying," my sister held up blistered palms.

"Me too." Tears of relief flowing now that I was home.

Dad walked right past her, his step quickening on the creaky stairs. When he came back up, his voice was sharp. "Haven't made much progress on your show. Do you always leave the door open down there?"

Emmy was born the following summer. What I remember best was the meanness in my father's voice, something we were meant to hear but not understand. Holding Emmy, he'd sing, "Wonder where she gets her dark, dark hair? Black, black eyes? Red, red lips? Our dear, dear Emmy."

Two years later, he died in a car accident. I hardly remember him now, except as someone who filled in the gaps left over by our mother. "Don't resuscitate," my mother said into the phone. "He wouldn't want that. I'm on my way."

My sister had been very close to our father, closer to him than to our mother. Helen seemed okay at first, but after the holidays she started cutting herself, and vomiting after meals. She was too thin, but thinness was celebrated in our family, thinness and straight posture. Helen wore our father's shirts over baggy jeans. She liked erasing her body under his old shirts, the body she stuffed with food, the arms she cut. When she ate my leftover birthday cake, I led my mother to the bathroom door so she would hear Helen retching. "That's my cake," I whispered, unfolding the handkerchief with Helen's razors, band-aides, alcohol swabs. "You should see her arms."

My mother led me back to my room, angry that I had tattled. "Can't you give your sister a break? She's grieving. She's in pain. She'll work through it."

"I met someone," Helen announced, after I'd returned from Mexico. We were sitting in a crowded café near her apartment. "His name is Richard."

I braced myself. Forgive me, but she had absolutely nothing to offer a healthy relationship—half a welfare check? And she had a long history of men: embezzler, gambler, alcoholic, several husbands, gun collector and ex-convict she met at the welfare office.

"Richard bought the building."

"Your building?"

She nodded. "He said he might buy some of my paintings for the lobby."

"What lobby?"

He's going to tear down the building and put in really nice

condos."

"What about the old lady who lives below you?" I'd never seen her but I could hear her television when I visited my sister.

"He's moving her into a nursing home. He's going to pay the bill. Believe me, he's doing her a favor." She ordered two croissants and a large cappuccino. She smiled, composed. "He's going to make the neighborhood better." This wasn't the way my sister talked, and already I saw her morphing into the kind of woman Richard might be attracted to.

"What about your dogs?" I asked. "What about Ray?"

"Richard bought me these so I could read recipes." She pulled out eyeglasses, expensive rims, same as mine, Anne et Valentin. "I told him I love to cook and he asked me if I would cook for him."

"How old is he?"

"Sixty-eight. He needs a healthier diet, and he offered to find me a new apartment in one of his other buildings, closer to him and to you."

"Draw a line *now*," my husband told me as soon as I got home. "She always lands on her feet. You're the one I worry about."

Years ago, I let her stay with us, "between apartments." Newly evicted, she arrived one Sunday night, end of the month. She'd spent the day looking for shelters that allowed dogs. Last Chance was a German Shepard, deaf, incontinent, shedding massive amounts of hair. My daughter Lucy had allergies, and within a day she needed inhalers. After that, I drew strict lines. "Two nights but no dogs."

"I don't have money for a kennel."

"There are pet friendly hotels." I handed her an envelope with two hundred dollars, money I'd argued about with Gordie who insisted once we started giving her cash, she'd come back for more. "Lucy has asthma. Try to understand."

She stared at me, waiting for me to cave. "You always put up walls now."

"Not walls," I said. "Lucy is studying for her SATs. She can't afford to get sick from allergies."

"I'm not going to jump over your boundaries."

"I don't expect you do."

She leaned toward me, her voice furious. "I guess I just love you more than you love me."

I didn't deny it, and she turned and walked away.

"Richard and I have an understanding," she said brightly, the next time we met for coffee. Months had passed since I'd last seen her. "He gives me a food allowance, and I cook for him." She leaned close, "I can siphon off enough to pay my rent, gas, and electricity."

"Does he know?"

"I'm sure he assumes." She sounded self-assured and that worried me. "He isn't paying me for all the time I spend shopping and cooking. I think he expects I will take a certain amount out for labor costs."

I tallied rent, electricity, and food in my head. "You must be taking out six hundred a month."

"Five hundred. I eat with him, take home the leftovers."

"You eat together?"

"Of course—candles, wine."

I pictured her like a worm, slowly making tunnels into the dirt of his life. "You stay all night?"

"He likes to sleep alone." She tore off sections of croissant, popping them in her mouth. Crumbs dotted her sweater and she brushed them off. "He takes me to the orchestra, center seats near the front."

Two years of Richard this, Richard that. But he wasn't going to marry her, offer her any real stability. I'd asked a realtor friend, and she told me all about Richard. He tore down old buildings, got variances, bypassed zoning laws. His former wives hated him. His children had moved away.

But those two years were the closest I came to freedom. I saw Helen less frequently, visits that dwindled to holidays and sometimes not even then. "Richard asked me to cook for his Christmas party. You're invited too."

The day my son got his driver's license, the phone rang late in the evening.

"Is he alright?" Gordie asked before handing the phone to me. "It's Helen." I heard my sister crying at the other end, "Richard collapsed. I'm at the hospital. His sisters are here. You have to come. They want me to leave."

An oxygen tank bubbled next to him. Richard couldn't move, couldn't speak. The only person he seemed to recognize was Helen. He blinked at her.

"See?" she said loudly to his sisters. "He's blinking at me." Then, sitting on the edge of his bed, she whispered to him, "When you come home, I'll make you lamb with mint sauce and rosemary potatoes."

He blinked again.

The nurse said, "Progress will be slow."

"But he's blinking," Helen insisted.

"Sometimes patients blink reflexively," the nurse explained. "It's the body reacting to light or sound."

The prognosis was grim, years of rehabilitation, and even then, he might never regain his cognitive skills. Social workers outlined programs, insurance policies, nursing home options. My sister slept in his room at night and only left to go back to her apartment to shower and change clothes. When the sisters realized Helen would be cheaper than assisted-living or in-home nursing, they hired her. They reorganized Richard's bank accounts and billing so my sister had no power to siphon funds. The eldest sister was the executor. She would pay Helen a monthly wage, and Helen would live in the spare bedroom of Richard's apartment, rent and heat paid, and in exchange, she'd spoon him food, wipe his butt, change his sheets.

"She's never been happier," I told my husband.

*

Selby, Richard died last night, and his sisters are trying to kick me out.

Selby, his sisters are selling his apartment. Call me.

Selb? Answer, please?

I didn't attend his funeral. I didn't even send a condolence letter.

"I hid from her," I told my husband one morning when I got back from the farmer's market. "I hid from my own sister. I crouched between two parked cars, pretending to tie my shoes until I saw her walk past. Twelve feet away, and I couldn't bring myself to stand up and talk to her."

"She didn't see you?"

I shook my head. "Thirty degrees and she was wearing that purple coat."

He knew which coat. Purple velvet, down to her ankles, fake fur collar.

She bought it to wear to the opera, and now she wore it to be seen. It wouldn't have kept her warm.

He was lying in bed, *Atlantic Monthly* propped on his belly. "Actually, hiding from her is healthy. It's the only thing you can do."

I lay on my back. "Her hair wasn't combed."

"Do you think she's worrying about you? I guarantee she isn't. She's probably milking some *new* friend or neighbor." He stared at me, worrying that I would call her. "Let her clean houses or dog-sit or cook for someone else. She wants to live this way."

"No one chooses to live like she does."

"Yes, some people do." He spoke softly, as if he knew how hard this was for me. "Sometimes you have to erase people from your life. Otherwise, they'll use you up."

I wanted him to keep reminding me. I wanted to believe she had only herself to blame. But my memory of her was my memory of survival, and letting go was like holding clouds in my hands, trying to separate air from water.

"What do you ever get from her?" he asked.

"She takes care of dying dogs," I said. "She doesn't hurt anyone."

"She hurts you."

Downstairs, my daughter was practicing for spring play tryouts, her voice breaking on the high notes. Across the street, my son and his friends skated across the frozen lake, slamming pucks between two stones. Next to me, my husband reached out his hand.

All my life I'd waited for my family to coalesce, the way my mother used to talk about clay and glaze coalescing, each sculpture becoming its own true form. But no matter how hard I tried to shape my own life, give it solidity, it never hardened enough. I couldn't pretend she didn't exist.

ICE BELLS

Half an hour out of the city, Willa parks her Prius at the top of the driveway, a space reserved for her mother so she won't have to climb steps. A large wooden stork points the way to the backyard where the baby shower is in full swing—Dixie Chicks belting "Wide Open Spaces," children shrieking, back door slamming.

"Hold on, Mom." Willa looks at herself in the rearview mirror: corkscrew curls, light brown skin, Peaches and Cream, her favorite new lipstick. She takes a Kleenex from the packet in her purse, wipes off most of the lipstick.

"Don't take it off," her mother tells her. "That color's good on you."

"Too bright for Eden Prairie," she says of the suburb where her aunt lives. *Capital of the Cul de sac* she calls its sloping green lawns, humming sprinklers, SUVs. *And white*, she thinks, as if stepping through a door, the day-ahead door. She is not fifth-generation Norwegian, not blonde-haired and blue-eyed like her cousins. Despite her family's desire to erase distinctions, she is a distinction, adopted as an infant thirty-four years ago.

"You give me a signal when you're ready to leave." Willa glances at her mother's bruised hands holding two baby shower gifts on her lap. Her mother is dying. The cancer has spread to her bones, and she has stopped chemo. Today might be the last time they're all together, her mother, her mother's sisters and their families. "Is Derek coming?" she asks about her older brother.

"I left a message." Her mother looks straight ahead. "In my day we didn't include men in baby showers. We invited only women, and it was much more fun. Personally, I think it's sad women your age have to do everything with husbands and kids."

"Did you tell Aunt Kate and Aunt Sylvie how you felt?"

"Of course not. The shower's for their daughters." Her mother takes a deep breath. "Unfortunately, *he'll* be here, and I'm sorry for that."

"We're all adults." The last thing Willa wants is for her mother to worry. "Maybe once he's a father, he'll finally grow up."

They never mention Willa's cousin by name. They call him *the Sleaze*, ever since the truth came out. Willa was five and Joe was eight when he first invited her to his fort. "Let's play pee-pee touch. You pull down your underpants," he told her, "and I'll pull down mine, and then we'll touch them." She did it once, feeling his penis touch her soft brown pubic skin, just a few seconds and then she pulled up her underwear and shorts and wanted the game to be over. But whenever their families got together, he found a moment when she was alone. "Let's do our game."

Even then, she didn't want to make a scene, didn't want to ruin the family gathering. She didn't tell her mother, not until she was twelve and Joe was fifteen, waiting Christmas Eve when she came out of the bathroom. He played hockey, and he was strong and muscular. He used his strength to push her back inside, pressing his hardness against her. "We could take pee-pee touch to the next level," he whispered, "It's okay since we're not related *that* way."

She pushed him away, but he grabbed her arms, turned her around, gripping from behind so tight she couldn't breathe. "Say please."

"Please."

She told her mother that night, and her mother told her father. They went as a family, except for Derek, who even at the age of seventeen didn't like to leave the house. They drove to Aunt Kate and Uncle Tom's, Joe's mother and father. Willa had never seen her father so angry. "You ever touch my daughter again, and you'll be sorry." His face was six inches from Joe's and his fists were clenched. "I won't think twice about hurting you right back. I don't care if I'm your uncle. I don't care if my wife's sister is your mother. You're a bully. You've always been a bully, and I will personally be watching you whenever our families get together. Willa is your cousin, and she deserves to be respected. All girls deserve to be respected. You touch her again, and I'll break every bone in your body."

*

As Willa opens the passenger door, Gwen puts her feet out first. "I feel bad I didn't make my rhubarb cake this year," then holds Willa's arm until she's balanced and standing. Catching her breath, Willa's mother stares at the flowerbeds spilling red, yellow, white petunias. "Mary has a done a beautiful job on this yard."

"We thought we heard a car door slam." Her aunts hurry to help their eldest sister. Big women, big hugs, wide faces, Aunts Kate, Sylvie, and Lilly wearing shorts, t-shirts, sandals, Aunt Mary in a long skirt. Louise, the youngest, is in Texas, meditating at an ashram. White-haired sisters, once blondes, they know how to cook for an army, tend the sick, talk to the dying, and Willa is glad her mother has them. But seeing her mother next to her sisters, she is stunned by the change, how diminished her mother has become, stick arms, sunken eyes, wig too thick for her gaunt cheeks.

"Don't forget the gifts," her mother calls to her.

As her aunts take charge of her mother, Willa uses the gifts as an excuse to lean against the car and check her phone for messages—two from Peter, one from Jonathan.

She opens the message from Jonathan. *Miss you.*

She texts: *Where are you?*

Toilet. Bangkok. Ha, ha. Cunting hours since your last text.

You mean counting.

Cunting.

Why him, why now, why did she resume their relationship the day her mother stopped treatment? Sitting in the dark hospital room, her mother drugged and sleeping next to her, she started it all up again, texting Jonathan far away in London: *Miss you.*

She hasn't told Peter. She is breaking their one rule: no secrets. She wonders if it's because Jonathan is far away and their sex is text sex. Very possibly, she is searching for something that doesn't exist. She has done this before in relationships, held back, kept secrets, lied. But not with Peter, never with Peter.

"My wife lied continually," he told her. "If you lie, it's over."

*

As soon as Willa places the presents on the gift table, Aunt Kate puts a sticker on her back. "Potential baby names. I looked up six generations of our family tree. You have to guess the name on your back by getting clues."

"Your name sounds like what sick people do." Kirsten, seven months pregnant, is married to the Sleaze. After glancing at Willa's back, she rocks back and forth, a pained expression on her face. "First syllable rhymes with groan."

"Joan?"

Kirsten shakes her head. "First letter is said with lips pursed."

Everyone is watching, waiting for Willa to guess.

"M? Moan . . . Mona?"

"You're always so smart at games." Kirsten hugs her. "Feel it kicking?" Kirsten places Willa's hands on her belly.

"Wow, big kicks." Willa tries to match her cousin's enthusiasm. Fun is the point, she reminds herself, thinking back to when she was young, running wild with her cousins, popsicle duels, skits, lemonade stands. She wonders when the fun stopped and the pretending began. She isn't sure what fun is anymore, if fun is attainable for someone who studies history. Or maybe she doesn't have the fun gene. At Carleton, she used to sit with her clique of college friends describing family holidays as if they were natural disasters. "My family still has Santa, and he comes down through the attic carrying a big bag of gifts," she'd explain. "One of my uncles actually looks like Santa and he dresses up. We all pretend we're still kids."

Her roommates insisted on coming to her house one Christmas, calling it an anthropological field trip. Afterward they said, "That was strange. Everyone laughs all the time."

"All. The. Time," she nodded. "Exhausting, right?"

Her cheeks already ache from smiling, from looking happy. She wishes she were in her office, getting a head start on the week ahead. She works in the education department at the Minneapolis Institute of Art, organizes classroom visits, leads school groups through vast collections of African masks, Egyptian mummies, Chinese vases, Impressionist landscapes. "In one tomb a child was buried with his toy horse. Can you find it?" she asks them. The fifth and sixth grade boys charge around the room, ruthless in their need to spot the horse first. The girls whisper, distracted by the hot security guard with dreads and huge arm muscles. She invents games, treasure hunts, methods of holding their imaginations, inciting curiosity. She spends hours on her search engine looking up histories of shoes, wedding rings, eyeglasses, hats, teddy bears, eyelash extensions, stories that will enthrall her students.

Aunt Mary is pouring drinks, swatting flies from the lemonade pitcher. "Lemonade, with or without?"

Willa sits at the long table. "With, please."

Her aunt pours a jigger of vodka into the glass, adds ice, lemonade. She sits beside Willa. "You have been so good through this. No one could ask for a better daughter." Then, resting her hand on Willa's arm. "How's Peter?"

"Fine. He's camping with his sons."

"Think you'll get married?"

"We've talked about it." She fingers the tablecloth—yellow teddy bears tethered to balloons floating through clouds.

Her aunts are polite. They don't pry into her life, asking why she is still single, why she stays with Peter who is not yet divorced, why she doesn't hurry up and settle down. They are not interested in museums or history, unless it's the Norwegian history of map-making which they love because her grandfather was known for his map collection. "You take after your grandfather," they tell her whenever she talks about her work. "He could spend hours studying the routes of Viking sailors."

Willa smiles and nods. Viking *slave ships*, she thinks. She has looked at his collection, done her research. But that is not the history they know or talk about.

Drops of water land on her shoulder. Nancy's sons spray one another with water guns, aiming irritatingly close to the picnic tables. She listens to uncles trading weekend scores, golf then baseball. They open another round of beers before contemplating meat, what makes it most tender, which kind of sauce is best, whether basting or marinating makes it more succulent, whether fat should be cut off or left on, taking turns basting chicken legs slathered in barbecue sauce while Willa's aunts assemble platters of potato salad, cold slaw, fruit salad, corn bread covered with cellophane to keep the flies away.

Nancy grabs her youngest son by the arm. "One more drop of water near this table, and you're losing those squirt guns for good." She leans over and hugs Willa. "Love your shirt. Nordstrom?"

"Vintage Bliss."

"Vintage? Really?" Nancy is a nurse at the university. "You can wear vintage because you've got a thin waist. You're a pear. I'm an apple." Nancy pulls out her baggy shirt, displaying a style suited to apples.

Willa wonders if pear is code for big ass. Nancy is Willa's age, thirty-four, a nurse and mother of three boys. They grew up together, and Willa has always felt that Nancy's compliments have an implicit condescension, as if Nancy is ahead of Willa in life.

"Pears live longer," Nancy says. "Apples get heart disease and are more prone to dementia."

Willa listens. Her yoga teacher tells her students to close their eyes and imagine their bodies as a house. "Where are you in your house right now," she asks. "In the attic of your mind? Living room of your heart? Are you staring out a window? Or lying in bed with your eyes closed? Notice the places you are afraid to go in your house." Whenever they do this exercise, Willa sees herself standing outside under a tree, looking in.

Aunt Sylvie puts two bowls of potato salad on the table. "This one has bacon, and this one doesn't. I used vegan mayo in the small bowl."

Willa gives her a grateful smile. "I could've brought my own."

"How do you know you get enough protein?" Kirsten is standing nearby, hands cupping her pregnant belly. "I would love to be vegan, but I'm not sure it would be good for the baby.

"I don't think everyone has to be vegan." Willa has been vegan since college. "It's a personal choice."

"But why?" The Sleaze stands next to his wife, casting a single shadow. "Because you love animals, or what?"

"My philosophy is do no harm," she says, trying to keep her voice from sounding preachy. "Methane belches from cows, pig manure in our rivers, antibiotics in chickens—"

"—Got it." He cuts her short, smiles at the chicken and hot dogs on the grill. "Personally, I love a little flesh between my teeth."

Willa glances at her mother sitting in a lawn chair, and they both smile, thinking the same thing, how much more fun it would be without men.

"Guess we shouldn't wait for Derek," the Sleaze says, with a laugh.

Kirsten jabs him. "Behave yourself." But it's a playful nudge.

Willa ignores them, pretending to be interested in her aunts' conversation about portable cribs. Derek, her older brother, is agoraphobic and rarely leaves his house. An Internet lawyer and hoarder, he orders items from eBay—clocks, elegant dishware, books, and furniture piled so deep you can't even see into the rat-infested rooms. When neighbors complain about raccoons in the garage or his un-mowed grass, bringing city officials to issue citations and fines, he files lawsuits against them, and, being a lawyer, knows how to draw out the lawsuits so that eventually they have to put their homes on the market. But no one will buy them, not with his house next door, and eventually they lower the price, and when they still cannot sell, they accept his offer. He owns four houses on the same block. One day, Willa thinks, she will find him dead inside one of his houses, tripped down stairs over his own junk or smothered under a fallen stack of magazines. Her phone vibrates. She excuses herself and goes inside to the bathroom.

Peter has texted: *Came home early. Can I come by later?*

She texts Peter back: *Family today. Not sure about tonight.*

He texts back: *Understand.*

Immediately she changes her mind, thinking it would be good to laugh about the baby shower barbecue with someone who sees it through her eyes: *Seven?*

He texts back: *See you then.*

ICE BELLS

*

Willa met Peter four years ago, the day her mother was first diagnosed with lung cancer. Fleeing the hospital room to cry alone, she stopped at Lucia's-To-Go to pick up soup to take to her mother later and, seeing the almost empty patio, decided to sit outside and eat a salad, drink a glass of wine. The only other person was a man with a golden retriever, and the dog's nose lifted toward her, milky eyes blinking.

"This is Henry. He's blind." The man jerked his chair forward so Willa had more room. "He can't see you, but he can smell a beautiful woman, can't you Henry?"

Henry's nose twitched.

Willa laughed. She needed the world to be shallow for a few minutes.

The man's beer glass was empty, his newspaper folded. She was hoping he might leave and then she'd have the patio to herself. Instead he ordered another beer.

She felt emptied of words, unable to chit chat. She ate her salad, glancing at her phone, not wanting to be rude, not knowing where else to look. She kept her sunglasses on even though dusk had arrived. Her eyes were swollen from crying and she didn't want the man to see her face.

When the waiter set down his second beer, he lifted it to Willa. "Kind of like being on an airplane seated next to a stranger, right?"

"Except I don't have my Bose."

"Ouch."

"I didn't mean it that way." She turned over her phone. "I just left my mother at the hospital. Not a good diagnosis."

"I'm sorry." He reached out his hand to shake hers. "Peter."

"Willa." She removed her sunglasses and ordered a second glass of wine. "How old is Henry?"

"Sixteen. Over a hundred in dog years. He's kind of a miracle."

Feeling the wine begin to take effect, she asked, "When you're not drinking beer with Henry, what do you do, Peter?"

"Veterinarian. Small breeds."

"That must be fulfilling."

He shrugged, stroking Henry under the chin. "Actually, veterinarians have the highest suicide rate of any profession."

He told her he'd recently separated from his wife and hadn't gotten used to eating alone. "Two sons. I get them every other weekend."

He kept two inflatable kayaks in the trunk of his Camry and began picking her up at the hospital an hour before sunset. They paddled the city lakes at dusk, sweeps of purple cloud, high-rises in the distance, windows reflecting swaths of orange. Afterward, they would go back to her place and sometimes they made love. Early in their relationship she debated whether to fake it, so it wouldn't become an issue.

"I've never been able to orgasm," she explained. "But I still love to feel you inside me." Right away that was the difference between Peter and other men. She told him the truth.

Peter kept trying, and each time, she lay back, feeling like damaged goods. "It's not your problem," she said. "It's like I'm dead there."

Sometimes he stayed the night. This was progress. Willa had

never been able to sleep next to men, next to anyone, not without medication. Sharing a room in college, she drank Nyquil for four years to fall asleep. She had lived alone since, had chosen jobs with offices that had doors and paid enough to rent a one-bedroom apartment, all with the goal of having her own space. Sometimes, when she traveled for work, the museum budget required her to share a room with a female colleague. She lay awake on her side of the bed, becoming more awake as night passed into morning. It was an old pattern, older than she understood.

Lying beside Peter, talking in the dark, felt closer than anything else, closer than sex. She talked about her mother's cancer, how her mother believed in God but she didn't, and the idea that she would not be able to talk to her mother ever again made her chest feel heavy, each breath trapped under a pile of stones.

"I've never loved her enough," she told him.

"I'm not sure you know what enough is." He stroked the outside of her arms, drawing little circles.

At a certain point, she said, "Let's get some sleep," and he moved far over to the other side of the bed and turned away. She stacked pillows between them, a soft wall, and only then could she sleep.

The first time he stayed the whole night, she made him breakfast the next morning, a victory breakfast she called it. "I actually slept!" She'd gone out to buy croissants and made a pot of coffee, brought it on a tray. She set it on his lap then moved around to the other side of the bed, lay down beside him, lifting pillows away. She smelled his skin, the lavender soap she kept in the shower.

*

Before sitting down to lunch, her family holds hands while her mother and aunts sing grace in four-part harmony honed from years of practice—"thank you, thank you, thank you"—eight rounds, climbing and falling, a chord of sisterly sound, her mother's alto voice hoarse but still on key.

Party favors: diapers with bows. They take their seats and unwrap them, "Tootsie Rolls!" Laughter, shrieks of it. "Who has the real poo?" Aunt Mary looks right at Willa as she opens her diaper to see caramel sauce smeared inside. "You got it, Willa!"

They all point at her diaper, the real-poo diaper, until one of the boys, Sven, grabs it and licks it, "Yum, real poo," and all the other kids say they want real poo too. They tug at her diaper until the diaper splits, caramel falling in clumps on the crotch of her white jeans.

The Sleaze is filming with his phone. Willa takes napkins, dunks them in water, and works the spot to dilute the stain. When it is gone, she glances up and sees her cousin. She frowns, "Really?"

He replays the video, grinning as he watches it. Then he looks up, catches her eye, and smiles. She feels enraged. He has her on camera, and that feels the same as before to Willa, like he can do with her as he pleases.

She gets up, walks over to the empty chair next to her mother. They sit side by side, watching Nancy's boys shoot water guns at spilled coleslaw, trying to clean off the patio. The Sleaze lights citronella candles, until Nancy, his older sister, waves her hand to clear the smoke. "Should pregnant women be breathing in those fumes?"

"Better than Zika," he says.

"We don't have Zika up here," she tells him.

"*Zzzzzzzz.*" He flies his finger right at her face. "All it takes is one."

"Isn't that the truth," Willa's mother whispers, mother and daughter laughing so hard they have to wipe tears from their cheeks.

The smell of citronella and bug spray always reminds Willa of camp.

She turned thirteen that summer, a few months after her parents learned what had been happening with her cousin. They sent her to a summer camp for adoptees, a teenage camp focused on issues of identity. Most of the kids were from Vietnam, Russia, and Colombia. She listened to therapists talk about how all teenagers grappled with issues of identity, but adoptees often struggled more.

"It's natural at your age to wonder about your origins, who you are biologically, to feel a certain loss. You have to grieve that loss even though most of you have never known your biological parents. That's not easy. How do we grieve what we've never experienced? How do we grieve what we've never known?"

Some adoptees cried and said they had always felt different, too fat, too thin, too stupid. Willa felt lucky. Even though Derek was her parents' biological child, he'd always made her feel like the normal one.

One boy kept trying to kiss her. He was darker than Willa, skinny with long legs and big buck teeth that pressed into his bottom lip. He'd wait for her to come out of the lake, and he'd wrestle her to the ground, sit on top, until one of the counselors told him, "Knock it off, James. No touching."

She tried to avoid him. Everyone did. But James followed her like a shadow. One night he began talking in multiple voices—his father's voice and his own voice. The girls heard yelling and hurried across the field to the boys' cabins. Two boys had been playing chess on the porch, and James picked up the chessboard and wacked it against the bunk beds, tossing pieces, his voice becoming a mean voice, telling them to pick them up or he'd cram the pieces down their throats. And when they did pick them up, he ran to the big rock overlooking the lake and threw the board into the water as far as he could wing it.

"If you want to play chess, little faggots," he yelled, "swim out there and find it." They all knew it must be the voice of his father, the father who raised him, and one of the girls ran to get their counselors, smoking in the boathouse.

They came running, and the head counselor grabbed James by his shoulders, "James, James," to calm him down. That night the same counselor packed James's bags and drove him home.

Willa came back from camp and tried to love her family more, love them with more kindness and appreciation. Her mother noticed how hard she was trying. "What's going on?"

Willa burst into tears. "I could've ended up in a different family."

"We all could have ended up in different families." Gwen

pulled her daughter onto her lap and hugged her tight. "Love is not a duty. You've nothing to be grateful for. You're our daughter. We'll always love you, always."

*

"I've never seen prettier baby sweaters," Kirsten and Judy hold up the tiny sweaters Willa's mother has knit for them.

"They're from both of us," Willa's mother explains. "Willa bought the yarn, and I knit the sweaters."

Kirsten and Judy lean over and hug Willa. "Where did you get this yarn? It's so soft."

"New World Yarn." Willa smiles at her mother.

That's where she met Jonathan. She drove her mother to New World Yarn four months ago, right after her mother's last round of chemo started. An old brick factory converted to an organic yarn shop: cement floors, chandeliers, yarn hanging from every surface. Willa eyed a table—champagne glasses, platters of cookies, smelly soft cheeses covered in cellophane.

"Poetry reading tonight." The owner, Charlie, flamboyant in hand-knit rose vest, black shirt and jeans, poured them each a glass of prosecco. "We knit while poets read their work. I have a friend who plays the cello between poems." Charlie touched Willa's sleeve, the sweater her mother had knit for her years ago when she'd finished graduate school. "Gorgeous."

"My mother knit this," she turned so he could see the unusual pattern down the back.

He turned to Gwen. "Did you use a pattern?"

She beamed. "I always make it up as I go along."

"Why haven't we met before?" He took her arm. "Let me show you some of my creations." He led her mother to a back room, lifting several striking sweaters from a rack.

"Oh my, that's wonderful." Her mother fingered the yarn, admiring angled pockets, wide sleeves, buttons made of keys, erasers, glass lenses taken from spectacles.

"All my buttons are found objects," Charlie told her. "I got this yarn from a woman who raises her own llamas near Rochester, spins and dyes it herself. Twice a year, Joyce brings me a truckload of her latest. Here." He handed her mother a pad, "Write down your name and number and next time she comes I'll call you. You'll get first dibs."

Did he know her mother was dying, Willa wondered? Could he tell the cancer was still growing, despite months of chemo? Surely, he must have noticed the wig, painted eyebrows, dry mouth, the way her mother worked her tongue.

"Gwen," he read her mother's name on the slip of paper. "I'm Charlie. Why don't you come tonight?"

Willa was deeply grateful for people who were kind to her mother. Deeply grateful, too, for places her dying mother could sit, knit, be part of the world. "Do you want to go?" she asked when they were in the car.

Her mother hesitated. "Wasn't he just being nice? I don't know."

"Mom, he's a yarn person. You're both knitters, exceptional knitters. He's probably lonely for someone who loves knitting the way he does."

They went back that night, and Willa met Jonathan. He read

haikus and left a silence between each short poem, his dark eyes glancing up to meet her gaze. She liked his British accent. Peter was in Florida with his boys. She dropped off her mother, circled back, telling herself, If he's still there, I'll sleep with him. She felt that familiar rush of adrenalin, the thrill of possibility. She had the faint sense she was hurting herself, but she didn't care. Sooner or later, she'd be too old to feel this free. She pretended she'd lost her scarf, had come back to look for it. "Did you see my scarf?" she asked Jonathan.

He gave her neck a hungry glance. "I'm quite certain you weren't wearing a scarf."

She wrote down the code into her condominium, explained where to park in the underground garage.

*

Afterward, when Peter came back, she told him everything.

She'd long ago confided her history of infidelity, fear of commitment, all the relationships she'd sabotaged in the past. That was why they had rules. She had to tell him everything. She watched hurt seep into his green eyes, nerves pulsing inside his cheeks, as if she were unearthing a beautiful flower by its roots. That's when she loved him most, when she could tell him anything.

"I'm sorry," she whispered. "I think I'm way more fucked up than you realize."

Still, he hugged her close. "As long as you tell me," he whispered. "That's what's important. No secrets. No lies."

A long tight hug, until she had the feeling he was hugging her so she couldn't see his face. "I'll be divorced soon." His voice was apologetic, as if he were to blame for her affair. His wife had met someone in AA. If Willa said yes, he was ready to move in together.

But Willa was afraid *yes* would feel like a cage. She often pictured them living together, connected beneath the surface, a subway system with only two stops. She understood euphoria wears off, the initial rush flattens, and habits are what you live with. One by one, her friends had settled down, married, started families. She knew there was closeness deeper than endorphins, but she didn't know how to get there, to that place that felt dead but wasn't. Sometimes, when Peter stayed at her place all weekend, she pretended to take long naps, lying in the bedroom with her eyes closed, hoping he would leave soon.

She doesn't tell Peter she sometimes gets photos of Jonathan's cock: *thinking of you.* She immediately erases them, but she cannot erase the feelings inside her, and sometimes after Jonathan texts, she goes into the bathroom and uses the shower nozzle, hard pulsing spray, trying to do to herself what he did.

She knows it matters—breaking the one rule she and Peter agreed to—but she tells herself it's not the same. She hasn't actually seen Jonathan since that one night, the night she had her first orgasm. Something about his skin, his touch, something electrical, easy. He pressed his hardness into her a little at a time, teasing her, making her want him more than anything else, warmth shuddering through her, collapsing distances between here and everywhere else.

ICE BELLS

*

Before dessert is served, Willa stands at the kitchen sink washing platters, glad to have something to do. Sunlight filters through shades, casting horizons across her hands. Birds fly across the sky, already migrating north. She thinks about her father, misses him. He counted birds in the spring and fall, kept numbers. Whenever they went for hikes, he stopped to stare at the sky through binoculars. She got impatient and ran ahead until he called out, "Where do you need to get to so fast, Willa?" She tried to slow down, but gradually her long stride sped up again, faster and faster, always trying to reach the highest point so she could see how far apart things were, see across the distances.

She misses him more as her mother gets sicker. He had a quirky sense of humor, jokes and puns about Norwegians. Heart attacks run in this family, big Norwegian bodies needing big hearts to pump blood. One day after pickleball at the community center, he walked to his car, leaned against the driver's wheel and died. He was sixty. Had just turned sixty. She was twenty-one, a month from graduation.

Her father used to tell her if she ever got lost anywhere in the world, go to a hospital. "They're open twenty-four-seven, and someone will help you." She is often at the hospital with her mother.

Through the window, she watches games of badminton and croquet taking place on opposite sides of the yard. She remembers a story on *Radio Lab* about how closeness is wired into genes, how second cousins have two times the diluted gene pool as first cousins. She can feel the closeness running through her blood-related cousins, something she has never felt, not just their round faces and bodies, not just their blue eyes and big teeth, but this desire to play games, sing songs, cultivate fun. She identifies more with the in-laws who have to learn how to *join in*.

This is my family, she thinks, but somewhere else my genes are lying on sand, dancing under stars, stirring big pots of fish stew. Or making love with someone darker, or lighter, someone who works in an office and drinks vodka martinis on weekends, or reads books about Buddhism, neuroscience, rewiring the brain. Somewhere, her genes might be saving elephants, wild blue herons, whales.

When she was sixteen, she tried to find information about her biological family. She asked her mother to take her to Duluth, the city where she was born. Built on hills, the small city was famous for its harbor, huge freighters beginning their journey across the largest chain of fresh water lakes: Superior, Michigan, Erie, Huron, Ontario—all the way to the ocean. Willa and her mother drove there late December, about the time she would have been conceived. Driving on icy roads through gusts of blowing snow, they circled St. Luke's Hospital where Willa had been born, then drove up and down Eighth Avenue past brick storefronts and offices, looking for the adoption agency.

"That's where we signed all the papers," her mother said, nodding at what was now an Internet café. "I remember it was next to the insurance building." Willa sat looking at the dreary building as her mother repeated what she'd already told Willa many times before. "Your mother wanted the records sealed. The agency told us your father was unnamed on the birth certificate, probably a sailor on one of the freighters. Unfortunately, they couldn't tell us where he was from."

They drove to the lighthouse and parked, looking out at the lake. The wind was too cold, and her mother waited in the car. Standing alone at the edge of the parking lot in her hooded down parka, Willa wondered if her particular combination of genes had sprung forth from this cold, two bodies trying to kindle heat on a lonely night after Christmas. When her fingers and toes began to sting from the cold, she went back to the car. They sat with the engine idling, heater turned high, watching a freighter move slowly, cutting a dark wake through chunks of ice until it reached open water and blew its horn.

Willa cried, glancing sideways to see tears running down her mother's cheeks too. When the ship was a tiny dot in the distance, Willa's mother rolled down the window to dump her coffee. "Hear the ice bells?" Ice shards lapping rocks. She reached out to warm her daughter's cold hands.

*

During dessert, the family divides into teams for Baby Trivia. Nancy is in charge, bossy Nancy.

"What percentage of babies arrive on their due date?"

Nancy's eldest son calls out, "Five percent," his pimples reddening.

Nancy shoots him a look, then moves on. "What is the heaviest baby ever born?"

"Twenty-two pounds, eight ounces, in Italy," Nancy's middle son calls out, laughing next to his brothers.

"You be quiet," Nancy tells her sons. "When are most babies conceived?"

Elbowed by his brothers, Nancy's youngest son calls out, "January."

"You've ruined it." She glares at her sons, rips up the questions, tossing the torn paper in the trash. "Proud of yourselves?"

Willa senses that moment when too much alcohol has been consumed. She watches aunts wipe frosting from toddlers' mouths, uncles chugging the last of their beers, voices louder than before. No one in her family articulates emptiness. They fill it up with the sound of themselves, with games and songs, recipes and advice. She has watched her aunts and uncles for years, mostly bickering, but still tender, the kind of tenderness that arises out of need: a deaf grandchild, a star athlete hooked on painkillers, her own brother afraid to leave his house. None of them, angels. Why then, she asks herself, do I even need to remind myself of this.

Later that night Peter texts: *Where are you? You said seven.*

She texts back: *Mom collapsed. We're at the hospital.*

Want company?

Tomorrow.

Four days from now her mother will take her last breath.

Before that, Willa does not leave her side. She sleeps on the sofa that folds into a small bed, machines beeping, soft-soled footsteps outside the door. She washes her mother's face, combs her hair, massages her feet. She wakes at three in the morning, listening to the silence between her mother's breaths, watches to make sure the blanket is rising and falling.

Each morning Peter comes with coffee, yogurt, Willa's favorite cheddar chutney sandwich for later. "What else can I bring you?"

"Clean underwear and bra, and my yoga pants, those soft ones. Gets so cold in here at night."

Peter writes a list on his phone, texts it to himself. "I work tonight but I have a break at four. I'll call first and see what I can bring you for dinner."

She squeezes his hand, kisses him on the cheek. "Thank you."

Willa spends hours sitting near the window overlooking the park, boys and girls playing soccer on the field below. Ambulances come and go, their sirens faint, eight stories up through double glass.

"You look exhausted," Peter tells her on the third day. "I'll stay and you can go home and sleep in your own bed. If anything changes, I'll call you right away."

But she can't risk it. What if her mother reaches for her? Tears roll down her cheeks, and Peter pulls her onto his lap, wraps her in his arms. His body feels warm, and they lean back together into the reclining chair. They stay like that for a long time, her head resting on his shoulder, and for the first time she falls asleep in his arms, something she has never done before, not with any man.

Later, after Peter leaves, her mother reaches across the bed for Willa's hand, her last words a thin whisper. "Peter loves you."

Her mother's final night on earth, Jonathan texts: *I have to be in Chicago day after tomorrow. Could make a side trip to Minneapolis after?*

She doesn't answer.

Another text comes in an hour later: *???*

Another text after midnight: a photo of a girl in his bed, a girl far too young to be his wife.

Willa turns off her phone, listens to a siren coming closer. Every few hours the nurse gives her mother another morphine drip to help with the pain. Willa watches her mother's face soften, feels her sinking into a place deeper than sleep. She misses her mother already, as if gravity has shifted, lost its center.

Her brother comes the next morning, but he cannot bring himself to kiss his dead mother's cheek. Derek is tall like their father, same long cheeks, bushy blond eyebrows, but unlike their father, he looks disheveled, shirt rumpled and stained, blond hair uncombed.

"Sorry, really sorry, Willa, but I can't stay." He hurries out the door.

Her aunts gather around her. "We're here for you, whatever you need." She promises to see them often.

Later that morning, she enters her apartment alone, doesn't know what to do with herself, whether to sit or lie down. Sunlight spills needles of light across her coffee table, art books piled high, modern furniture bought piece by piece, framed photos on the wall, her senior thesis, black and white photos of alleys in Minneapolis, meant to signify what remains hidden, marginalized, unexplored. Her mother loved these photos, told her she had an eye for finding beauty in places no one else looked. But staring at them now, Willa sees the stark, empty stillness, nothing moving.

ICE BELLS

Her mother's funeral takes place the following Saturday at dusk, and that will always be Willa's sad hour, the hour when she feels a certain terror of what comes next, of not arriving anywhere, of days emptying through her, never landing.

Peter stands beside her at the church, holds her hand, sits between Willa and her brother in the black car following the hearse. Afterward, in her apartment, he holds her in his arms. "I'll stay tonight if you want me to."

Outside the window, she watches clouds pass over, forming shadows that darken buildings. The sun is bright through the window, wind chimes ringing on the neighbor's balcony. Every time the wind wraps around this side of the building, she hears them, but today her mind is a catalogue of losses, and she thinks of ice bells, of sitting beside her mother in the car that day, watching the last ship leave the harbor.

Her breath is tight with sadness. She leans back, rests her weight against Peter. She is tired of holding on to distances. He deserves to know the truth.

She stares into his gray eyes, flecks of sun around the iris. Even before she speaks, she can hear her own voice, words she won't be able to take back. "Only that one time, but I had an orgasm." She watches him flinch, knows it is a risk. She doesn't want him to interpret her orgasm as the most important thing.

"We've been texting, but it's over. I've stopped. I think of him as an ending to that part of my life."

She wants something deeper, something that will catch her.

Peter steps back, shakes his head, and begins to laugh, a deep angry chortle. "Jesus, Willa, I trusted you."

She reaches for his arm, but he pulls free, his whole body bent over, a long deep groan pushing to reach open water.

NEAR MISSES

After a year together, I still hadn't told him I loved him. I'd warned him though. "I have a memory of needing help and not getting it. That's my baseline."

Still, he convinced me to come with him. "Middle of Idaho, most beautiful valley in the world, a great place to spend your thirty-fifth birthday."

We ate dinner late, sitting around wooden tables with men and women who seemed to have plenty of money from jobs that didn't impede fly-fishing vacations.

"Ever fished New Zealand?" Rita passed a platter of roasted chicken on a bed of wild rice. Cropped hair, chapped cheeks, a Scottish accent, she dressed just like her husband—corduroys with embroidered flies, turtleneck, wool sweater with wooden buttons.

Her husband Angus had the ugliest hands I'd ever seen, scarred stubby fingers, one sporting a big turquoise silver ring that grabbed my attention every time he refilled my wineglass. I'd never liked men who wore jewelry, another bias acquired from my mother. I still heard her voice in my head, and sometimes I wondered if it would always be the deepest voice: *Women her age should not wear headbands with painted fish. He talks with his mouth full. I've never understood why Europeans don't get their teeth fixed.* Mostly, I heard her asking, *Why on earth are you dating a man who accepts invitations to private fishing lodges?*

The fly-fishing people all knew each other from other rivers, other fishing camps. "We just got back. Six weeks on the southern tip near Dunedin. Saw the albatross hatching. Bigger than you," Rita said, nodding at me. "Wing span of eleven feet. They can circle the globe in forty-six days, stay at sea for five years."

I felt a kinship to the giant albatross circling the earth.

"They only land for sex," Angus said, with a wink.

She lifted the wine bottle out of his reach. "Drink more water." And, looking at me, "What do you do?"

"Patrol the school lunchroom and playground."

"Jenny teaches." Will pressed his knee into mine under the table. Only spouses and intended spouses were allowed to stay at the lodge. I wore a fake diamond ring he'd bought at Nordstrom Rack. "You should see her apartment, full of books. She graduated from Stanford."

They looked at me differently then, as if I were made of something they'd previously missed. It wasn't who I wanted to be.

"She writes poetry," Will said, smiling at me. "But she won't let anyone read her poems. She keeps them locked in one of those metal cabinets."

"Mental cabinets?" Angus asked, squinting at me.

"*Metal*, like what you have up here." Rita knocked on his head. She looked at me, her small eyes red and watery from fishing all day in the sun. "Ever been published?"

"A few."

Angus smiled. "You should write a poem about me."

"That would be a boring poem." Rita shook her head.

After dinner, Will led me into the lounge and introduced me as his fiancée to Elijah, one of four Mormon sons who ran the fishing camp. Elijah smiled and shook my hand—"Hope you're making yourself at home"—then disappeared into the kitchen. The lounge was a large, oak paneled room spanning the width of the lodge with two fireplaces either end, black leather couches and chairs arranged in constellations, Indian rugs, walnut tables, lamps with painted ducks. Across one wall mounted fish were displayed. "Replicas," Will explained. "We're all catch and release."

Will poured two round glasses of brandy from the row of bottles on the honor bar, then signed our room number on the sheet. "Wouldn't mind being up there someday." He nodded at the wall with Hall of Fame photos, men who'd caught the biggest trout for each decade, starting in 1900. "I love the sense of tradition."

"Really? I find it creepy."

He laughed, his arm circling my shoulders—his ability to listen without taking offense often left me feeling unheard. Upstairs, our room had a view of the mountains and a firm queen bed. I stared out the window, the whole valley a single shade of night. I was turning thirty-five in three days, and I wondered why I was here. Death still felt close—a childhood premonition—and sometimes it clouded my judgment. The lodge had many rules: no cell phones, no televisions, fishermen off the river by sunset, back by dark. But the strangest rule was that guests were not allowed to disclose who had invited them. Will liked having a secret. It turned him on to have me want something from him, to keep me guessing.

"Rita and Angus?" I ran a finger up his thigh. "Donald Heeley, the guy from San Francisco? Was it Heeley?" Each time I tried to narrow it down, he pulled off a piece of my clothing. "Cecil? He doesn't say much . . . Cecil, the bald guy?"

Will made love the way he fished, drawing me closer, backing off, until the line between us was taut. At a certain point, he rolled on top, and our bodies lost their edges.

We lay back, flushed and breathless. Death always felt closer after sex. I stared at his blond curls. I wondered what it meant to *fall* in love, more like lifting something heavy into a smaller space. I wondered if he was too good looking, if his passion for fly-fishing indicated a lack of depth. I could feel the panic rise up inside when I thought of the future, and I did what I always did when the first waves of panic surfaced. I picked him apart in my head, and then I picked apart his older sisters who didn't like me. They said I was a handful. I didn't know why he'd told me.

His body cradled mine. "Tell me a story. One of your near misses." I knew what he was doing. His love was like a toolbelt, and over time he thought he could fix me.

Near Miss #1

I don't remember the farm, except from the photo my parents kept on the mantel, my father standing in a field holding stalks of brightly colored Indian corn. After graduating from NYU, they bought the farm in Minnesota—their niche: decorative organic Indian corn sold to fancy grocery stores around the country.

"When we bought the seed, we didn't realize Indian corn had to be hand-harvested. That's how naive we were." My mother loved to tell this story, "We wanted to be part of the back-to-nature movement. Then we learned the neighbor was a pedophile, a school bus driver before he went to prison."

She explained they never would have known about the pedophile if the pedophile's father, an old farmer who lived across the road, had not come over to warn my parents his son had been released from prison. Nothing he could do about his son, the old farmer told them; he'd served his time and had no place else to go. He told them they should move, and he offered to buy their farm. At first my mother thought maybe he just wanted the land. But one morning the son dropped by, bringing me a wooden doll he'd crafted himself and asking if we needed help harvesting corn. As soon as he left, my mother called the local church, a church she'd never attended. She explained to the pastor she needed someone to tell her if she should sell.

"He's an evil person," the pastor said of the farmer's son. "Sell the farm."

Growing up in Minneapolis in the eighties, my brother and I heard this story many times, how close we'd come to danger, how lucky we were to be spared.

The way my parents talked, it was important to know the truth about things. Life was full of near misses, and the more you knew, the better you could protect yourself.

"Lot of luck in this world." My father always spoke with admiration for the old farmer. "He wasn't afraid to face the truth about his son, painful as it must've been. If it hadn't been for him, I wouldn't have gone to law school, and your mother wouldn't have started the Montessori school."

I listened, seeing two paths—one with tragic consequences, the other unfolding the future, a future that required constant vigilance. Danger lurked everywhere, shuttered windows, men sitting in idling trucks, a babysitter missing a finger on one hand. Each night when my parents read to us in bed, I always wanted to hurry the story forward to the last line, somehow feeling the most brutal endings were the truest ones: *Her eyes were pecked out. Her hands were cut off. She wasted all her wishes.*

Genetics, they'd say now, about children like me, children born seeing what's underneath; more than they can hold inside. Lying in bed each night, I stared at the ceiling fan, knowing it could fall on me at any moment and kill me in my sleep. I slept at the very edge of the bed, slept with one foot on the floor. I was always looking for ways to stop being afraid.

On my eighth birthday, I announced to my parents, "I'm going to die before thirty-five." I thought of death like sleep, a relief from all my worries.

"Why would you say that?" my mother laughed, stirring the cheese into the macaroni. "Every one of your grandparents has made it past eighty."

We were gathered in the kitchen, my five-year-old brother moving his tiny Matchbox ambulance and fire engine underneath the table—"*vroom, vroom*"—driving over my father's shoe, undoing his shoelaces, digging his fingers down into my father's sock, pretending sick people were being evacuated. My father turned the page. "Saving a lot of people down there, Zach?"

"*Vrooom, vroom*," my brother growled, his voice switching to siren noises, "*Ernnnn-nnn, ernnnnnnn-nnnn*."

"Thirty-five, max." I licked leftover frosting from the bowl with my finger, and when my brother stood up and wanted his own lick, I pushed him away. "You're allergic."

My father pulled my brother onto his lap. "Let Zach have a lick. This frosting is made with coconut milk."

My mother smiled at me. "What's your preferred way to die?" Challenging me to think about death before I spoke of it so casually.

"Not by lightning," my father said. "That's what happened to your Uncle Dick when he went to check his boat during a storm."

"Or a long slow illness." My mother glanced next door where our neighbor Sarah, diagnosed with MS, had recently put in a wheelchair-accessible ramp.

Death by imagination became my parents' method for leaning into my fears, a method my brother exploited as he grew older, imagining death scenarios and pestering me to choose. "One, plane crash over the ocean. Two, sinking in a bog while mosquitoes bite your face. Three, falling through ice on a frozen lake."

Six a.m., mountains blue in the distance, moon a faint sliver across the valley, Will stood midstream ten feet away, trying to decipher ripples, whether fish were rising.

"Do you think I should go back to school and get my MA?" I asked.

Glancing up, he smiled. "You think too much. Watch the water. I think you have a big one."

Judging by his wide grin and the lack of movement near my fly, he was referring to himself.

I sat on a rock and rested my arm. "Don't you think catch and release is a little cruel? What if someone were dangling food in front of you and, driven by hunger, you bit it, then were pulled out of your most secure place, your natural habitat, only to be unhooked and thrown back. I'd never bite again."

"Wouldn't the fish appreciate his freedom more?"

"I think the fish will live the rest of his life with anxiety and fear of making the wrong choice." I'd been a psychology major in college. "Negative experience forms grooves in our brains much faster than positive experience. You have to actually reaffirm positive experience several times before it overrides the flight and fear response in the brain."

Will sloshed through the water, removed his brimmed hat, and kissed me. "I'm making new grooves in your brain."

"Too bad you have your waders on." I patted the rubbery material.

"I won't tonight." He turned and waded back into the current, working his rod back and forth so that when he finally released the line, the fly landed exactly where it was supposed to, a pool of still water surrounded by rocks. "See? It's all in the wrist."

The sun was on his back. Aspen leaves shimmered in the wind, like the rising and falling of whispers. The current splashed steadily. I saw how happy he was standing in the middle of the river, blond curls visible beneath his brimmed hat, eyes shaded, all his senses tuned to the movement of water, as if it were right there, everything he needed to be happy.

I remembered the first time Will came to my apartment. He stared at the stacks of books. "You've read all these?"

"Most."

"Smells like books." His nose crinkled. He stared at Henrietta's photos on my refrigerator. "How old was she?"

"Fourteen."

"Old, in dog years."

He didn't tell me she had great ears. He didn't say she had a great face.

I didn't know why it still bothered me.

When I told him I'd rather have a dog than a child, he looked at me with disbelief. "Maybe you haven't met the right man."

"Maybe I've met too many men."

He studied me, his blue eyes unwavering, then glanced at the photos of famous bridges spread across my kitchen table. "This for your class?"

"We're doing bridges this week. Bridge as metaphor. Language bridges, thought bridges, time bridges. We'll write poems in the shape of the bridges."

He frowned. "You're not building anything?"

Even then, our words were parallel flights, thousands of feet apart.

Near Miss #2

I transferred to Stanford my sophomore year of college, 1997, the same year the Moonies abducted two coeds. They didn't say they were Moonies. They said they were the transitional housing committee, and they had a big farm thirteen miles from campus with extra rooms for students. The transitional housing committee consisted of two girls and a boy who wore shorts and Stanford t-shirts and looked like us, like transfer students. The boy had dimples and deep blue eyes. "Free rooms in exchange for chores. Anyone interested should be here tomorrow morning, nine a.m. We have a van that will pick you up, and you can come tour the farm and then we'll bring you back."

Stanford had sent a letter explaining there might not be enough on-campus housing for all the transferees, and we should be prepared to find off-campus apartments. Gathered on the lawn for the welcome-picnic, a student rock band playing on stage, I sat in group D with Elizabeth and Mary, from Iowa and Wisconsin, Midwesterners like me. The TA, Monica, had an artificial leg fully displayed below white shorts, metal knee-hinge glinting in the sun. "Welcome, everyone. We'll begin by going around and introducing ourselves. I'm Monica Talbet from Anchorage, Alaska. I'm a senior, majoring in psychology."

"I'm Lee Hwang. From L.A. Political Science major."

"I'm Cindy Carston. Seattle. Pre-med."

Eleven of us, defining ourselves by where we were from, what we wanted to do. Until we reached Greg, who raised his dark glasses so we could see his bloodshot eyes. "I'm Greg. I'm a vet." He held up his wallet displaying a photo of himself in Marine uniform with a shaggy-haired girl. "I'm Miggy's boyfriend. She's over there. A Junior." He nodded at a girl with huge breasts working behind the table. "Fucking gorgeous, isn't she?"

Mary leaned close and whispered, "Is he supposed to be here?"

"Transfer law student," Greg shot back, his eyes drilling into us as if he'd been trained to hear whispers across distances.

"Nice to meet you, Greg." Monica moved her gaze to the next person.

The idea of the picnic was to make friends and find potential roommates. The tables and band were set up in a roped-off section of the quad. Two huge tables stood on one side of the lawn, and as soon as platters of sandwiches and salads arrived, the groups disbanded, some students hurrying to get in line, while the rest of us waited, sprawled on the grass, trying to figure out the best options for housing.

The transitional housing committee approached our group, circulating photos of a beautiful white mansion on a hill. The girls had their hair pulled back in ponytails. The boy smiled through smudged glasses. "We're here to support you in finding housing. We can answer all your questions."

"What kind of chores would we have to do?" Mary asked. "I'm on a swimming scholarship so I have to be here at six-thirty every morning."

"That wouldn't be a problem," the blonde girl said. "Someone could drop you off. And you could do your chores on weekends."

"In exchange for free rent?" I asked.

The other girl nodded. "We love it there."

"We're a family." The boy's forehead glistened with sweat. "You should come tomorrow and visit."

After lunch, Greg and I joined the students dancing on the lawn. Between songs, the transitional housing committee approached me with their sign-up sheet.

"Your friends said you're interested?"

I had planned to sign up with Elizabeth and Mary, but Greg waved the clipboard away. "Plenty of fucking housing if you're patient." He nodded at the street lined with dormitories. "Just give them time to figure out who flunked out and who's on mental leave of absence."

A month later, *Time* put their faces on the cover of the magazine, Elizabeth and Mary, the girls who were abducted. The article said they were brainwashed, kept from sleeping for forty-eight hours, kept dancing and chanting day and night. When their parents finally were allowed to speak to them over the phone, their daughters said they didn't want to leave the Moonie farm, didn't want to see them. A year later, there was another article about how their parents hired former military Green Berets to kidnap them back. Stanford began issuing warnings during every orientation not to leave campus with strangers.

I kept the *Time* article in my suitcase under my bed. Sometimes, I took it out and stared at the photos—probably a reporter had climbed a tree—blurry images taken from a distance, women leaning over garden rows, scarves around their heads. I wondered if Elizabeth and Mary were happy, or if they'd been emptied of themselves and maybe happiness didn't matter anymore. I wondered if they were allowed to be friends, sharing a room, whispering late at night. I thought about Mary's wasted swimming scholarship, her huge arm muscles, whether she could figure out a way to escape. I wondered if they dreamed about their parents when they were asleep and woke with feelings they had to hide. Maybe they had fallen in love with Moonie men, were pregnant with Moonie babies. The article said Reverend Moon assigned spouses and did mass marriages twice a year.

"I knew those girls who were kidnapped," I told my parents the Sunday after it happened. "I was sitting with them at the picnic. I almost signed up."

"You're smarter than that," my mother said. "Listen, honey, we just got back from your brother's hockey tournament. Can we call you back tomorrow night? We still haven't unloaded the car."

The Mormon wives were good cooks, and dinner at the lodge was served family style at long tables—platters of trout, green beans, pilaf, cornbread, blackberry pie for dessert.

"If you eat trout, why do you throw them back?" I asked, glancing at the platter of Trout Almondine being passed around the table.

"These are farm-raised," Rita said, picking a bone from her mouth with two fingers. "Sustainable. Keeps the sport alive."

Angus looked at me. "I agree with you. We should be allowed to keep one."

Rita glanced sideways at her husband. "You'd cheat."

Angus smiled and shrugged.

They talked about restoring wetlands in the same breath as the stock market, my judgments about the fishing camp's exclusivity confirmed and challenged. I was surprised on the third night when John talked about going to the moon. A former astronaut in his early sixties, he spoke with a slight southern accent, an educated lilt. Square jaw, graying hair, ruddy skin, he told us about *the overview effect,* a theory of profound change that happened to astronauts in outer space.

"You look at Earth from out there and it changes your heart." He spoke softly, with a kind of reverence. "You understand how small and fragile our planet is, how important every part is, *every* living thing—plants, insects, oceans, and rivers."

Will reached his hand under the table and held my hand.

"Does it leave, that feeling?" I asked.

"No, it doesn't." John smiled. "It's the closest thing to God. That oneness."

After dinner, in our room, I sat on the edge of the bed. "I want the overview-effect in my life."

Will began pulling off my pants, waiting for me to guess who had invited him, but I was tired of the game. "I hope it wasn't Rita."

He pulled off my socks. "You should be nicer to her. She invented a fly rod for women."

I undid my bra. "Why do women need a different fly rod?"

"Smaller wrists. It's shorter and lighter. I'll get you one."

"No, don't," I said, my tone harsher than intended.

He stopped undressing me and silently pulled me onto the bed, his movements infused with anger, a little rough, confident, the way I liked. Our bodies instinctually opened to each other. It confused me, all the realities that co-existed, flesh and bone sparking heat that expanded beyond the limits of feeling. He clutched so hard I could feel his heart beating. Afterward, as we lay breathing side by side, feet and hands touching, our physical closeness disturbed me, the way my body could separate from my heart.

"We belong together," Will whispered. "I don't know why you can't accept that and let our bodies do what they're meant to do."

"Don't ever tell a woman what her body is meant to do."

"That's not what I meant." He pulled me closer, his body cupping mine. "I love you."

I felt cruel, not saying anything back, but also safer. I suspected this trip meant something different to him, and lying there in the dark, I was glad I'd paid my own way.

He fell asleep first. I lay awake, facing the window. His feet were sticking out from under the blanket. I wondered how much feeling was enough. *You'll know when you meet the right one.* My mother said this about a boy I was dating who wore sandals to my cousin's bat mitzvah. Her advice changed when I hit thirty: *Nobody's perfect. You're not getting any younger.*

Near Miss #3

Two months before graduation, I started thinking about death again. Counting down to thirty-five eased the anxiety I felt as my friends waved letters of acceptance—Peace Corps, graduate school, internships in Washington, D.C.

"What are your plans after graduating?" my mother kept asking when I called home Sunday nights. My father spoke on the other extension. "You should be sending out applications. You're graduating in two months."

One afternoon during finals, I opened my email and found a letter from Sherri, a Stanford friend who had graduated a semester early. She was in Spain on a junior Fulbright, writing poems about Gitano still living in caves. Her letter said, *Come to Spain. You can stay with me. I have my own cave.*

I called my parents and told them I thought Spanish would really widen my employment opportunities. My brother was premed at Carlton, and my parents often complained our tuitions were going to push back their retirement by at least a decade. They were so glad that I was thinking realistically about the future, they immediately offered to pay for two months of language study in Spain as a graduation present.

By the time I arrived in Malaga six weeks later, Sherri had moved out of her cave. "The bats returned," she said, pushing the scarf up her forehead. "Besides, the Gitano family needed my cave back, so I decided to study tango with what's left of my Fulbright. I might write a book about tango, instead."

Every day while I studied Spanish at language school, Sherri tangoed at the dance school next door. At night we went to a nearby disco where women danced alone in front of mirrors while men watched them from the bar. Only later, when the men were drunk, did they actually approach us, pressing their groins against us, kissing our necks.

Sherri became a big thing at the bar. Tango lessons had freed her body. She had a word for it, for the sexiness she felt when she danced. *Duende.* All the men wanted to dance with her. But she preferred to dance alone. Men doused in sweet cologne, wearing white and tan suits, reached into their pockets and placed bets on who would finally get lucky. One of the waitresses spoke English and warned her, "Don't dance with anyone, because if you do there will be a fight."

No one bet on me. I studied my friend's sexiness, which was hard to copy—her wild curly hair and blousy shirts with tie-strings at the top. Mostly, it had to do with her not caring about the men. They could sense that about her. They could sense she wasn't dancing for them. She was dancing for herself. I could see that made them want her more than anything, made her absolutely necessary to them.

I wanted to be absolutely necessary to someone.

I am sure he thought me an easy conquest. In those days, American girls had a terrible reputation. He was handsome in a rough way, ravaged skin, intense blue eyes, a scar across his chin that deepened when he smiled. I liked to feel his arms circle my waist, pulling me against him. I asked him questions, but his Spanish was a dialect incomprehensible to me.

He danced with me three nights in row. The third night, I let him lead me down the street to a seedy hotel not too far away from the house where I was living with Sherri and two Russian women. I did not see myself as promiscuous. I was willing to search high and low for that one great love that would make all the other choices fall away.

The room was sparsely furnished, little more than a creaky bed with faded linen. As he undressed, he leaned over and unstrapped a gun he carried around his ankle. He did the same with the other ankle, positioning one gun on the chair, the other on the bed table. He did not explain and I didn't ask, but it was clear to me he had positioned the guns at particular angles in case someone burst through the door. I understood he was either a policeman or a gangster, and given the recent reports about police corruption, I wasn't sure there was any difference.

The Spanish man told me I was too wet down there. He wanted me to be drier. He kept taking the sheet and wiping me between the legs, interrupting sex to wipe again, and each time I felt ashamed of my own excitement. He not only wanted me to be dry but also quiet. He took off his condom and when I began to protest, he told me, “Silencio!” After being told to stay dry and shut up, I lay like a corpse, and that is when he became really excited.

Long after he rolled onto his back and fell asleep, I lay staring at his face, half-lit from the streetlight outside the window, eyes like black caves. Why was I here? Why was I in Spain? Why was I in bed with a man who strapped guns to his legs? I could possibly die in this room. He might kill me or someone might come and kill both of us. I couldn’t move from the bed, not even to use the bathroom. I was afraid he might wake up and, thinking me an intruder, shoot at the bathroom.

The next morning, I left while he was in the shower. I didn’t go back to the disco, didn’t get my language certificate. At the American Express agency, I exchanged my return plane ticket for a standby ticket, then I waited at the airport for two days, going gate to gate, hoping for a seat, until a KLM Airline attendant took pity on me and found me a flight with three layovers that would get me home in twenty-eight hours.

“I know you’re awake.” Will kissed my forehead. “Happy birthday.”

Thunder rolled across the sky, and a minute later, rain pelted the roof and window. “Best weather for fishing.” He reached into his duffle, unfolding a poncho. “I brought you rain gear.”

I snuggled deeper under the blankets. “I might stay in today and read.”

He looked disappointed. “I’ll be gone all day. You sure?”

I nestled under the covers. "Positive."

After he left the room, I stood at the window, watching him disappear into a stand of aspens. The poncho was draped over his backpack, making him look like a hunchback, except for his athletic walk, a bounce to his step, even in mud.

I fell back asleep. When the maid, a young pregnant Mormon wife wanting to clean the room, knocked, I quickly dressed. I found a corner in the lounge where I could read near the fire. But as soon as I opened my book, Angus came up and sat in the big leather chair across from me. He placed a bottle of whiskey between us on the table, big stubby finger to his lips—*"shsssh"*—nodding at Rita across the room, playing bridge with Mary and Keith and John. "I'm on a short leash after yesterday." He opened the bottle. "Fell asleep by the river. Vultures circled above. Rita followed them to me."

"That was you?" I didn't encourage him, but I didn't stop him from pouring either. "We saw the vultures."

Reaching for a handful of peanuts from the bowl, he scattered a few into his mouth. "You want to be a member?"

"If it's important to Will," I said, imagining what a good fiancée would say.

"You don't seem like the fly-fishing type." Angus took a big gulp of whiskey and smiled. "You remind me of our daughter."

"Where does she live?"

He stared into his glass. "Died eight years ago. Pancreatic cancer." His knee moved up and down. "Our son-in-law took our grandkids and moved to Nova Scotia." He lifted his gaze. "He's a Buddhist. Nova Scotia's filled with Buddhists, did you know that?

'Do no harm,' he tells the kids." Angus shook his head. "Wasn't thinking about us."

"I'm sorry for your loss," I said, staring at his hand swirling whiskey in his glass.

Angus coughed, his eyes settling on my fake diamond ring. "I hope you're not going to break his heart."

Near Miss #4

I found a job as a classroom assistant and took night classes to get my teaching certificate. I lived in a studio apartment in a sketchy part of Minneapolis. At first, I thought it was a coincidence—the man was always near my mailbox whenever I entered the building. Late thirties, black curls, jeans and sweat-shirt, maybe the janitor or building engineer. *Gleglllellllelll.* That's how he sounded. Maybe he was learning disabled or had a speech impediment. I nodded politely and hurried away, pulling Henrietta's leash, but Henrietta resisted my pull until he gave her a treat.

Same thing the next day. "*Gllellllegllll.*"

I began varying the time I checked my mailbox, and sometimes I avoided checking my mailbox for two or three days. But he was always there, dog treats in hand for Henrietta. "*Glllellleglllll,*" he'd say, scratching behind her ears, feeding her treats.

One day I parked a block away and searched the windows overlooking the parking lot. He was in the stairwell window, big smile on his face, waving to me.

Ray, the building manager, lived in the basement. He always

seemed impatient with me. I had complained twice about my Murphy bed getting stuck and not being able to fold it into the wall.

"You try oil?"

When I shook my head, he threw up his hands. "Well, try some, and if it doesn't work, I'll loosen the screws."

His wife did laundry for the old people in the building. Their apartment always smelled like bleach. Every time I went to the basement to get my bike from the storage room, I could hear their television blaring soap operas inside the apartment. I had to knock loudly to be heard.

Ray opened the door. "*Another* problem?"

"There's this guy in the building who's always waiting by the mailboxes—"

"Brad?"

"I'm wondering if he's safe."

Ray laughed, "Yeah, he's safe. Retired cop. Been here six years."

"He seems drunk."

Ray scowled, jowls pressed to his neck. "Punks cut out his tongue in some kind of drug bust. Got disability now. Believe me, he's harmless."

I felt like Ray wasn't listening. I was afraid to come home, afraid to get my mail, afraid to use the stairs and elevator for fear of running into him. "He's always, *always* there . . . I get the feeling he's waiting for me."

Ray shrugged. "I'll have a conversation with him."

Brad stopped waiting by the mailboxes, and I didn't see him for a few days. A week later the elevator doors opened, and he was there, riding up from the basement. He smiled at Henrietta but didn't say anything to me. He backed up to the wall to make room for us. He was careful not to speak or stand too close. I kept my back to him the whole way up, hairs on my neck and arms rigid, Henrietta's tail wagging as she waited for him to give her a treat. When I got off, I turned to make sure he wasn't getting off too, and he flashed me a peace sign.

A few days later, I woke and heard a scraping sound. Henrietta lay collapsed on the floor, gasping for air. I pulled on blue jeans, sweatshirt, and slip-ons and carried her to the elevator. Brad was parking his SUV, just home from his job as night security guard. He saw me trying to lift her into the car and took her in his arms, nodding at me to drive. He sat with her in the backseat, speaking softly the whole way, "*Gliieggh, gliieggh.*"

The vet took x-rays. "She's got a huge mass in her lungs. She's bleeding out."

I stood next to the table where Henrietta lay, sedated, eyelids fluttering closed. I stroked the little ridges behind her ears, and when her tail stayed limp, I took that to be a vote for a painless end.

The phone was ringing when I entered my apartment an hour later. I thought it might be the veterinarian calling to tell me Henrietta hadn't died after all. She'd actually fought off death because she loved me so much. That thought crossed my mind.

"What's wrong?" my mother asked. "I can hear it in your voice."

"I had to put Henrietta to sleep this morning. She couldn't breathe."

"Oh honey, I'm so sorry. I'll call you another time. I have something I need to talk to you about."

"What is it, Mom?"

She hesitated. "We can't take another Minnesota winter. We bought a condo in Florida."

I held the receiver away from my ear—my childhood home, the place I could return to holidays, birthdays, if I got cancer.

"You sound far away," she said.

"No, I'm here."

"You better set up a time with your brother to come over and decide what you each want. The house is going on the market next month."

"Where would I put anything?" My voice trembled. "I live in one room. I have no space."

After I hung up, I hugged Henrietta's reindeer. My life felt weightless, no head resting on my lap, no tail wagging by the door. I stared out the window—rain spots and dust from road construction. For a year, they'd been rebuilding the highway entrance ramp below my window.

I heard a knock on the door. Brad was standing next to a little girl. She handed me a drawing she'd made of Henrietta. "Daddy and me are sorry your dog died." I put the picture on my refrigerator next to Henrietta's photo.

In the days and weeks after Henrietta's death, some part of me died too. I went to work, came home, and slept. Brad and his daughter came by often in the late afternoon, bringing soup and casseroles and homemade pumpkin bread. Brad's daughter, Ellie, stayed with her father two nights a week and every other weekend. He was careful to come only when his daughter was with him. She was a chatty little girl, not nervous at all, and she interpreted her father's speech for me. "Daddy and me are going to Costco. Do you need anything?"

I began to notice his muscular build, black curls, shiny brown eyes. He always smelled good in an ironed button-down shirt and jeans. I also began to understand his way of speaking, and after a month, I didn't need his daughter to explain. I wondered if I could love a man without a tongue. I searched on my computer: *tongue transplants*. It had worked once or twice, but in each case the patient's immune system had to be suppressed so the transplant wouldn't be rejected. Apparently infections set in, too many nerve endings, complicated by the mouth's unsterile environment.

One night, after his daughter had gone to bed, we sat in his apartment watching reruns of *Frazier*. Maybe it was the wine, and maybe it was the smell of his soap. I stroked his arm. He sat very still for a moment, and then he leaned in to kiss me. That's when I panicked, wondering if we could have rules—no kissing, no mouth-related intimacy. He must have felt me recoil, his body going rigid.

I sat back. "Could we just not kiss?"

His eyes grew hard, unblinking, and he opened his mouth wide, as if he wasn't going to hide who he was or feel ashamed. I refused to look and stood up, hurrying toward the door. I felt deeply ashamed of my behavior, asking myself why a tongue was so important, telling myself I should have figured out my own feelings before I ruined our friendship. Two weeks later he moved out. When I saw him loading a U-Haul in the parking lot, I went outside to apologize and to see if I could help, but he walked past me, back and forth, carrying boxes, as if I weren't there.

The rain stopped. Evening fog settled over the tops of trees. The grandfather clock on the landing bonged seven times. I went downstairs and poured myself a glass of wine, then found Caleb, the youngest Mormon brother, behind the front desk. "Have you seen Will? He hasn't come back to the room yet."

He glanced at his watch. "Let's give it a little longer."

But a half hour later, Will still hadn't returned. The four brothers gathered flashlights, pulled on waders. Rita stood beside me, nodding at Emmett, who was checking his square duffle for supplies. "He's the local EMT."

I headed into the lounge to pour myself another glass of wine. Upstairs, I sat on the bed and drank the wine fast. A year ago, we'd met under a meteor shower. A sales rep for Patagonia outdoor clothing, Will had offered me space on his thermal blanket. He'd also brought a thermos of hot cider, ginger cookies, and bug spray. I hadn't met many men well prepared for life.

Afterward, he had invited me to his apartment in a new building, *Seven-Fifty*, each apartment seven-hundred-fifty square feet. One wall was covered with photographs, rivers he'd fished all over the world: Ireland, Chile, Nova Scotia, Argentina. In the corner of each photo, he'd inscribed the name of the fly he'd used—*Gold Ribbed Hare's Ear*, *Royal Wulff*, *Sparkle Dun*, *Black Ghost*. Standing in front of floor-to-ceiling windows, I'd stared at traffic below, surprised it was so quiet inside. I'd hoped the double windows were bird-proof, but I didn't say so. For years, my mother had been chiding me, *Nobody likes Debbie Downer.*

Two months later, he had handed me the invitation embossed with a single gold trout leaping across the top of the card. "It's kind of a big deal, getting an invitation. You have to fish ten of the world's best streams before you get invited. Only members and guests of members are allowed. You should come with me."

"Seriously? A fishing frat?" I'd opened the card, four nights in September at Temperance River Lodge, signed *The Board*. "That's my thirty-fifth birthday." I'd told him about my childhood premonition. "Not sure I want to travel that weekend."

He'd laughed. "Not many people die fly-fishing."

Now, hours after he was due back, I remembered his words. I heard a knock. Angus had that old man way of noisy breathing, breath filtering through too many nose-hairs. "They're back."

They'd wrapped Will, naked, in a thermal blanket, carried him on a stretcher. His clothes were wet, and they handed them to Becca, one of the wives, to wash and dry. His eyes were closed, and when I took his hand, he squeezed my fingers. "I'm sorry. I ruined your birthday."

"He's been in water for hours," Emmett explained. "Maybe lightning, maybe he fell and hit his head. His vitals are fine. We could take him to the hospital, but it's a three-hour drive. If it's a concussion, they'll just send him home. You'll need to wake him up every two hours. We need to get him warm. Room next to yours has a bathtub. We'll get him into a hot bath and bring him a stiff drink. Does he have a spare set of pajamas?"

"A sweat-suit. I'll get it."

The velvet box was tucked inside the folded sweat-suit. Inside was a gold ring. I stared at the amber stone, feeling the same panic I always felt when I imagined making Will happy, giving him the life he wanted. Maybe I had used up all my innocence. Maybe I had run out of wishes. Maybe something inside me was missing, like those hollow chocolate bunnies that crumbled when you took a bite.

I didn't tell him I'd found it. I knelt down next to the tub, sponging away the dirt and sand, streaks of blood along his hairline. His cheek was beginning to darken into a bruise. I moved the warm washcloth over his shoulders, around his neck, and he reached up and took my wrist. "Take off your clothes. Come in here with me." I undressed and climbed in, the water rising to our shoulders. He cupped my body from behind, his inhale pressing into my back. "Rita and Angus," he whispered, his chin on my shoulder. "Next time we'll go wherever you want. No fishing, I promise."

It's hard to shed our stories enough to feel something new.

My mother used to say, "Be careful what you wish for." She said this standing next to my father who was tearing up kitchen linoleum to put in hardwood, uncovering four layers underneath.

My mother also said, "You wait too long, the good ones are gone." But then she added, "There's someone for everyone. But that's not necessarily a good thing."

Recently she told me, "My friends who live alone have very full lives." Her voice grew soft. "Anyway, we all end up alone sooner or later. Believe me, your father's memory isn't what it used to be. I have to give him a list every day."

I worried she saw things in me I couldn't see.

I'd never told her about Will. I knew what she'd say. "That's a career? Selling jackets and sleeping bags?"

By the time we returned to our room, they'd delivered a cake and champagne in a bucket of ice. Will reached into the drawer and took out the velvet box. "Happy birthday. Thirty-five and you're still alive."

I felt the same emptiness I always felt when I realized I might not die soon, and I had my whole life ahead of me. I could feel it rising up, coming toward me, air trapped inside a huge wave. Maybe this was the emptiness we all shared, made of our own choices, imbued with our own meanings. Possibly, love was a matter of translation. Or needed something to adhere to, like pollen or commitment.

I took off the fake diamond ring and held out my hand, letting him slide the new ring onto my finger. I thought how easy it would be to marry a man I didn't love, marry for reasons more important than love. I set the alarm for two hours. I listened to the river's distant rush, moths batting wings against the screen, Will breathing next to me. I lay awake a long time, asking, *What is love anyway?*

All my life I had been inventing ways not to be afraid.

My toes were cold, and I pressed them between Will's warm legs.

WINNING

A certain kind of freedom only happens once.

Across the street, across horizons of highway, windswept hills calculated by longing. No place else to go with it, except forward, and the forwardness was my own. I was thirteen. I needed to believe in my own possibilities. I hadn't yet accepted the ordinary.

Each morning I left the house on my bike, descending the steep hill through St. Mary's Hospital parking lot, crossing Second Street, past smaller houses, shaded yards, until I reached the dead end—Rochester Outdoor Tennis Club.

It wasn't a *clubby*-club. Anybody could join as long as you paid the small monthly fee and followed the rules—tennis shoes on the courts, voices lowered in the bleachers, phones turned off, handshakes after a match.

I parked my bike next to Randy's blue Saab, as close as I could without actually touching, as if my bike and his car were commencing our relationship. I could hear his voice out on the court. "Keep your eye on the ball, ladies." I waited for the juniors' practice to begin, my headphones blasting Mariah Carey's "We Belong Together." I hummed it, believing in telepathic communication, believing if I hummed and stared at Randy, I could stir his cells in my direction with my thoughts. On the courts, old women played doubles, arms browned and loose like tea bags, dogs barking in the park, fire lilies edging the fence, balls bouncing back and forth.

The clubhouse smelled like resin and new tennis balls. Two

refrigerated vending machines buzzed along the wall—one for sodas, one for snacks. The showers were cement block squares with a drain in the middle, plastic curtain in front, one each, men's and women's locker rooms. I fed quarters into the machine to buy grape soda, a cold bottle to hold to my forehead between games. I lived on Salted Nut Rolls, pretzels, frozen Snickers from the freezer in the pro's office. Chairs lined the three-sided porch, but I preferred to sit in the bleachers that overlooked the courts. Large oaks kept them shaded, and I could see all eight courts if I sat high up.

Home from Stanford for the summer, Randy demonstrated how to volley, his voice carrying from the court. "Knees bent, Mrs. G."

"My artificial knee bends better than my arthritic one," Mrs. G. called back.

From my perch on the bleachers, I admired Randy's muscled biceps, copper skin, red curls under the brim of his visor. I heard the nearby trill of songbirds, clatter of empty bottles in the bed of the soda delivery truck. Further away, trucks beeped on Highway 52, laying tar. Occasionally, we heard the drone of medical helicopters coming closer, delivering patients or transplant organs to St. Mary's Hospital two blocks away. The blades made a wind. The women on court waited to serve until the helicopters passed overhead.

At ten a.m., Randy announced, "Juniors," and we took our seats on the first two rows of the bleachers, seventeen girls between the ages of twelve and fourteen, junior ladder tennis players, waiting to be paired for our matches. Winners moved up the rungs and played other winners. Losers moved up, too, only more slowly, playing other losers.

"Visualization is a huge part of tennis," Randy explained. "You can do almost anything if you put your mind to it. This is where tennis becomes more than a game. It can become a method for training your mind."

He told us two stories, one about a prisoner of war who visualized playing golf while in captivity, and after he was freed, became a champion golf player. Another one about a woman who was paralyzed from a boat accident but visualized herself swimming. Eventually she swam across the Hudson River.

"There are two kinds of practice. Out there," he nodded at the courts. Then, tapping his head, "And up here. Up here is more important because there will always be great players, but the difference is mindset, your ability to concentrate and be fully present, moment to moment, so you don't undermine yourself with doubt." He paused, "Okay, close your eyes."

Most of the time when he led us through these visualizations, I was the last to open my eyes. I always added more, more than perfect serves and great backhands, more than winning. I visualized Randy falling in love with me.

"You done, Julie?" he asked. "Ready to play?"

Any time I caught his attention, I believed my visualizations were working.

Every day at noon, Joey Picciannini sat behind me on the bleachers eating his lunch. I didn't know him personally. He was an adult, my parents' age, forties maybe. I assumed he was a family member of one of the patients at St. Mary's. He started showing up, sitting under the big oak shading the top of the bleachers, sports coat folded neatly on the bleacher next to him. Often, he leaned back, his beefy arms sprawled on the seat behind him. Flat nose, pockmarked cheeks, shiny black hair combed back with gel, so I could see the grooves when the sun hit his head. "Hey, kid, you like potato chips?" He held out a bag.

"No thank you." I was hesitant to talk to strangers.

"Keep it for later," he insisted, holding the bag out to me.

I took it and thanked him.

"You good at tennis?"

"Not really."

"Can't think like that." He leaned forward, his huge gold ring glinting in the sun. "I ask, You good? You say, Yeah, I'm the best."

"Tanya Ellison beat me last year. She's better."

"Yeah?"

I nodded, watching the older girls hit balls back and forth. "She practices against her garage all day. Her brothers won state doubles last year."

When I went inside to get a grape soda, the assistant tennis coach Meghan asked me, "You know that guy?"

"No." I glanced at Joey Picciannini reading the newspaper on the bleachers.

"Sounds like a thug." She mimicked his Chicago accent. "Wheyse the batt-room?" She stared at him. "Let me know if he's bothering you, okay?"

Joey Picciannini always kept a safe distance, two rows behind me near the top. His suit was a brighter version of navy, his black shoes shiny, and he always wore a black t-shirt and dark glasses. Every day he brought turkey on rye with mayo and lettuce. "My diet," he said, "turkey instead of pastrami." He talked with his mouth full.

"My father," pronounced *fadduh*, "died of a heart attack when he was forty-two." Each day he handed me the bag of chips that came with his sandwich. "Gotta watch my weight. Italians are the longest living people, but not if they eat pastrami."

He offered me the dill pickle but I shook my head. "No thank you."

"Good manners," he nodded. "Wish you could teach my kids."

He often brought magazines—*National Geographic*, *Time*, *Sports Illustrated*—paging through them when the matches were boring. Once, he showed me a photo of his wife and kids. His wife had thick black hair pinned on top of her head, pretty eyes. His kids looked like him, round faces, flat noses, wide-set eyes. The girl had bows in her hair, and the boy's hair was greased back like his father's. They were standing by a Christmas tree surrounded by presents. "Spoiled rotten," he told me.

Meghan didn't like Joey Picciannini. She gave him dark looks when she took the beginner groups onto the court. She called him *Mr. Pedo* behind his back. After a couple of weeks, she approached him. "Do you play tennis? Or do you just come to watch."

"Might wanna' play. I'm thinkin' about it." He shrugged. "Relaxes me to watch."

"Seems like you have a lot of time to watch."

"Yeah, I do."

She folded her arms across her chest, stared him in the eye. "Well it's a free country."

Joey Picciannini smiled. "Yeah, it is."

He showed up the next day wearing white shorts and Lacoste t-shirt. His arms and legs were covered with thick black hair. "Champ," he started calling me. "I was thinking you could give me a lesson."

"I'm not good enough."

"Sure you are. I'll pay you."

I stared at his brand-new racket, brand-new can of balls, brand-new white tennis shoes. Even then, thirteen years old, I was always alert to the first sign of loss, my own or someone else's. Joey Picciannini was losing something too. I felt his sadness—the way he looked out at the courts not because he loved tennis, but because he needed something to distract him from his own life.

"Okay, first you have to learn to control the ball." I bounced the ball off the strings of my racket.

He tried to imitate me, but the ball kept flying off.

"Smaller movements." I kept bouncing, even after I closed my eyes.

"Show-off," he said, his big arms tensed as he tried again and failed.

I changed tactics. I showed him how to grip the racket and bounce the ball on asphalt. But his muscled arms couldn't make the small repetitive movements, and after five minutes, he was sweating and out of breath. "Enough, champ."

I laughed. "Meghan taught me. She's really good with beginners. You should take lessons from her."

WINNING

Joey Picciannini signed up for three privates from Meghan.

"Picks up his own balls at least," Meghan told me after his first lesson. She tucked her blonde bangs inside her visor, pulled down the tennis skirt that rode up her wide hips. "Not like some men." She nodded at Dr. Nesbith zipping his racket into the cover, "Like I'm his ball boy, right? Like he can't break a sweat?"

Joey Picciannini rarely sent a ball over the net, and when he did, turned and raised his racket to me, a victory sign. I clapped from the bleachers.

Afterward, he took a shower in the men's locker room and put on his regular clothes. Then he'd climb the bleacher to the top row behind me. "Whadda' 'ya think?"

"Much better."

"Yeah?"

"Yeah."

I didn't tell my parents about Joey Picciannini. There was already enough tension in our house.

"Wash your hands." My father turned a page of his newspaper when I came in from the garage and set down my racket before dinner.

My mother handed me a paper towel. "Your father has had a rough day, a girl your sister's age with an inoperable brain tumor."

"Can anyone get a brain tumor?" I felt a throbbing behind my right ear. "Could I get a brain tumor?"

"Not this kind. It's inherited." He spoke from behind the newspaper.

"Did her mother or father have a brain tumor?" I always wanted to know my chances. My father was an oncologist. We talked about illness the way other people discussed weather.

"Her grandfather." My father turned the page.

Outside, my sister's boyfriend revved his motorcycle up the hill into our driveway, delivering Annie home for dinner. My father hated motorcycles. He referred to Jared's motorcycle as a *death wish.* He referred to Jared as a *future organ donor*, and he told my sister she was foolish for riding behind him.

Seconds later, Annie entered the door, smelling of cigarettes. "What's with the donkey?"

We all looked up from what we were doing. My first thought was she's on drugs, hallucinatory drugs.

"On the front lawn," my sister nodded, "tied to the tree. A real, live donkey eating Mom's wild grasses."

We hurried outside. We lived on Plummer Circle, a quiet residential street, Craftsman bungalows and mid-century modern homes, sprinklers pulsing rhythmically to keep the grass green, flowers blooming.

"Donkeys are mean," Jared said, straddling his motorcycle.

My parents ignored him. They were barely on speaking terms with Jared.

The donkey was tethered to the lamp post—long ears, short legs, sloped back, tail swishing away flies. My little brother Billy ran around it, braying "*heee-haw, heeeh-haw*," causing the donkey to lift its head, flatten its ears, pull back its lips.

"Stop running, Billy," my mother called to him. "You're getting her excited."

Jared laughed, and climbing off his motorcycle, wrapped his arms around my sister's waist.

"Is this from that mafia guy?" My sister leaned back against Jared. "He gives my parents really expensive gifts."

My father glared at her. We weren't supposed to talk about his patients outside the family.

My mother looked up and down the street. "How do *they* know Annie loves horses?" her voice climbing toward outrage. My sister worked at a stable during the summer, teaching children how to ride ponies around the corral. My mother glared at my father. "I thought you were going to tell him doctors aren't allowed gifts—"

"I did."

First a Rolex watch. Then a diamond bracelet. Now a Sicilian donkey tied to a tree outside our kitchen window. Each time, my father returned them.

"So, I can sell it, right?" Annie wanted to buy a Jeep with big wheels and roll bars.

My father walked toward the house. "I'll ask Mr. Culotti to send someone to pick it up tomorrow."

My mother took Billy's hand and followed him inside. "Couldn't you get him assigned to another doctor?"

My parents went to their bedroom and closed the door so we wouldn't be able to hear their conversation. I settled onto the couch for an episode of *Star Trek*. My brother had built a Lego space station on the stairway landing, and now he was sending his fleet of spaceships to their doom, exploding them near my feet. "*Splaaaach-boooom!*"

"Hit her, not me." My sister plunked down on the sofa next

to me. She kicked off her sandals and put her feet on the couch, pushing her heel into my thigh. "Wonder what he's going to give you?" Push. "A personality?" Push. "An original thought?" Push. "Actual boobs?"

"You smell like horse manure." I moved to my side of the couch and turned up the volume on the television.

"Babe," she imitated the way Jared talked. "Your face is one big frickin' freckle." She moved her arms in a swimming motion, as if to swim through my freckles to find my real skin tone. "Oh, here's your face."

"How long has the Eiffel Tower been planted on your chin?" I stared at her pimple, waving to the people at the top.

That was how we talked to each other.

Before that summer, we were the kind of family that said goodnight to one another. Even Annie, furious with our parents for having a curfew, knocked on their bedroom door before midnight. "Night," she'd whisper in her cold, angry voice.

All that had changed. I was aware of gravitational forces, family silences that hadn't been there before. Aware of my father's back pain, my mother's exhaustion, parental bickering behind doors, and afterward, funnels of anger spinning through the house. I didn't know if it was Mr. Culotti's gifts or my sister's choice of boyfriends. Or if it was me changing, feeling airless pockets in my family that I'd never noticed before.

I didn't trust what my parents told me anymore, understandings lodged in meaningful glances, their silence a thin tablecloth protecting the surface. I had my own life and I was lonelier for it, but loneliness felt necessary too, closer to the truth of things.

WINNING

"When will you be home?" my mother asked each morning, but when I came in the door late, she'd say, "Where were you?"

"I told you I was staying for the seniors' tournament." The tennis club was my escape, and I stayed there as late as I could before returning for dinner.

My sister mocked my tennis skirts, my preppy shirts, my strong leg and arm muscles. She laughed at me. "Is Tennis-*Bawwwwbie* in love with *Wandy*? Wouldn't *Wandy* love Tennis-*Bawwwbie's* bed-*woom*?"

She never lost an opportunity to remind me of my fake room. While I was at French camp the previous summer, my mother, thinking I was entering adolescence, remodeled my room to look like a French café—royal blue walls, white and blue checked curtains, bedspread to match, my desk replaced with a wrought iron table and chairs, striped umbrella above. My sister had taken one look before sinking to the floor in a fit of laughter. "*Oooh-la-la*, *Bawbie*-doll *woom*."

I waited all week for my private lesson, Randy standing behind me, gripping my wrist, drawing back my arm, his Juicy Fruit breath. "Just let me do the work," his arm swinging my arm in a smooth stroke. "Feel the difference?" I breathed in his scent, Life Buoy soap and salty sweat. He brought several shirts each day, changing them out, hanging the damp ones on a line out back. Sometimes, I walked underneath just to catch his smell, just to feel the shirts brush my shoulder.

Between lessons, Randy restrung rackets. I sat on the counter, watching him. He had beautiful hands, calloused and strong, hands he hoped to use as a future orthopedic surgeon. He pulled strings tight with the crank, asking Meghan, the assistant coach, "Did Dr. Pitt call back?"

"No."

"Shoot. I have to charge him for the lesson then." Randy often complained about doctors who forgot their lessons but claimed they'd had an emergency, expecting him not to charge them for the hour they missed.

"So, how's the studying going?" Meghan asked him.

"Fine."

"Sí Señor?"

They laughed. I didn't understand the joke, why he cocked his head at the door indicating she should be more discreet.

"How old are you?" He glanced at me, assessing whether I should be overhearing the conversation.

"Thirteen."

"You seem older."

A senior at Stanford, Randy was studying hard for his MCATs. He'd go anywhere, he told me, but his first choice was Mayo. I visualized him going to Mayo for medical school and coaching me all through high school. I visualized him showing me how to swing my racket, reaching his arms around me, unable to hold back his desire.

Mrs. Oliveira had a lesson after me. She drove a convertible Porsche and parked away from other cars so her car wouldn't get scratched. Argentinian, married to an orthopedic resident, she'd been a star tennis player in Buenos Aires. Long dark hair braided down her back, visor shading her eyes, gold earrings, peach lipstick, she played beautifully, muscled calves flexing when she volleyed at the net. She paid Randy to play two sets and sometimes, if he won, fed quarters into the machine and bought Randy a root beer. I heard Meghan tell him he still had to charge her for the lesson.

Joey Picciannini sat beside me, watching Randy and Mrs. Oliveira play their sets. He saw things no one else did. "Wait a few years and you'll have him eating out of your hand."

I flushed, embarrassed, turning my head away, glad I was wearing a visor.

"You gotta best friend?" Joey Picciannini asked.

"Sometimes."

"*Sometimes.*" He laughed like a steak sizzling, little pops of fat. "Ain't that the truth."

He was the first adult to become my friend. I told him all about my family, how my sister was wild and rode Jared's motorcycle all over country roads, how my brother loved toy cars but never picked them up, how my father had tripped over a Matchbox fire engine coming home late from the hospital and had hurt his back. "He might have to have surgery."

Joey Picciannini always had Tic Tacs in his pocket, and he reached forward and shook a few into my hand. "You know birds got two sides of their brains, just like us? You hear the term bird brain? Not true. Their brains are actually bigger per body size. Got their own radar. Way smarter than us that way."

"What's your favorite bird?" I asked.

"Crows. I got a lot in common with your basic crow."

"Like what?"

"Like knowing who to trust. People think you get born with instinct, you know? But it comes from watching people." He grinned. "You got good instincts, champ. I can tell."

Arriving home one afternoon in July, my mother and Billy found a brand-new child-sized motorized Jeep in front of the garage. My brother jumped into the seat, but my mother grabbed his arm and hurried him inside the house. "Don't touch it. It's going back tomorrow." When my father walked in the door early evening, she didn't even wait for him to pour his Scotch. "How do they know Billy loves cars? You have to put a stop to this."

My sister sat beside me on the couch. "Why Billy and not you? You realize you're the only one who hasn't received a gift?"

"So what?"

"They skipped you. Makes you wonder, doesn't it?"

I thought maybe Joey Picciannini was my gift. Week by week, he cheered me on. Week by week, I won my matches. It occurred to me Joey Picciannini might be one of Mr. Culotti's men. But he could also be an FBI agent, one of the agents guarding Mr. Culotti's room day and night to make sure he didn't disappear before he was well enough to testify in Chicago. I didn't ask my father about Mr. Culotti's men because I didn't want to arouse suspicion. This summer would be my only chance to win. Next summer, my family was going to Europe. My mother had been saving up for years—a family trip to Europe before my sister left for college. She talked about it all the time. "We'll rent a car, drive through villages."

"Aren't villages just towns?" my sister asked.

WINNING

"Villages are old. We don't have villages in Minnesota." My mother had spent hours reading *Best Small Hotels in Europe,* earmarking castles and chalets. "It will broaden you." She said this in a certain tone, the same tone she used to talk about people who didn't change bed sheets for guests or put clean towels in the bathroom.

Sitting near Joey Picciannini on the bleachers was like visiting a foreign country. All summer he reminded me, "Call me Joey. Everybody does."

I called him Mr. Picciannini, and that made him laugh. "Okay, champ."

As I moved up the rungs, he bought me grape sodas to celebrate my wins.

Only four of us had made it to the second rung from the top.

"She's pretty good." Joey Picciannini nodded at Tanya Ellison, walking off the court, wiping her face with a towel. "But you're better. All bets on you."

"Her serve is hard to return."

My sister was friends with Tanya's brothers. Her mother was black, her father white. Tanya looked just like her brothers, dark curly hair, almond skin, wide nose, blue eyes. Her dad worked for IBM, and her mother had lupus. They'd moved here so her mother could be part of some new trial medical treatment. The mother's autoimmune system attacked her own body: mouth, eyes, toenails, lungs. Mrs. Ellison couldn't be in sunlight, not at all, so she could never watch her daughter play tennis.

"Her brothers train her," I told Joey Picciannini. "They hit balls with her every day."

"You can beat her."

"Maybe not." I recognized she might have something I didn't have. She might be motivated because her mother was sick or because her mother's medical bills required her to get a scholarship to college. I sensed her desire to win came from a different place, a place where winning was not something acquired through hard work but wired into her body like survival. I recognized some motivations were higher than others.

August arrived. I didn't see Joey Picciannini for three days because of steady, heavy rain. I practiced my serve in my bedroom, throwing the ball in the air, little throws, swooping my arm forward with an imaginary racket.

"Don't bounce the ball in the house," my mother yelled up the stairs.

I was so bored, I went two houses down to see Sarah Lewis. She spent most of the summer preparing for next year's spelling bee. Her mother was a dermatologist and gave me sample tubes of Vanicream sunscreen. Her father was a specialist in tropical diseases. He was in Mali for a conference, so Sarah suggested we look at his book on parasites. As we sat thumbing pages, Sarah's cat crawled into her lap.

"Tilly is a very narcissistic cat." Sarah always tried to practice her vocabulary. She took the cat's paws in her hands and made the cat stroke its own face. "I am the most beautiful cat in the world. I am the most intelligent cat too." She kissed the cat's nose, releasing its paws.

WINNING

Sarah showed me a photo of a Malian family with streaks of white lines covering their arms and legs. "Guinea worms, my next science fair project. When they draw out the worms with tweezers," she explained, "the worms release larvae that make people's skin burn, so they run to the nearest pond to cool their skin. Then other people drink the water, and that's how guinea worm spreads. Dogs are getting it now."

For lunch that day she asked her babysitter to cook spaghetti. We sucked in the noodles. "*Mmmm*, guinea worms, delicious."

I went home that afternoon and did my visualization. Even with my eyes closed, I could see the light between curtains, shaped by an opening. I focused my mind on the opening until it became something else, became me winning, became Randy loving me.

Second week in August I had my last private with Randy before the final match. Only two of us left, Tanya and I had made it to the top rung.

Randy took the bag of balls to the opposite side of the court. "We'll work on your volley."

The sun was hot, and sweat stung my eyes. I kept hitting balls too hard, hitting them out. Then I softened my return, lobbing them over the net, and he slammed them back to make a point.

"Still doing the visualization?" Randy asked me.

I nodded. But I felt a sharp pain radiating through my shoulder

"Concentrate. You're taking your eye off the ball."

I wiped my eyes with a towel, pretending the tears pricking my eyes were sweat.

"Happens to everyone before a big match," he told me. "Don't put so much pressure on yourself. It's a game. Just remember that."

Later, off the court, Randy warned me that wanting something too much would sabotage the game. I had to loosen the wanting, undo it. "You know it doesn't matter in the big scheme of things. This whole ladder thing? It's just a way to make sure you keep playing. Keep it fun."

His words diminished my effort. I didn't know how to rest into nothing.

The next afternoon, bulbous black clouds blew in and erased shadows, turning the sky dark, making the day seem like night. The air had a yellowish tint, thick and heavy. No wind. Ninety-two degrees. We didn't even have to hit the balls to feel sweat dripping down our temples.

"I feel a tornado." Meghan turned on the radio and looked out from the porch.

"You think?" Randy stared at the sky over the strip mall along the highway. He hung the tarp over the tennis ladder so the little circles with our names wouldn't get blown off. After about fifteen minutes, the wind picked up and rain began to fall. He closed the club, sent us all home.

I had ridden two blocks when tornado sirens sounded. The wind came in huge gusts, trees swaying at impossible angles, angles that made me afraid branches would break off and fall on me. Cars splashed through puddles. Rain blew sideways. I could hardly pedal against the wind, so I turned my bike around and cycled back to the club.

Randy's Saab was still there. So was the red Porsche parked behind some bushes. I locked my bike to the bleachers and pounded on the wood screen. The whole club had been locked down, shutters closed. I knocked harder, yelling "Randy? Randy!" to be heard above the sirens.

He unlocked the door and opened it, startled to see me. "What're you doing here? I sent everyone home."

"I can't make it home," I said.

He glanced into the room, "We have a visitor," and waved me inside. Mrs. Oliviera stood with her back to me. She wore a short black dress instead of tennis clothes. The radio was on, announcing eighty-mile winds moving north along the I-90 corridor.

Randy nodded toward the women's locker room. "Go into the shower and stay there, Julie. That's the safest place."

"Aren't you coming?" I glanced between them.

"Go in the shower." Mrs. Oliviera said, not bothering to hide her irritation.

The club had thin walls and their voices carried.

"I have to leave," she said. "I can't be here when someone comes to get her."

"You can't drive in this weather," he told her. "Trees are falling. We can say you had a lesson."

I heard footsteps and the screen slammed. A second later Randy called to me, "Just stay there, Julie. You're safe in there, okay?"

I sat on the floor in the cement shower, my back to the wall, and waited for him to return. But when I heard the car engine start and Randy still didn't return, I knew I was alone. I closed my eyes and hugged my knees to my chest, storm raging around me, tornado sirens sounding through the city, rain drumming metal bleachers. The wind roared above sounds I'd never heard before, snapping branches, blowing chairs, metal gutters twisting. I thought of my mother, certain she was on her way to get me. Lightning flashed, followed by loud cracks of thunder; then a thud, and the whole building shook. I opened my eyes. One of the giant oaks had fallen across the roof, leaves pressing against the small rectangular window above the sink.

Minutes later, ambulance and fire engine sirens sounded through the streets. The sky through the small window lightened. Birds sang.

I heard a voice. "Julie? Julie Watson?"

Joey Picciannini had seen my bike chained to the collapsed bleacher. "You here?" He hurried into the bathroom and lifted me off the floor. Glancing at the door of the office, he shook his head in anger. "Randy left you here alone?"

He picked up my backpack and led me outside. "Gotta be careful of downed wires. Killed a friend of mine."

We stood together looking at the debris. Trees were down, porch chairs blown into the park, fallen trees covering the end courts, bleachers collapsed, half the porch crushed under the huge oak.

"My mom will come soon."

"If she can. Lotta trees down. I'll wait with you."

I looked across the park and saw a huge fallen pine blocking the red Porsche at the edge of the parking lot. It would take me years to understand the nature of wanting—the way we wrap ourselves around a feeling, the way it inevitably dissolves into nothing—but that day I felt it for the first time. "There are people in that car," I told Joey Picciannini.

The following day, Randy was fired from the club. My mother received a phone call from one of her doubles' partners who had spoken to Meghan. Dr. Oliviera had apparently hired a private investigator to follow his wife.

The day before my final tournament, my father arrived home with big news. The FBI had transferred Mr. Culotti by ambulance to Chicago to testify against his boss. Before Mr. Culotti left, one of his men handed my father an expensive leather briefcase with my father's initials engraved.

"He told me I might want to lose my old one," my father told us that night when he got home. "He said, 'We mighta got it bugged.'"

"Isn't that illegal?" My mother shook her head, furious.

That evening, my father performed surgery on the kitchen table, taking apart his old briefcase with my mother's kitchen knives. My mother stood beside him, watching him dismantle the case, piece by piece, pulling out the lining, cutting away the buckle, separating the bottom liner, carving leather off the handle. But he couldn't find anything that looked like a bug.

"Was he joking?" my mother asked. "Does he think that's funny?"

"Who knows?" My father shook his head and placed the remnants in a grocery bag, assuring my mother he'd send both briefcases to the hospital incinerator, just to be safe.

The next day I played my final match.

Dried yellow grass rustled in the wind. Flocks of geese flew overhead. I didn't want to play. I didn't care about winning anymore. But my father had taken half a day off work to watch my match, and my mother told me he'd been waiting all summer to see me play. The club had been cleaned up, and Meghan was running the tournament.

I played hard, but tennis had stopped being fun. I could feel my best out there in the future. I could imagine it. But I couldn't land it, couldn't make it happen. Tanya beat me 6-0, both sets.

I shook her hand. I was relieved it was over. While Meghan took photos, we held our trophies high, hollow gold plastic, lighter than I'd imagined. I kept looking for Joey Picciannini until Meghan said, "Oh, I almost forgot," and handed me a tennis can full of quarters. "Mr. Picciannini told me to give this to you. He was sorry he couldn't be here." Under the plastic cover was a note. *You're a champ!* She leaned close and told me, "He was the guy hired by Dr. Oliviera."

The next day I cleared out my locker. This world, too, had begun to feel small.

When I got home, I put my tennis racket on a shelf in the garage.

That night my sister set it back inside my bedroom door. I was lying on my bed in the dark, and Annie stood there in the doorway, light pouring around her from the hallway. "*Bawbie's woom* is *pwetty* in the *dawk*." She was trying to be funny, trying to make me laugh.

I didn't laugh. I didn't care about my room. I wanted to love larger things.

She stood there a moment longer, staring at me with a worried smile. "Just have fun while you can."

THE DOG

When they bought the dog, they were a different family. The family they would become was there, inside them, waiting to show itself the moment the daughter, about to turn ten at the end of the summer, would begin to see her parents as people who could fail her at various, crucial moments in her life. But they didn't know it yet. The parents didn't know they would fail their daughter, and the daughter still felt safe, especially in the car, listening to her parents plan a dinner party.

"Why should we include them?" the mother asked. "We've had them twice, and we've never been to their house."

"Maybe they don't have parties," her father replied.

"Maybe they don't like us."

They were driving south from Minneapolis on an empty four-lane highway, staring at farms, fields of ripe corn waiting to be harvested. It was late August, mist rising off the Mississippi. The family had just returned from Paris. The father and daughter missed the excitement of living in a foreign city where everything felt new. The flatness of the Midwest resonated with the flatness they felt inside, coming home to the same neighborhood, same grocery store, same English language, flat and dull as the highway stretching before them. Only the wife was glad to be home. She was tired of feeling fat among the slender French women, tired of hanging laundry to dry, pushing jeans, t-shirts, nylons through wooden slats, pulling cords to raise the dry rack, socks on radiators, sheets over closet doors. She had learned not to complain about the small kitchen, thin walls, rats scurrying around dumpsters below their balcony, vibrations from the metro waking them at night. The husband and daughter adored Paris and refused to hear anything bad about it. If the mother pointed out the metro smelled of urine, they defended the uriney scent, declaring Americans had a sanitized version of the world. Then they would find something to dislike about Minnesota. Gas-guzzling SUVs. Toothpicks after meals. Orange cheese.

The daughter had no idea they were going to pick up a puppy for her tenth birthday, a promise they'd made before moving overseas. The parents wanted to surprise her—a good breeder five hours away, a farming family in Marshall, Minnesota, who raised standard poodles, good family dogs.

"My uncle left me some land." The father liked to invent stories, this one about Jewish relatives fleeing Russian pogroms who came to Minnesota to farm. "We're going to look at it and decide if we want to keep it or sell it."

The daughter was surprised to hear her father speak of relatives in southern Minnesota. He was from New York City and he referred to Minnesota as Siberia.

"Combien de temps, Papa?"

"Deux heures, Chérie. Calme-toi."

The mother rolled her eyes. She felt these conversations were slightly incestuous, this bond of language that excluded her. The mother had tried to learn French, four years in college and again at Centre de Langue Française, but when she practiced at home the daughter and husband corrected her accent. "Pas comme ça," her daughter said, repeating the correct pronunciation, delighting in her mother's failures.

As they continued driving, the daughter stared at the fields of corn, wondering what it would be like to grow up on a farm, far away from other houses.

Basically, everything you believed could change according to where you lived. She felt it in her bones, and it made her slightly uncomfortable, as if everything was light enough to blow away. And maybe what didn't blow away didn't matter much, either.

"Speed limit is seventy." The mother glanced at the father. "Tired?"

"I'm fine."

"Sure? I can take over." Two years before, he had fallen asleep at the wheel on their way to visit cousins in Rochester. "*Just in time*," she liked to remind him, referring to that moment when she'd opened her eyes to see their car careening across the highway toward the ravine. Just in time for the father to grip the wheel and stop the car five feet from a cement drainage pipe. Even after the car had stopped moving, the mother kept screaming, "You almost killed us . . . you almost killed us!" That is what the daughter remembered best, not the father's momentary lapse in consciousness, but her mother's shrill voice that wouldn't stop.

She stared at the back of her mother's head, brown frizzy curls tied back in a ponytail. The mother turned sideways to look at the father, her voice filling the car. "If she's a vegan, I could make a vegetable curry with coconut milk." Mouth-wrinkles pinching, unpinching. The daughter was glad she looked like her father—blue eyes and blonde hair. The mother could talk about the smallest, most insignificant things: whether bagged carrots were chemically treated, how long eggs were safe, whether nail polish was toxic. She had this amazing ability to make a big deal out of everything. The daughter worried she would inherit this trait. She had huge feelings, feelings that moved inside her like birds crossing oceans, no land in sight. She sensed she was on the verge of understanding truths that would cause her pain, would make her angry, particularly at her mother who, having had four miscarriages, loved her daughter with an urgency that confirmed the daughter's importance in the family, but also frightened the daughter with a sense of unending responsibility.

The mother reached back, touching the daughter's skinned knee lightly. "You should take the bandage off so it can air."

The daughter left the bandage on. She began speaking French with her Barbies. She felt too old for dolls, but not too old to design clothes, wraparound dresses cut from the mother's old scarves. "Je suis de Paris." The daughter strutted Barbie across her thigh. She was starting middle school in the fall. Having lived in another country, she felt smarter than the two Jessica's who lived down the block in Minneapolis. The two Jessica's had become best friends in her absence, calling each other Jess and Jessie to stay separate. Except they weren't separate, not when the daughter was around them. She told them about France even though they didn't ask. Cheese could be served for dessert. French bathrooms had two toilets. French ate horse and rabbit and eel, which is why she had become vegetarian. French women wore high heels, even with bathrobes. She told them about Madame Gonçalves, the beautiful Portuguese concierge who lived on the first floor and wore high heels to mop the courtyard.

The father turned on the radio. They fell silent, the family listening to *Car Talk*, Click and Clack, talking to a woman whose husband had caught Valley Fever after buying a car that had been shipped from Arizona. Was it possible the car carried dust with Valley Fever, the woman wanted to know. The daughter noticed whenever the father laughed, the mother laughed, too, as if she couldn't let him laugh alone. The daughter saw things she hadn't noticed before. She could hardly wait to be old enough to stay home alone.

When they arrived at the farm, gray prefab with aluminum siding surrounded by patchy yellow grass, the daughter stared at the rusted porch, gutter hanging from the roof, a child's tricycle turned on its side. "C'est la maison, Papa?"

"Oui, c'est ça."

The door of the farmhouse opened. A heavy-set woman in blue jeans and t-shirt handed a black furry bundle to the daughter. "This one's yours. She's eight weeks old today. Just waking up."

"We wanted to surprise you." The mother stroked the puppy's ears.

"She's mine?" The daughter glanced between her parents.

The father put his arm around her shoulders. "You'll have to walk her and learn how to take care of her."

The daughter smiled at the puppy. "This is the happiest day of my life." It was the only thing she could think of to say, and it sounded canned, and she knew it, and the parents knew it, too, but they were still a family that could say canned things and feel the truth behind the words, that who they were together, no matter how fragile, was still the closest they would ever come to giving existence a center. But also, and this was something they would never have admitted to each other, each harbored a sense that a family of three was not a real family. A family of three lacked gravity. They imagined bigger families pulled together like metal to a magnet, filling kitchens and dens with laughter. They pictured big families as fun families. They could divide into teams, fill benches at swim meets, help each other with homework, dispel insecurities about familial traits—big ears, buck teeth, hair that would never lay flat.

They couldn't have named the loneliness they sometimes felt with each other, the sense that who they were together wasn't enough. But it was the same feeling every holiday, Easter or Passover, when the mother set the table with good dishes and silverware, and the three of them made an effort to have a real discussion about public education or media literacy or individualism versus collectivism.

Sometimes, the father would arrive at the table in an old t-shirt and blue jeans, and the mother would say, "Why do I spend all day cooking?" And the father would say, "Why do you?" And the mother would say, "Families need rituals." And the father would say, "I'm fine going out." And the tension would remain until after the meal when they went to a movie, which was actually their most consistent holiday ritual, and only then, among strangers more alone than they were, did they feel like a real family.

The family sensed they needed something else to love, something beyond themselves. They stood close, smiling at the small furry bundle curled in the daughter's arms. The puppy yawned, blinking sleepy eyes.

Driving home, they stopped for gas in Corville and bought Subway sandwiches next door. The sun was warm and they sat at a picnic table, the wind off the fields strong, blowing trash out of bins, cups and straws and sandwich wrappers flying across the highway. The family watched the puppy sniff their feet as they talked about names.

"Claire?" The daughter suggested the name of her best friend in Paris.

"Antoinette," the mother said. "And we could call her Nette."

"Remember what your bubby called you?" the father smiled. "Sheynah meydeleh. Yiddish for pretty little girl."

"Sheynah meydeleh." The daughter had made her choice.

In the first three years of the dog's life, the family experienced smaller, less important deaths. The daughter's grades, for instance, mobile pings kidnapping her attention, eyes focused on the screen, fingers clicking, glacial replies. "I *am* listening."

Under fleecy clouds, clammy air, a northern cold, three sets of shoulders, chins, lungs, breath full of clutch and brake around the kitchen table, cautious voices, worn treads driving over hills, swerving around potholes. Mother, father, daughter passing toast and jam, yogurt and honey, feeding bits of cheese to the dog under the table, trying to locate the sadness, its exact point of entry, like running a finger over a map on which the smaller streets are unnamed, distances hard to measure, hovering between them.

"Feral," the mother said of the daughter. Hormones or chemical imbalance, the way salt induced water to boil. At night, lying in bed, the mother turned over worries like spiritual compost consuming itself, until everything she believed could be buried in one tiny, tiny hole. The mother wondered if they'd had more children, would the daughter still be so angry at her, so moody and short-tempered? Maybe, she thought, her own sadness had spilled over.

"We have to pick our battles," the father said. "Let her make her own mistakes." He worried more about the mother, doughy now with thinning hair, bloom long gone from failed pregnancies. She had not forgiven him. He'd been willing to a point, the point being all sense of desire extinguished. No more thermometers, timed ejaculations, sperm tests in paper cups. If anything was hurting their daughter, he told her, it was trying and failing. "She feels your sadness."

"Sorry I can't compartmentalize."

One advantage to being a small family, the father believed, was they could live abroad again, one more time before their daughter left for college. If they couldn't be a big family, they could be an interesting family, a worldly family. Just as they had moved before, they could move again, another sabbatical, nine months overseas. Hadn't the mother always wanted to live in Rome, where, he'd read, the fertility rate was 1.37 children and a family of three the norm?

It had been four years since they'd left France. The daughter, four years older, four years angrier, shoved her chair back. "I'm starting high school. I don't want to go." She marched upstairs and slammed the bedroom door. Then she opened the door and clapped her hands, the rhythm she always used—*dutt-duttah-dutt-dah*. The dog came jogging up the stairs and sat beside her on the bed. The daughter tried to picture another new life, and instead felt this one unraveling, seconds and years flying out of her like confetti, nothing to adhere to.

Downstairs the father cleared the table while the mother rinsed dishes. "Maybe she's right," the mother said. "Maybe we're expecting too much of her."

The father put the leftover bread in a plastic bag. "She's so dramatic. I would've given anything if my parents had lived abroad. She doesn't know how lucky she is."

"Maybe it's not about that."

"It's always about that."

The dog, nose to crotches and armpits, lived among these smaller deaths, unaware, black eyes staring, nose twitching . . . treat? Popcorn? Cheese? Peanuts? Licking tears, nudging hands, delicate lashes blinking, pet me, pet me, demanding a simpler love, of physical presence, warm fur, weight of bones, occupying whatever space was empty, whatever space needed to be filled.

Security was tight at the girl's new school, cameras posted along the twelve-foot steel fence covered with barbed wire. Entering, she had to ring a bell and pass the gatehouse where the guard, Rodolfo, glanced up from his soccer magazine and waved her through. Inside the gate, the school inhabited two elegant villas and an old chapel. Half the students were Italian, the other half children of parents working next door at FAO, the United Nation's Food and Agricultural Organization.

At the first assembly, the headmaster welcomed new students.

"Many of you are fourth-world children. You have lived all over the world. Sitting among this freshman class," said the principal, "are children of ministers of agriculture, scientists, transportation experts. Some of you are from the naval base in Gaeta, others from Naples."

Laughter broke out. Someone made the sound of a gun, "*Pop, pop, pop.*"

The girl sitting next to the daughter wore a nametag, Valeria, and underneath, Naples. Valeria turned around, pointed her finger at the boys, clicked her thumb. That shut them up. Her skin was sun-darkened, and she wore thick black eyeliner around her dark eyes. She was very thin in tight blue jeans, long-sleeved t-shirt, legs crossed, heeled boot kicking air.

"Some of you are here because your families fled violence in your home countries." The principal paused to let this sink in. "We have eight new boarding students who will live in the dorm next door. The rest of you are commuters. Those of you who commute might think about reaching out to the boarders on weekends and inviting them for a home-cooked meal. We, myself and all the faculty," he nodded at the adults standing around the edge of the chapel, "will do everything possible to make you all feel at home."

"*Blah, blah, blah,*" Valeria whispered.

The daughter felt expanded, but not in a good way. The truth changed from one country to the next, but always the same sense of competing lives, competing places. The daughter's truth, the biggest truth she knew, was that she had to keep adjusting her life until there were so many different versions of herself in so many places, she had no idea who she really was. She was so tired of searching for what mattered here versus what mattered there. Nothing mattered, if you kept widening your perspective.

She began smoking that first afternoon, after Western Civilization, a class excursion to the oldest bridge in Rome. "Pons Aemilius, Ponte Rotto, now," said Leif, the school's new history teacher. "Started in one-seventy-nine B.C. and completed in one-fifty-one B.C., rebuilt by Augustus in two-eighty A.D."

Walking past the American ambassador's house, a German student, Jochen, gave the finger into the security camera. Leif herded the group across the scraggly field. "Imagine Caesar leading battles on his chariot." The students crowded around him, trying to hear above the drone of traffic. "Etruscans were pagans," Leif explained, "and when they built the bridge, feared the wrath of the river god, so they made sacrifices, one or two children, along with a third of the year's harvest." This was said with a smile. The daughter didn't know if he was joking.

All the other students were taking notes, so she took notes. She scribbled *179 – 151 B.C.* But the dates were backward, and the daughter was lost, her brain a drawer too small for the timeline to fit, a whole civilization forty feet underground, buried in volcanic rubble or burned after plagues or mummified after invasions.

The daughter's head was full, her brain softening like candle wax, shapeless globs of knowledge. The daughter didn't ask questions. She was afraid of sounding stupid, aware that the students here were of another caliber than students in Minnesota.

Same in astronomy, later that afternoon, the class she'd opted for instead of calculus. "The really interesting questions don't have answers *yet*." Mr. Larsen, a Dane with thick wrists and square jaw, pointed to a map of orbiting planets. "A new quasar just discovered that formed six-hundred-and-ninety-million years after the Big Bang, traveling toward us for thirteen-billion years."

Valeria raised her hand and asked, "Are we supposed to know what a quasar is?"

"Light and energy in extreme, distant space," Mr. Larsen told her.

The daughter remembered things she could actually feel. She could not feel light and energy in extreme distances of space. She could not feel any distances except the ones between here and the places she missed. Everything inside was disrupted, a cloud inhaling memory.

After the final bell, Valeria offered her a cigarette outside the gate. "Maybe we could go shopping sometime."

The daughter nodded, "Sure, great," and blew smoke as they stood together, watching class-mates straddle motorini, kicking engines into a communal roar.

"How was your day?" the mother asked each afternoon when she entered the apartment. The daughter shrugged and peeled a banana. It was absurd how despite everything, some people were always optimistic. The mother believed everything depended on attitude and perspective. "No feeling is final," she told the daughter. "You'll adapt, and your life here will seem just as good. It just takes time and patience."

But as soon as the mother spoke those words, *time* and *patience*, they became empty for the daughter. Everything the mother touched became empty. Once, that first week, she looked at the mother and shook her head. "You are like a really ugly wallpaper all over my brain." The daughter hated the mother. It was maybe the only thing the daughter was sure about—*hated her, hated her, hated her.*

The mother was studying Italian and spent her mornings at a language school filled with nuns and priests. It soothed her to be around childless adults who still found meaning in their lives. The nuns were from India and would go back and start schools for girls. One of the priests, an Irishman named Danny, had OCD and didn't want to take the wafer during communion, didn't like to hug or shake hands. He worried he wasn't suited to the priesthood. The mother felt like a mother to them all, buying the younger students coffee during break, glad they confided, and amazed at how profound conversations could be in rudimentary Italian. Sometimes she wished her daughter and husband confided in her the way these foreign students did. They could tell her anything because they'd never see each other again after the course ended. She thought maybe this was the way to approach life from now on, no expectations of the future. Maybe this was what she'd been meant to learn.

The mother began praying in Italy. She prayed for the daughter to make the right decisions. The mother worried the daughter was choosing the wrong friends, the ones whose texts pinged after midnight, who didn't shake hands or look her in the eye when they came to the apartment. When she found butts in the daughter's coat pocket, the daughter shrugged. "I don't smoke, but my Italian friends do. I pick up the butts so they don't wash into the river."

THE DOG

The daughter had learned how to bend the truth, how to make almost any situation sound true, how to say enough about her life to make the parents think she was confiding.

"Huge argument at lunch today," she said at dinner one night three months after they'd arrived.

"About what?" the mother asked.

"Valeria asked what gives Americans the right to have military bases in Italy." The daughter's eyebrows lifted as she glanced between the parents, her voice full of a new kind of authority. "The Americans said anyone in construction in Naples is mafia, and Valeria's dad is one of the biggest builders. They laughed and said she's only here so she won't be kidnapped, and the way they said it was like they want her to be kidnapped."

"It's probably true about the mafia," the father said. "Garbage and construction, from what I've read."

"Stay away from her, from Valeria," the mother warned her. "They might take both of you."

The daughter pushed back her chair. "If you didn't want me to make friends with Italians, we shouldn't have moved here."

Alone in her room, she leaned out the window, blowing smoke toward the sky, looking at stars and listening to disco music from nearby bars. The terrace next door smelled like cat piss and basil, and the old woman kept the television turned up loud. Cars honked on the Lungotevere, sirens in the distance. Stubbing out her cigarette, she heard her father's voice carry through the kitchen window. "Can't we stop talking about her? I'm tired of it. She's all you talk about."

"But she's getting in with the wrong crowd—"

“We can’t do anything. Don’t you understand that? We can’t do anything more for her. We’ve done all we can.”

The dog was easy in comparison. The dog was a giver. “Amore mio,” the daughter practiced, pressing her face into the dog’s fur. “Ti voglio bene.”

The daughter felt much closer to the father, mostly because he left her alone. He often traveled to conferences in other parts of Europe and wrote her emails from airport lounges, long letters about his own childhood, things he could have told her when he was home except he wanted to put them in writing. *Suffering is necessary, even normal, in a perverse world*, for instance. He always ended the letters by likening her to him, her strong will and perseverance, telling her she would pull through the difficult moments and use them to build wisdom. The daughter read these letters, feeling her breath tighten. She had the vague sense that she was meant to keep them in a box to remember him after he was gone.

After his most recent trip, the father brought home a cartoon from *The New Yorker* and taped it on the daughter’s door. It showed a cemetery, and the biggest gravestone belonged to the dog, the second biggest to the daughter, the third to the wife, the last, the tiniest, to the father. When they sat down for dinner, he asked the daughter if she’d noticed the cartoon.

“Poor you,” the daughter laughed, but it wasn’t her real laugh. It was a new Italian laugh, sharp and hollow.

THE DOG

*

After dinner each night she walked the dog. The daughter often crossed the Ponte Sisto, passing homeless drifters and immigrants, some selling purses on blankets, other holding out hands, begging for money. "Bella, per favore. Ho fame." They had sad-looking dogs with red eyes and dull fur. These dogs, lying still and looking up at her through droopy eyes, scratched at fleas until patches of pink skin showed through their fur. The daughter felt a deep pity for these dogs.

One of the boys, handsome with black curls and pale-blue eyes, always stood in her way, blocking the bridge, trying to sell her jewelry he'd made from twine. She bought three bracelets, hoping the money would feed his dog but knowing it would probably be used for wine and drugs.

She had trained her own dog to lift its paw whenever it heard the Italian word *piacere*, and Luca, introducing himself, knelt down and shook the dog's paw. "Che bella cane."

She started going there each night, taking scraps of leftover food for the dogs.

She hung out with Luca and his friends, sometimes going to meet them after school with Valeria who spoke a dialect with the boys. Luca and his friends didn't play soccer and study for the IB exams. They had no dreams to go to hotel schools in Switzerland or engineering colleges in France or the London School of Economics—everyone at her school wanted to go to the London School of Economics. Luca and his friends had no plans for tomorrow or all the days after. There were no jobs here, Luca told her. He'd gladly go to America with her, if her father could find him a job. Some afternoons he picked her up at school, and she rode behind him on his motorino. She hugged his waist as he steered switchback roads over the hills surrounding Rome. As dusk fell, and the streetlights below came on, vesper bells ringing, they sat on walls and looked over the city, feeling above the rest of the world.

Pigeons cooed on the roof, garlic grew heavy on the shelf, peppers turned red. The daughter grew wilder. Wilder in a way she might not recover from. Even she knew it. Most people her age had dreams of starting over someplace new, away from their families, places like Paris or Rome or New York. But the daughter had lived in those places, and, living there, they had become part of her life already. Nothing felt new anymore. She understood that everything she would experience would just be that—another experience. She felt so much pressure, and she could look at her life ahead and see nothing but the same pressure, because it was life itself pressing in upon her, making her desperate from the effort.

Her grades were barely passing, gaps in understanding growing too wide to ever catch up. The other American students were talking about her behind her back, calling her Valeria's bodyguard. She could hardly be near the mother who, having posted the daughter's high school applications for next year, was now focused on getting the dog home again.

"We just got here," the daughter said.

"It takes six months to process the papers, and if we want to go back in June, we have to start now. Italy is such a bureaucracy," the mother complained. "The veterinarian requires an appointment, weeks in advance at his office near the airport. Pages to fill out with the dog's history. It's ridiculous."

On the day of the appointment, the mother went with the dog in a special taxi to the building near the airport, complaining to the veterinarian about all the paperwork. A bald man with small eyes and moist cheeks, he examined the dog in less than two minutes and handed the mother a receipt. "It is not our country which demands all this. It is yours, after 9/11. If we do not oblige, we are fined."

"I could see the ocean from his office," the mother said that night, slicing onion, wiping her eyes with the back of her wrist. "I had no idea Rome was so close to the ocean. We should go by train one Sunday when it gets warm. Eat at one of the open restaurants along the water?"

But the daughter had no intention of wasting a Sunday on the parents.

Instead she went to Valeria's bathroom in the dorm and dyed her hair maroon. Afterward, the daughter and Valeria walked to Porta Portese, a huge market where they bought sexy lingerie that smelled like drapes in old houses, slightly gassy and metallic. Later that afternoon, she met Luca at the Ponte Sisto. He ran his fingers through her maroon hair and laughed. He laughed often when she sat beside him, selling stolen discs to foreigners who trusted her English.

Always before, Luca had driven her around Rome's winding streets, delivering her back to Piazza Trilussa near the family's apartment. But that night, the night she told him they were already making plans to return to Minnesota, he drove her to the ocean, middle of nowhere, a patio of an abandoned restaurant. She could hear planes landing and trains rumbling in the distance. They kissed and smoked pot and listened to waves. He kept touching her hair, yanking it harder each time to pull her down beside him. It was already past midnight, and twice she asked him to take her home. He laughed, shaking his head. He told her if she wanted a ride home, she had to make him happy. At first, she laughed, thinking they were still flirting. He lay there beside her, his legs hanging over the ledge, heels kicking the wall.

"I need to get home," she told him in Italian. "My parents will be waiting."

"Genitori." He smiled, keeping his eyes closed.

She studied the darkness around them, looking for lights or buildings. But it was all shadows and waves and tall grass and boarded up windows. No signs of life. She brushed his hair with her hand, pleading, "Per favore. Devo tornare."

He unzipped his pants. He refused to look at her.

He had known exactly where to turn off the road, exactly where to park his motorino, where the path began through tall reeds, leading to this beach lined with cement restaurants, all of them boarded up. The waves kept climbing toward them, growing louder. No one would hear if she yelled. She could run away, but where to? How would she get back? She looked at him, his zipper open. What else could she do?

Afterward, she sat behind him on the bike, arms around his waist on the highway, relieved to see cars, people nearby. When she saw the city's lights coming closer, she thought, My parents and dog are waiting for me. Tears stung her eyes. Piazza Trilussa was littered with drunks, broken bottles, mangy dogs sleeping under the lip of the fountain. She washed her face and hands, then walked the narrow streets past the Basilica Santa Maria in Trastevere, its gold mosaic lit at night. She had studied the famous basilica in class, built in the 1600s, bombed in the revolution of 1848. Women had picked up cannonballs launched by the French, and after extinguishing fuses by dipping their fingers in wet clay, carried them in their aprons to republican soldiers who launched them back at the French. She remembered more than she realized, and she found comfort in this knowledge, comfort in knowing how far back history went, that something always survived. She prayed she wouldn't catch a disease, and if her prayers were answered, she would study harder, would fill herself with knowledge.

Opening the door quietly, the daughter stood still, listening to see if her parents were still up. The dog growled then barked as if she were an intruder.

"It's me, dummy. It's me." She waited until the dog jumped down from the couch, tail wagging, then stepped inside.

"Your own dog doesn't recognize you." The mother was sitting at the kitchen table in the dark. "Where have you been all night?" Tears rolled down the mother's cheeks, tears of relief and fury. "Your father's still out there walking the streets, looking for you."

The daughter had lived through something, and it felt like an oil slick across her chest, something that couldn't be washed away. Part of her wanted to tell her parents so they could absolve her, tell her she was still the same daughter, their little girl. She wanted to be young again, nothing to hide. But she also knew that if she confided what had happened, she would have to contend with the mother's fears, the father's advice. The mother would take her to the doctor. The father would lecture her about life. Easier to tell the dog, lying next to her, breathing steadily, each exhale a little circle of warmth on her ankle.

She cried until her body felt empty. Other-ness pierced the daughter's heart, small invisible separations, the way wind collected dust, covering everything, combing surfaces, and the only consolation was she would be leaving soon. Back to snow, blue hours, air like tarnished dimes. She felt older now, from tears and sighs and waiting, from the *sheer-ness* of sorrow.

Twilight. The daughter avoided the same streets, same bridges. Walking the dog, she moved with a vigilance that reminded her of the mother, the mother's way of trying not to be overwhelmed. It didn't matter. What happened with the boy didn't matter, not in the long run.

Each morning the world turned over, taking the daughter further away from that night. The silences in the family were no longer empty silences. The daughter believed secrets were necessary. She already understood from living in other places that everything she loved and despised would be supplanted by the life ahead. This knowledge freed her, made her feel she could become someone else all over again.

The mother and father circled the daughter's distances, knocked on her bedroom door. "You okay?"

"Studying for finals."

How to speak of these things? Not easy and flowing like a

river, but heavy and weighted as rocks on the bottom, slowing the current.

*

Grief did not settle like dust. It was a vine, green and alive, blooming endings as the daughter outgrew childhood.

The dog collapsed the day after the daughter left for college. The parents didn't tell the daughter right away, not until parents' weekend when they could be with her. They still thought of their daughter as fragile, someone who could descend under certain circumstances.

Visiting her dorm room, the father noticed her wall covered with photos of the dog. "More photos of the dog than us," the father teased.

"You're in a few," the daughter smiled. "Where does she sleep now?"

The father nodded at the mother to explain, and the mother told the daughter the veterinarian had found a large tumor in the dog's stomach. The dog was not in pain, not yet, but the tumor was growing fast. A month from now the daughter would be home for Thanksgiving and they could do it then, when the family was together, help the dog die a peaceful death. If that was what the daughter wanted.

A month later, the daughter's boyfriend drove her home from Madison. He had round, gray eyes and short hair that stood up on top of his head. He was tall and very thin, and when he smiled, dimples creased his cheeks. He wore blue jeans, flannel shirts, and thick-soled hiking shoes which he removed when he came inside the house. He watched the family weep over the dog, and because he was vegan and loved animals, his own eyes welled with tears. The daughter had described the parents as huge, overpowering people. But the boyfriend was surprised to find the father short with rounded shoulders and a soft, filmy voice. The mother had kind eyes, but her face was full of gravity especially when she smiled and the lines around her mouth deepened. He'd heard about the father's publications, the mother's causes, but they were shy with him and much more accommodating than he'd been led to believe.

Afterward, after the vet carried the dog to the car, the house seemed dark and quiet. The mother warmed a pot of soup. The father opened a bottle of red wine. The daughter set the table. The boyfriend offered to help, but was told by the father to sit down and enjoy his wine. "Already too many cooks in the kitchen."

The family moved about the kitchen, each feeling the dog's absence. And because they were a small family, they thought the absence belonged only to them. They thought if they had been a bigger family they might not miss the dog so much. They couldn't be sure, but they imagined bigger families had a different kind of love, more diluted and spread out. They had come through something, not just the dog's dying, but also their life as a family. They missed the dog, and they missed each other, but they also realized the dog had never erased the loneliness of being a small family.

When the soup was served, bread sliced, wine poured, they sat down, mother and father facing each other. The boyfriend evened out the table, a great comfort to the mother who kept offering him more cheese. "Would you prefer blue?" She leapt up, pulled out smoked blue, set the wedge on a cheese plate in front of him. "The blue is local."

"I warned him we're a quiet family." The daughter looked at the boyfriend.

"Quiet's good," the boyfriend nodded. "I like quiet."

When the dinner was over and the daughter and her boyfriend went out to a local bar to listen to music, the mother and father cleaned up the kitchen and, after watching the news, lay in bed, feet touching where they used to feel the dog above the covers. Since the daughter had left for college, the dog slept on their bed, between their feet.

"Glad I got a twenty-pound turkey," the mother said. "He has an appetite."

"I'll see if he wants to go with me to pick up the pies." The father reached out, took her hand. "He might prefer pecan instead of pumpkin."

"Get both. Better to have too much."

Each felt the silence of the house, the silence underneath everything else.

They circled it. They did not name it, this understanding—their whole life together, moving back and forth across it like the hands of a clock turning mechanically. The world was full of hollow places. Things came undone. Closeness thinned. Endings arrived. Even now they listened, waiting for their daughter to come home.

Somewhere else, a neighbor chopped ice from his driveway, a car door slammed, someone else's dog barked.

SARGASSO SEA

Even before they board the plane, Lilly knows this trip is a mistake.

Each time her daughter's cell pings, Lilly glances sideways, watching Tessa read the texts, thumbs tapping quick responses, eyes focused, mouth curled up at the edges. Lilly knows by the way Tessa's face becomes softer, younger, that it is him, *Mr. Married*, that he is still in her life. She suspects her daughter misses her former boss, the same boss who refused to fire Henry, her daughter's colleague, for stalking her, and, instead, gallantly offered to drive Tessa to and from work to make sure she was safe, which is how they got involved in the first place.

As soon as the plane lands, new pings, new texts, her daughter's face lighting up, thumbs working the keys.

Outside the airport doors, drivers call to them: "Madam, can I help you?" "We drive cheap." "Hello, hello!" Men in crisp cotton shirts and slacks hold signs: *Dreams Resort, Erma and John Hitchcock*; *Encantata Resort, Gillian and Scott Truitt*; *Azulik, Smith Family Reunion*. Passengers pour through the exit doors behind them, Lilly feeling puffs of cool air on her neck each time the sliding doors open. Dialing the hotel, hearing a voice speak English on the other end, Lilly shouts to be heard. "Lilly Moore. We're by the main door."

"Wait there, madam. Your driver is close. Ten more minutes."

Thirty minutes pass. They are hot, dehydrated, and tired. Tessa's phone keeps pinging, her thumbs tapping quick dashes of connection.

SARGASSO SEA

Lilly calls the resort again. "We are still waiting."

"He is almost there," the woman at the hotel tells Lilly. "Ten more minutes."

A Mercedes bus parks in front of them, Americans climbing aboard, a woman in a white suit handing guests cocktails as they take their plush, high seats, the guests looking down on Lilly and her daughter. On the side of the bus, blue waves: *Sandals, Cancun.*

As the bus drives away to passengers' cheers, Lilly says, "I've always disliked pampered Americans wanting things to happen on American time." She remembers reading about Sandals, Cancun, #1 on Trip Advisor—all-inclusive meals, cocktails, side trips to caves and Mayan ruins, four different pools, one for adults only.

"Let's take a cab," Tessa suggests. She has two weeks of vacation a year. Off the clock, she feels entitled to indulge: pedicures, manicures, facials. She would never waste time waiting for a car that didn't show up.

"I already paid for an airport transport," Lilly explains. "The hotel is three hours away. We got a special deal." But maybe it wasn't a special deal. Maybe it was a rip-off. She isn't sure about pesos to dollars. She doesn't speak Spanish. Lilly wonders if she made a huge mistake booking an eco-yoga resort.

The crowd of drivers changes, old signs disappear, new signs arrive. *Ritz Cancun*; *Hilton Cancun*; *Intercontinental.* The cab drivers seem to sense Lilly's desperation. "Where are you going, madam. I take you cheap." Lilly dials the hotel one more time.

"If someone doesn't come right now, we'll take a cab and demand our money back. We've been waiting an hour!"

"He is there," the woman on the other end tells her.

A small man appears, holding up a handwritten sign, *Maya*, on a piece of cardboard. "Moores?" He pronounces it *Morez*. "Come," he tells them. "The driver will be here soon."

"You're not the driver?" Lilly asks.

"Soon." He hands them each a bottle of water, leads them through the crowd to an open space along the curb. When the van pulls up twenty minutes later, Lilly and her daughter climb into the back seat, adjust the air conditioning vents on their faces. They lean back, looking out at passing scenery, scruffy grass and dense jungle on one side of the highway, expensive hotel entrances with tall gates and guardhouses on the other.

Across the seat, Lilly listens to Tessa's blue fingernails click. From thousands of miles north, Mr. Married reaches her. Apparently, her daughter has the expensive international cell plan that extends to the far edges of the Yucatan peninsula where the yoga resort is situated between jungle and ocean.

"What, Mom?" Tessa looks up from her phone. "You're staring at me with that look."

"Nothing."

"I hate when you don't say what you're thinking."

Lilly shifts her gaze out the window as they pass the entrance to a monkey sanctuary. She remembers the one time she met Mr. Married. Tessa brought him to the house for a Sunday night dinner. Lilly watched through the curtains as he got out of his Tesla, opening the passenger door for her daughter. "Too good-looking," Lilly whispered to her husband, referring to his brown buzz cut, graying sideburns, and deceptively warm smile.

As they came through the door, Tessa called out, "We're here," and Lilly stood in the hallway, thinking his teeth were too white, not knowing what to say to a married man courting her daughter.

But Mr. Married didn't hesitate to hug Lilly. "So nice to meet you," he said, before shaking hands with Tessa's father. "You have an amazing daughter."

"Then why haven't you fired Henry?" Lilly blurted.

"—Mom!" Tessa cut her off.

"I understand," Mr. Married nodded. "And, believe me, I'd like to fire him, but it's almost impossible to prove stalking between colleagues, and this guy, Henry, he's a brilliant prosecutor, one of the best in the state."

Remembering that night, Lilly fumes silently as the van passes through Tulum—bars painted orange and blue, souvenir shops with woven blankets hanging in front. Four years, Mr. Married strung her daughter along, promising to marry her, insisting his divorce was imminent, using up her fertile years, until now, as Tessa approaches her thirty-ninth birthday, he has become a habit, Tessa's fallback when other relationships don't pan out. By the time they reach the resort, Lilly thinks of this trip as an intervention.

Eight months ago, the dentist found the lump in Lilly's husband's jaw, a little lump. "Probably a cyst," the dentist said. "We find a lot of cysts in the salivary glands, small benign blockages."

But it wasn't a cyst. "Mucoepidermoid carcinoma, third stage," the otolaryngologist told them after the lump was removed. "He'll need surgery right away to remove the salivary gland and lymph nodes on that side. Then he'll need radiation every day for three months."

"Is it related to the melanoma?" Lilly asked, holding her husband's hand.

"We don't know," the doctor admitted.

Every morning while they strapped the mask over her husband's face, customized with a hole for neck and jaw, Lilly sat in the waiting room, turning pages of *Travel and Leisure*, the issue with "Best Adventure Vacations." She kept returning to "Best Yoga Spa," an eco-resort in Mexico, photos showing beaches and thatched roofs, sandy paths, open-air yoga studios overlooking the ocean. *Return to yourself with our five-day rejuvenation package.* Looking up from the magazine, she watched the patients on trial drugs clearly losing the battle but willing themselves to keep trying. Rotating wives and husbands, daughters and sons, sometimes paid caregivers, sitting quietly in the waiting room. She understood vulnerability better now, how genes were a matter of luck.

After radiation, when they returned for the six-month follow-up, Tessa came to sit with Lilly while her father was taken to another wing of the hospital for a CT scan.

"Tinder? You're on Tinder?" Lilly couldn't believe her daughter was swiping at the hospital. "Have you seen the *Law and Order* episode? It was based on a true story."

"Hot single doctors." Tessa laughed, showing her mother a very handsome orthopedist. "Don't worry. I rarely meet anyone, and if I do, it's at a coffee shop."

"But he can follow you back to your car." Lilly fought the desire to say, *You've already been stalked once!*

"I usually Uber."

"Uber! You can be a stage-three sex offender and get a license to drive for Uber." Lilly believed she had a responsibility to inform her daughter since Tessa didn't read newspapers. "Did you hear about what happened in Michigan? First word. *Uber*. Second word. *Decapitated.* Third word. *Trunk—*"

"—Enough, Mom." Tessa shoved her phone into her purse. "I should get to work." Leaning over, she gave her mother a brisk hug. "Call me with the results."

Despite occasional setbacks with her daughter, Lilly has been trying to let go of her need to be in control, under the guidance of her therapist. Years of Lilly telling her therapist, "I was very good. I kept my mouth shut." But then, explaining to her therapist how nobody talks about the fallout from smart, independent daughters. "All the studies focus on the lack of educated men, the impact of available sex, hookup culture, which, by the way," Lilly added, "*is* rape culture. No articles talk about mothers worrying as their daughters breeze into their forties alone, still dating strangers on online websites."

At their last appointment, Lilly reminded her therapist about the phone ringing at eleven p.m. the previous weekend, her whole body adrenalized when she saw her daughter's number. "I texted her, *Everything okay?* And she texted back, *Sorry, butt dial.*" Lilly shook her head, "How was I supposed to sleep? What if Henry was holding a knife to her throat, and she'd managed to call for help?"

The therapist always told Lilly the same thing. *Detach. Detach. Detach.*

That morning, after Tessa left the hospital, Lilly's husband found her in the waiting room and hugged her. "Clean bill of health." They both choked up and kept hugging until he nodded at the magazine he'd noticed her reading every morning. "You deserve a vacation. Take Tessa with you. She loves yoga." He smiled. "You both need a break."

Lilly did need a break. All the doctors' visits, prescription pickups, grocery runs, soups and puddings and smoothies that went down a radiated throat, every flavor of popsicle and gelato filling their freezer, kitchen counter lined with medicines. For six months, she'd felt the need to prepare, her brain forming neuronal connections that would withstand loss, as well as arranging the help she would need if her husband's health deteriorated (dog-walker, handyman, snow removal, lawncare). His snoring was worse now that he'd lost a salivary gland, waking her at four a.m., her fears and worries gathered into a tight little ball of wakefulness, a ball that bounced forward, out of her grip, empty house, empty bed, empty future, concentric circles expanding, as if life were one long hyperventilation with no paper bag in sight.

"I'm not going on a vacation without you," she told him, as they left the hospital. "I'll wait until you get your energy back, and we'll go someplace together."

"Go to Mexico with Tessa. You need to have some fun." He handed her the keys to the car. "Honestly? I could use a little time alone without anyone hovering over me."

Climbing out of the van, they feel engulfed by the strong odor. "What is that smell?" Lilly whispers to Tessa as they pull their bags-on-wheels over the sandy path to the reception desk, a large open-air lounge under an elegant, sweeping thatched roof. She parks her bag before a long desk, and gives her name to the hotel manager. He hands them each a bottle of water and checks them in.

"Your cabana is ready, madam." He unfolds a map of the grounds. "Number eleven, just beyond the restaurant."

Arriving at their cabana, overlooking the ocean, they see the source of the pungent odor—hills of thick, rubbery Sargassum seaweed decomposing on the beach. Lilly closes the windows to lessen the intensity, and immediately realizes they can see nothing but salt fog. She opens them again. They turn on the ceiling fan, but the smell remains, absorbed into the thatched roof, bamboo furniture, contents of the purified water container.

They unpack, each taking one side of the room—two single beds draped with netting, two small side tables. Near the windows sit two bamboo armchairs and a table, facing the sea. The bathroom has a compostable toilet with a sign: *No tissue in toilet please! We respect the earth's ecosystem.* The shower has another sign: *Do not drink! This seawater has been desalinated and is safe for showering.*

Lilly crawls under her net. The resort is a shoes-optional environment, bowls of water placed strategically in front of each cabana. She has rinsed her feet, but sand still clings to her ankles and calves. Too tired to get up and wash them, she lies on top of the covers and closes her eyes, holding the sheet over her nose. "What if the smell lasts the whole week?"

"We're here, Mom. Let's just enjoy it." Wearing her bikini, Tessa comes out of the bathroom. She is tall and thin with long blonde hair. "See you later." She heads toward the beach to catch the last rays of sun.

But right away, Tessa returns to the cabana, her voice registering alarm. "Mom, come see."

On the beach, below their cabana, English words written in seaweed: *I raped a girl*, each word the length of a car, spanning the beach beneath the eco-yoga resort. Yoga people gather on the hill, arms around each other. A television helicopter hovers overhead. Police gather in a group taking photos. Nearby, two Mexican men shovel seaweed while the hotel manager talks to the police. He gestures to them to shovel the words.

Lilly stares at her daughter. "Have you heard from Henry recently?"

"I've asked you never to say his name."

"But have you?"

Putting in her ear pods, Tessa shakes her head and heads toward the beach.

Lilly lies under her cabana net, remembering all the months Henry drove by her daughter's house, left messages of heavy breathing on her phone, hacked into her cell calendar and arrived at restaurants where she was meeting people. He sat nearby, staring at her, sending drinks to her table on his bill. Sometimes, in the middle of the night, he rang her doorbell until a light went on, then he left. Once, after a huge blizzard, Tessa arrived on the street to find her car completely cleared of snow, tires dug out, a message left under the windshield wiper. *Forever.* Roses arrived weekly, and when Tessa called the florist, she was told they were from an anonymous sender. He'd paid in cash for a year's worth of weekly bouquets. "Wow, he must really love you," the florist said.

After six months of his stalking, Lilly and her husband

convinced Tessa to file a report at the police station. But Henry was a criminal lawyer and brilliant at covering his own tracks. Only when Lilly and her husband called Henry's family and asked them to intervene, did they discover that Henry had been diagnosed with schizophrenia in college. "He's done it before, stalked women," his mother confided. "He's fine when he's on medication. He'd never hurt anyone. I wish we could help," she told Lilly. "But he doesn't speak to us anymore."

Before dinner, Lilly and Tessa sit in hammocks, looking at the sunset. The only sign of the rapist's message is the increased number of guards, three uniformed men strolling different sections of the beach. Further away, the same two Mexican men wearing back braces are still swinging pitchforks of seaweed into the wheelbarrows. In the days to come, Lilly will see them working from sun-up to sundown, pushing their loads along the sandy paths and across the busy road, disappearing into the jungle, coming back with empty wheelbarrows.

As the sun sets, mother and daughter watch guests pass by on the beach, shoeless men and women with *Om* and *Presence* written across their t-shirts. A family walks by, speaking German, parents and children all with blonde dreadlocks. Lilly says, "Maybe they lost their comb."

Tessa laughs as she gazes at the ocean. "I love the sound of waves."

Lilly can't stop searching the beach for Henry. Lanterns light bars packed with tourists. She hadn't expected the beach to be so built-up—fancy hotels, bars, restaurants, wooden shacks with signs out front: *Astrology*; *Tarot Readings*; *Massage*; *Wind Surfing Classes.* As dusk falls, rocks and fishermen become a single silhouette. The moon rises, casting its reflection across water. "Is there any way he could've found out we're here?"

"Jesus, Mom." Tessa gets up from the hammock and heads toward the restaurant, and Lilly, sensing she has once again crossed a line, gathers her shawl and follows.

Dinner is over by seven. No television, no Wi-Fi in their room. In frigid Minneapolis, the simplicity of a cabana without television had sounded great, but Tessa wants to take a walk. "I'll stay on the premises," she promises her mother. "The paths are well lit."

Lilly reads in bed, vigilant to sounds outside, waiting for her daughter.

Tessa returns right away. "It's so dark here at night. No one's on the beach except for the guards."

It is only eight when Tessa gets into bed. Lilly lies under her net, aware of scratching sounds in the thatch above—Roof rats? Scorpions? Iguanas? Aware, too, of crashing waves thirty feet away, her body responding, not with the calm promised in the "Best of the Best" article, but an inner erosion, waves loosening earth. Lilly had pictured mother and daughter sitting in hammocks under stars and moon, talking late into the night. She turns off the light. She doesn't know why she thought sharing a cabana would be fun. She and Tessa are both introverts, and introverts don't share rooms easily. She can feel her daughter two feet away, Tessa's movements entering Lilly's space like invisible paper airplanes landing on her forehead. Tessa yawns, *airplane!* Plumps her pillow, *airplane!*

Flings open her net, *airplane!*

"Maybe the nets are there to catch the iguanas falling from the ceiling," Lilly says.

Tessa turns over, away from her mother. "Feels like we're camping."

"Don't tell your father that. He paid a fortune. This trip is my birthday present."

"Goodnight, Mom."

The next morning, they wake to a loud banging. Tessa opens the curtain. "The cooks are chopping coconuts." Half an hour later, they walk barefoot over sandy paths to the morning yoga class in the main hall overlooking the ocean. On the door is a note: *Reserved for Lynn Terry's Ashtanga group.* They hurry to the second hall further down the beach. *Reserved for Lotus Vinyasa Teacher Training.* It is ten to seven, and the resort classes start at seven. They hurry to the front desk. "Is there any morning yoga for guests who aren't part of a group?" Lilly asks.

The man at the front desk points toward the road. "Small studio, madam."

By the time they arrive, the small cement slab under a flat, thatched roof is crowded with mostly older women and a few younger couples. They squeeze in at the back. Behind the hedge, trucks rumble by, delivering purified water, horns honking, making it difficult to hear the yoga teacher.

The teacher, Ingrid, is from Germany. She sits cross-legged, chanting in Sanskrit. When she is done chanting, she demonstrates a sun salutation. Gradually, it becomes clear that the entire class will be sun salutations.

"Maybe the afternoon classes are better," Tessa says after class, heading back to their cabana.

"On that dinky square of cement?" Lilly asks, noticing Tessa's quickened step, a warning her daughter doesn't want to take care of her mother's feelings.

Lilly glances toward the office. "I might sign up for the snorkeling trip."

"You should," Tessa says, a little too encouraging.

At the open-air concierge, Lilly stares at a posting on the large bulletin board: *Note to Guests: Please know that we are doing our best to remove the Sargassum seaweed and make your stay as pleasant as possible.*

While a couple pays their bill, she reads the information underneath: *The Sargasso Sea is the only sea without a boundary, a region of the North Atlantic Ocean one thousand miles wide and three thousand miles long. Recent changes in climate and increased environmental destruction have caused massive sargassum blooms along coasts.*

Lilly stares at satellite images of seaweed blooms. They remind her of her husband's cancer when the doctor showed them the MRI. Even though she knows he is fine at home without her, Lilly feels there is a valve inside her, a worry valve, that won't turn off.

"Madam," the manager turns the book so Lilly can see the empty sign-up sheet. "Unfortunately, no one else has signed up, and we need at least four people for the trip to go. I can give you the name of a private guide." He has soft brown eyes, a patient smile. "If you wish to go tomorrow, we must notify him right away."

"How long is the trip?"

"Eight hours. You will want to see everything, no?"

Lilly doesn't want to leave her daughter alone for a whole day, not after the seaweed message. "Thank you," she says. "I'll have to think about it."

When she doesn't move away from the desk, the manager asks, "Anything else, madam?"

She looks toward the beach. "Do the police have any idea who it is? Did anyone report a rape?"

"I am sorry, madam, we do not have any information. We are increasing our security, of course."

"But no one here has reported seeing any strangers? Men who aren't supposed to be here?"

"No, madam."

She finds Tessa lying on a lounge chair. "The trips are canceled because no one else signed up." Lilly pulls out her tube of SPF-70 and sets it next to her daughter's shoulder. "Your father had melanoma and throat cancer."

Tessa looks up at Lilly's colorful beachwear and bursts into laughter.

"I bought SPF clothing at Coolbar," Lilly says of her flowered serape and SPF-50 full bodysuit. "You're welcome to borrow."

Tessa takes photos of her mother in beach clothing, every inch covered, including a wide-brimmed SPF-50 hat flapping furiously in the wind.

"Do not post any photos of me on Facebook," Lilly says, sweating under her SPF clothing.

"I can send them to Dad, can't I?"

"Only him." She stares at the women next to them on break from their yoga studies, sipping coconut milk through straws. "Do you want a coconut?"

Tessa holds up her water bottle. "Coconut's fattening." Tessa exudes good health. She drinks liters of water and protein smoothies, abstains from all forms of mind-altering substances. She has many rules, but none of them apply to her phone. She goes back to scrolling.

A few feet away, two yoga women on break lather sunscreen over bared ankles. "I never remember the Sanskrit, do you?" asks the younger one.

"I don't need to know what the chants mean," says the one with thin gray braids. "I feel so calm afterward."

Twenty feet in front of Lilly, a Mexican family arrives with a large umbrella. The father plants the pole in the sand, and the son, a teenager, sets two pails underneath. The father and son take a large net and wade out to an island of rocks the size of a house. The other two children follow their mother into a shallow pool behind the rocks, the mother holding a baby in her arms. From the rocks, the father casts the net. When the wave passes, the son gathers it, wades to shore, and dumps mussels into the pail.

Tessa's phone pings.

"*Ping*," Lilly says. "*Ping, ping, ping, pi—*."

"—Stop." Tessa cuts her off.

"I thought you were going to disconnect."

"Work stuff," she says, without looking up.

"Can't you do one of those automatic out-of-the-office things?"

"Not talkie time yet."

Touché. Lilly used this line when Tessa was a little girl, and Lilly edited books at home for a living.

The same bird keeps cawing. Lilly's heart caws in response.

Her daughter's shoulders are burning, but Lilly has to choose her battles. It is the kind of love that requires constant pruning. Her daughter's phone is pinging the way it did when Henry was sending hundreds of messages each day.

"Who's pinging you so much?" Lilly asks.

"A client."

"Really?"

When Tessa ignores her, Lilly gets up and walks to the restaurant. She drinks two signature mojitos and orders her own bowl of signature guacamole. Her daughter joins her for lunch and sips lemon water, sticking to the bowl of salsa. The buffet is mostly vegetarian, rice dishes with vegetable medleys, ingredients listed on cards. Lilly makes it through her salad before she asks, "Why, when you know he's not going to leave his wife?"

"We're just online friends. He's going through a hard time. His son was diagnosed with autism."

"Be glad you're not married to him."

Tessa, too angry to look at her mother, rises from the table, "I'll get a smoothie for lunch," and leaves Lilly sitting alone.

"Do you mind?" A woman sets down her tray across the table from Lilly. "Was that your daughter who just left?"

Lilly nods. "She's sick of me already."

"I'm Ann."

"Lilly."

"I have a daughter. She just turned thirty." Ann digs into her coconut curry.

"Is she married?" Lilly asks.

"Sort of." Ann leans in, confiding, "She's polyamorous."

Lilly stares at her, shaking her head. "I don't know what that means."

"She loves three women in three different, committed ways. She calls it ethical non-monogamy." Ann shrugs. "She says it's the only way a person can really fulfill all the parts of herself."

"Didn't we do that in the sixties and call it a commune?" Lilly asks.

"They don't all live together," Ann explains, taking a sip of water.

"What about jealousy?"

"Apparently, this generation doesn't feel jealous. Social media has changed all that. There's just so much of everything available on their phones." Ann wipes her mouth with a napkin. "I heard a story on *Science Friday* that elephants are evolving without tusks because that's what they're killed for. It's the species' way of avoiding extinction."

Lilly doesn't see the connection. "What if they want kids? Who pays for college?"

"Don't ask me. You should see her calendar. Exhausting." Ann nods at Lilly. "You're lucky. My daughter would never have time to take a vacation with me. She has to plan three different vacations with her partners."

Checking her watch, Lilly excuses herself from the table. "I should go call my husband before he takes his nap." Walking toward the lounge, the only area her cellphone works, Lilly wishes Tessa had three committed partners to look after her. Tessa lives alone, working long hours at her new job at a law firm in downtown Minneapolis, coming home late at night to an empty house.

"Which would you prefer," she asks her husband when he picks up the phone. "A daughter who lives alone, or a daughter who has multiple partners?"

"Whatever makes her happy."

"You're probably equal to three partners," Lilly teases.

"I hope that means I fill all your needs."

"Yes, yes, yes," she laughs. "I miss you."

After they hang up, Lilly walks along the beach. It takes her about three minutes to see Henry—curly red hair, preppy pink Polo, sailor shorts, wide calves. She hurries toward him, heels digging into the sand, but just as she's catching up to him, he turns—a birthmark along his cheek, not Henry. The seaweed fronds are big as plates, and as she turns back, Lilly weaves to avoid the mounds, sometimes stepping through, sometimes circling, saddened by the plastic bottles and diapers trapped in the ropey vines. What a relief rain would be, Lilly thinks, any excuse to stay under her net.

Day three, another seaweed-message appears: *Stop me, please.*

Lilly stands on the hill next to her daughter, staring at the beach. "This is Henry's modus operandi. He always leaves messages—"

Tessa leans down to tighten her shoelaces.

"You *know* it is."

Launching into a run, she waves goodbye to her mother with

the back of her hand.

Lilly tries to construct a routine: read and sketch. She unpacks her beach bag filled with sketchbook and old *New Yorkers*. But the constant breeze makes it difficult to concentrate—flapping hat and umbrella, gusts of sand when people walk by. She feels unsettled, agitated, wind swaying fronds of palm, feathery bushes, pages flashing light and dark with moving shadows. Coconuts fall with a thud. She cannot force relaxation, cannot force herself to unwind. She puts her magazine away, stares at the waves.

Overnight, the seaweed carpets have collected into small hills. The five-star hotel next door uses an army of men and an ATV with a large trailer attached. The men shovel the trailer full of seaweed, then the truck heads across the road to deposit the load in the jungle. Two loads, and the hotel's beach is cleared by ten a.m. Their guests are sipping coffee without the pungent odor filling their nostrils.

"Our guys are burying it right over there," the woman sitting behind Lilly says to her husband. "Yesterday they were taking it into the jungle. Maybe the jungle's full."

"Every invention was motivated by a problem," the husband says, dismissing his wife's observations.

"You've lost your sense of smell," his wife says. "It's not a problem for you."

"They'll probably learn how to make antibiotics out of it. Or bombs. There's energy in every kind of decomposition."

Mr. Married talked like that, Lilly thinks, recalling the night they met him. He represented pharmaceutical firms in lawsuits. "You can tell a lot about a country by the way it administers medicines," he told them. "Italy gives you shots you administer yourself. France, suppositories you-know-where. Germany is all homeopathic. Spain is packets of powder you mix in hot water. The U.S. is pills. Easy, right?"

"I wouldn't say easy," Lilly said. Her husband was taking a pill form of chemotherapy and pill bottles lined their kitchen counter.

"He makes me laugh," Tessa told her mother in the kitchen.

Lilly leaned over the sink, rinsing dishes. "Can't be seen in public together? Huge, *huge* red flag."

"He's protecting my reputation at work."

Lilly kept rinsing. "They're not even separated yet."

"It's complicated." Tessa unwrapped the dessert they'd brought. "Because of the children."

"Just protect yourself." Lilly faced her daughter. "Don't let him think you'll wait forever."

Then last fall, three years after they'd begun their affair, Mr. Married told her daughter he had too much debt to divorce his wife. He thought it best if Tessa looked for another job.

"It's over," Tessa told her mother. "We've both agreed it's over."

Lilly sees her daughter in the distance, walking toward her wearing a pink bikini. She remembers when Tessa was four and wore a pink tutu for a whole summer. She loved to eat Goldfish, and sometimes Lilly would pick one out of the pink netting, telling her daughter, "Your tutu is magic. It's growing Goldfish." Giggling, Tessa would shake to see if there were more Goldfish hidden there. "Part of me believed that skirt was magic," Tessa once told her mother. "I really thought Goldfish grew there." That same part of her wants to believe he will leave his wife, Lilly thinks, even now.

*

By the third evening, they are already tired of the resort's healthy cuisine. Tessa googles local restaurants and finds an authentic Mexican restaurant up the road.

"That side." The hotel manager points toward the jungle. "Ten-minute walk."

Arriving just after five, they find only eight tables, and most are already filled. As they take their seats, the waiter sprays insecticide around the perimeter of the dining area, then lights citronella torches, pungent smoke filling the air.

"Should we be breathing that?" Lilly whispers.

Two dogs lie at their feet. Tessa loves dogs and rubs behind their ears.

"It's the Zika outbreak," Lilly says. "You're not planning to get pregnant in the next year, right?"

"I'm never planning to get pregnant. I'm thirty-eight, Mom. I've decided."

"Maybe you should consider saving your eggs." Lilly believes if her daughter met the right man she would want to have a child.

Tessa sips her mango water. "The last thing this world needs is more people."

"That's a cerebral approach to life."

"So is saving eggs." Tessa shrugs. "I was raised by cerebral people."

"What about adoption?" Lilly asks. "Those children are already here."

"I sometimes work with mothers who give their kids up for

adoption, and they never get over it."

"What's a future without children?"

"What's a future with half the planet burning up," Tessa says, shaking her head, "the other half at risk for flooding when the oceans rise?"

They eat in silence.

When they get back to their cabana, the Mexican family is still there, gathering mussels under the moon. Lilly notices how affectionate the children are with their mother, one girl laying her head on her mother's lap while the other braids her mother's hair.

Lilly sits in the open-air lounge and calls her husband while Tessa showers.

"She doesn't want children."

"That's okay."

"I keep thinking I see Henry on the beach."

"You always see Henry."

Lilly fights back tears. Women's bodies carry extinction inside them. She knows this, just as she also knows she is responsible for her own suffering, platitudes of hope, ski jumps of feeling, no place to go but down. She has never felt such powerlessness, in all directions. It's the kind of knowledge she doesn't want, like wading into water until her face is submerged.

She tells her husband, "I'm never going to be a grandmother."

He says, "Could be much worse."

He means their daughter could have breast cancer. He means their daughter could give birth to a baby girl who dies six days later. He means their daughter could die of a heroin overdose. These things have happened to their friends. Lilly meets a group of women for wine and cheese Sunday afternoons, telling each other braggers aren't allowed. Meaning the grandmothers at book group who pass around photos of their grandchildren.

Day four. Lilly does not leave her net except to walk to the restaurant to get breakfast, lunch, and dinner. Then back to her cabana where she crawls under her net. She reads two books, a Swedish mystery and a collection of short stories by William Styron.

She loves her net. She imagines people asking her, *How was Mexico?* And she will tell them, *I loved my net.*

Outside, the birds are loud. Everything moves in Mexico, wind, shadows, water. Nature is under her sternum, stirring up all the feelings Lilly has kept contained during her husband's cancer treatment. She wants to relax. She wants to unwind and breathe in the wind and waves, the beauty of the ocean. Instead, everything overwhelms her, the brightness of sun, crashing of waves, shrieks of birds; nothing familiar, nothing that lets her rest.

Beyond the window, the same two Mexican men continue to shovel seaweed, their eyes cast down, as if they've been told not to look at guests. Lilly cringes with shame, her own sadness self-indulgent, imagining what they must feel as they shovel seaweed in front of tourists drinking cocktails out of coconuts.

Late afternoon, Tessa comes in from the beach. "You're still here? You've barely left the room."

Lilly hears it in her voice. Tessa wants the room to herself.

"Are you having a breakdown?" Tessa stares at her mother.

Lilly curls into a ball. Islands in her chest sink under water.

"Not a major breakdown," she tells her, "a little breakdown, a vacation breakdown."

On their last morning, the third seaweed message appears: *I'm sorry.*

Lilly stands on the hill above the beach, holding her coffee mug in both hands. "First guilt, then a plea for help, now an apology. You know it's him."

Tessa nods, shocking her mother. She opens her phone and shows her mother the email she received from Mr. Married the first day: *Henry is on vacation this week. I've asked around, but no one knows where. Just thought I should warn you.*

Lilly stares at her daughter, mouth agape.

"You would have insisted we leave," Tessa says. "I don't want to give Henry that much power over my life."

"But you give Mr. Married that much power."

"He's been checking in with me every day to make sure we've had no Henry sightings."

"He feels guilty." Lilly shakes her head. "How could you not tell me?"

"I've learned it's better to ignore Henry," Tessa tells her. "Besides, the law doesn't apply here. If you saw him, what could you do?"

"Snip, snip," Lilly makes a scissoring motion with her fingers. "If he ever comes near you again, he'll be speaking in a very high voice, if he speaks at all."

Tessa laughs, wrapping an arm around her mother's shoulders.

"I'll visit you in prison."

Their final afternoon, Lilly is reading in the hammock when Tessa, returning from her swim, steps inside the cabana and screams, "Mom, quick!"

Hurrying to her daughter's side, Lilly sees the iguana sitting on Tessa's pillow, small threads of iguana shit staining the pillowcase.

"Do something, Mom. Get it out."

"I told you the nets were there for a reason."

The iguana's throat pulses.

"You're the mother. You have to get it out of here." Tessa runs into the bathroom and won't come out.

Lilly picks up her plastic toiletry kit, empties it on the dresser, and gently puts it over the iguana. She lifts the reptile and sets it outside the door, where it scurries away.

Tessa removes the pillow from the case, "So disgusting," and exchanges her pillow for Lilly's clean pillow.

"No way." Lilly grabs it back.

They both tug, until this pretend battle takes on a life of its own, and everything they are pulling against is inside them, too, one of them stronger, one of them refusing to let go, some primitive anger shaping itself.

Tessa twists the pillow. "I'm your child. You're supposed to give me your pillow."

Not today, Lilly thinks, not when she has warned her daughter to keep her net down.

"You're not a child anymore." Lilly releases the pillow, and

Tessa falls onto her bed. "Those days are long, *long* gone."

Tessa picks up her phone, heads outside.

"Go call Mr. Married," Lilly calls out. "Ask him if he's fired Henry yet. Ask him that!"

Dusk has begun to fall, the sun a pearl under cotton. The restaurant they've chosen for their last night is built like a tree house overlooking the beach. The scent of grilled pineapple fills the air, and Andrea Bocelli sings in a continuous loop.

Next to them, a man stares into his cell until his wife says sharply, "Couldn't we at least order first?"

The waitress in tight shorts and midriff t-shirt places two mojitos in front of Lilly and her daughter. "The gentleman over there ordered these for you."

They turn in synchronized dread toward the bar. The waitress stares at the empty seat. "He was just there."

Tessa sends the drinks back and, looking at her mother, shakes her head. "Believe me, if it's him, the best policy is to ignore him."

"Order me a margarita. I have to go to the bathroom," Lilly tells her.

She hurries down the stairs and leaves the restaurant, glancing along the beach. This time she is certain it is Henry, a hundred feet away, walking at a fast clip. Lilly is running, adrenalin pulsing through her legs and arms, pushing her to move faster. Gaining on him, she weaves through couples walking the beach at sunset, hills of seaweed giving way under her feet. She never loses sight of him, never looks away. When she is almost at his side, she yells, "Henry, stop," and is surprised when he does.

He turns and stares at her. Lilly has seen a photo of him among the lawyers' portraits hanging in the office where Tessa used to work. He is tall and sturdy, a rugby player, according to her daughter, thick arms and calves, his muscular build on display in Hawaiian shirt and khaki shorts. Lilly might have found him handsome under different circumstances, red curls blowing in the breeze, sunburned cheeks, his unshaven chin catching the last of the sunset, bristles aglow. He digs his hand into his pocket, and for a moment, Lilly is terrified he will pull out a knife and lunge for her. But he pulls out an inhaler and takes two puffs. "Asthma," he tells her. "All the pollen."

Lilly is breathless, her voice strained with anger. "I'm Tessa's mother."

He smiles. "I know. I sent two drinks to your table." His confidence verges on swagger.

Lilly is unprepared for his unruffled demeanor, as if it were entirely normal for them to run into each other on a beach in Mexico. It is his calm veneer that alarms her, his disconnect with what is real.

"I know it's you leaving the seaweed messages." Lilly's voice rises, her fury unleashed, causing passersby to stop and stare. "You're stalking her again, and it has to stop."

His face settles into a small, tight smile. "I would never hurt Tessa."

"But you *are* hurting her," Lilly cries out. "You need to leave her alone."

"Or what?" Henry's eyebrows bob up and down, his mouth

a smirk, as if he finds Lilly's anger amusing. Shaking his head, he erupts into laughter, chortling in a way that makes Lilly understand—he is truly ill.

Shaken and outraged, Lilly has a sudden glimpse into her daughter's strength, the courage it has taken for Tessa to live her life in spite of Henry's menacing presence. But Tessa is right. There is nothing Lilly can do, nothing in Mexico, at least. Trembling and outraged, she walks away, half expecting Henry to follow her. But when she reaches the restaurant and glances back, Henry is nowhere in sight.

"What took you so long?" Tessa eyes her suspiciously.

"Long line for the women's bathroom." Lilly, breathless, takes several sips from her margarita, sparing her daughter the truth and refusing to give Henry the power to ruin their last night together.

Tessa glances at the tables around them, most occupied by couples her age. "You know what I was remembering today?" her voice cloudy, holding back. "*The Velveteen Rabbit*."

Lilly smiles. "You wanted me to read that book to you every night."

"Remember how Velveteen Rabbit asks Old Toy Horse, *What is real?*"

Lilly nods.

"And Old Toy Horse answers, *Once you are real, you can't become unreal. Real lasts forever*." Tessa takes her napkin and wipes tears from her eyes. "The Velveteen Rabbit needed someone to love him to become real. I haven't found that."

There is an anchor of sadness in her daughter's voice Lilly hasn't heard before. She squeezes her daughter's hand. Lilly understands,

understands better than her daughter realizes. She used to think it was important to hold onto dreams. But the question that has eaten away at her all these years is when to let go, and once you do, what replaces the dream? Certainly not every dream will come true. When do you just say, *This one's a lemon.*

Later that night, their last, Lilly wakes in the dark to see her daughter texting under the net. The light illuminates the net and makes it look like a beam from a spaceship is abducting her. Irritated, Lilly wraps a shawl around her shoulders, goes outside, and sits in the hammock. She hears voices on the beach and thinks of Henry, glad her daughter is safe inside, even if she is texting a married man in the middle of the night.

"Sorry if I woke you." Tessa joins her, sitting in the hammock next to her mother. Her voice is hoarse from crying. "I've ended it. I've blocked him on my phone."

Lilly would do anything for her daughter, anything at all. But tonight, sitting side by side under the stars, watching the tide rise, pounding the island of rocks until there is no island, she knows to remain silent.

SOMEONE LESS PERFECT

After ten years together, one grief pulled on another like a string of lights circling our marriage.

Elizabeth was a medical librarian at the university, pale skin, gray eyes, slender fingers with manicured nails. Early in our marriage, she used to tickle my back at night in bed if I let her keep the light on to read. She would hold her medical journal on her knees and keep her fingernails dancing over my skin.

"Did your mother have a C-section?"

"I'm not sure," I mumbled.

"Says here children born by C-section are more likely to have asthma."

She often became so absorbed in an article she would stop moving her hand.

I'd jiggle my back to remind her. "Light-on, equals tickle." She'd laugh and resume tickling.

We had many bargains like that. I didn't even realize they were bargains. I thought we were giving to each other, making each other happy.

The back-tickles ended after the children were born.

"I'll read in the living room," she told me.

"No, I'll wear an eye pillow."

Sometimes, rarely, she would let me take her hand and place it on my groin, my hand moving her hand, and then I would pull off her nightie and underwear, and we would both try to feel the passion we thought we were expected to feel. I would close my eyes and try to remember who I was before, who I was when I actually felt desire. I had to go far back in time, to a pillow in my basement, those early years of discovery. Often, that part of me felt like a ten-hour plane ride away, a slight pressure between my legs, and I would work that pressure for all it was worth. I assumed she was doing the same, fantasizing that we had just met or that I was someone else, a stronger man, a man who left each day in a suit. We would both keep our eyes closed, concentrating on pleasure; on abandoning who we had become.

One night she withdrew her hand and moved onto her back. "I don't know how to please you anymore."

I didn't hear the disdain in her voice. Maybe I didn't want to hear it. I did take a while, sure, but I would give her equal time. I always made sure she had an orgasm.

"Is it something I'm not doing?" She was careful not to hurt my feelings, to make it seem as if it were her technique, which we both knew it wasn't.

"I like everything you do." I placed her hand back on my penis. "Just keep doing it a little longer."

Something I didn't tell her, something I never would've admitted: my softness denying her, me in control, made for a fantastic orgasm.

"Just tell me what turns you on," she sighed. "I can't tell."

I resented all my wife's expectations, not just for me, but also for our children—good grades and good manners and a certain amount of obedience.

SOMEONE LESS PERFECT

"Wash your hands before you sit at the table."

I would stand behind her, winking at the kids, pretending to wash my hands and instead, just wiping them on my pants, making my son and daughter laugh. Standing my ground when she caught me. "Germs are good," I insisted. "They build resistance."

"Don't do that," she said. "Don't undermine me."

Or the time she told them to put napkins in their laps, and I tucked my napkin into my collar. "I want them to understand there's more than one way to do things."

"That's what you do if you eat lobster," she told them, nodding at me. "Or, corn on the cob or spaghetti."

I refused to remove the napkin tucked into my collar.

"Or, you're a baby," she added with that familiar edge to her voice. Beneath her skin were nerves that pulsed and eyes that strained to find something, anything, to like about me. Despite sunhats and nightly retinol cream, lines manifested around her mouth and eyes, lines I am sure I put there, just the stress of living with someone less perfect.

She didn't ask about my work anymore, no doubt tired of hearing me mourn my unfinished paintings, or the paintings that didn't sell, or the show that didn't even give me honorable mention. The agreement we'd come to a decade before—I'd stay home with the kids and paint while they were napping—had, in her mind at least, expired last year when our youngest started kindergarten.

"If I were you," my wife told me one night. "I'd make my neuronal connections spark a bit more than they are sparking now. Maybe you should get a job outside the house." She said it in a jokey way, but I could hear the fear in her voice.

I told myself she had no understanding of the creative process. I drew or painted a few hours each day. But since the gallery that carried my work had closed, I'd lost momentum. The basement walls were covered with drawings of paintings I'd yet to begin. "Who will meet the kids' bus and take them to soccer and swimming?" I asked, facing her in bed.

"You don't have to get a full-time job. Just *something.*"

"Isn't doing my art something? Isn't helping the kids finish their homework something?"

"I'm not criticizing you." She sat up in bed and looked at me in the dark. "But do you even enjoy painting anymore?"

She saw things in me I didn't want to see in myself, and I hated her for it. Not true hate, just a little hate, the kind that seeps in slowly when you live with someone over time.

"Do you like spending hours finding obscure articles on moles for medical students whose earnings will one day quadruple your salary?" I asked her, my voice antagonistic, the way my son sounded when I insisted he tie his shoes before running to the bus. "Do you like filing books on shelves when your work-study students don't show up? Do you like packing up books and sending them to professors too lazy to come get them themselves?"

"Yes," she said. "I actually do. I love my work."

I felt like every conversation ended up with her on top—only, not in bed. She said she had no desire for that kind of closeness, not when she felt distant from me emotionally. Verbally on top, her sense of certainty pressing down on every discussion, like a lid sealing my voice inside a jar.

The following spring, I began teaching watercolor one night a week at the local community college. My students arrived with their supplies, culled from an expensive list I posted on the college website, an investment in their talent as future painters. Their average age was sixty. I broke the process down into what I thought were doable steps, but many of my students had never learned how to draw. They didn't understand color or perspective, or even how the weight of paper affected their paintings. They hid their work from me as I passed, pleading, "Don't look," even though I always found one good thing about each painting. "I like your shadow." "I like that tree." "Good barn."

But deep down, I wasn't convinced art could be taught. You can teach technique and art appreciation and art history, but in the end, an artist has to see something that needs to come to life. Most of my art students wanted to imitate what they saw and the closer the imitation, the happier they were with their paintings. I began to think of most peoples' lives as imitations. I shared this theory with my wife.

"So, what?" she said. "At least they're trying something new."

I liked my students though, especially the older women who brought cookies and iced tea to keep us all awake. As they sat painting, they discussed their children with amazing frankness. One of them had a son who had been in and out of treatment. "Meth," she told us, looking up from her first wash. "Terrible drug. He's a different person now. His wife won't let him see the kids."

Another nodded, mixing a puddle of Payne's Grey on her pallet. "My son has three children by three different women. Sometimes he can't make child support, and the women ask me for money. What can I say? They're the mothers of my grandchildren."

They made me feel better about myself. They made me feel every family had its issues.

That same spring, my wife insisted we see the therapist who had helped a friend of hers. The idea, according to Michael, was to train us how to really listen and be present for each other. Elizabeth wasn't allowed to interrupt, and I had to start every sentence with *I feel.* Once the rules were established, he nodded at me to go first.

"I feel like I always disappoint you," I told her. "And maybe if I hold back, there will be less for you to criticize."

She listened, arms folded across her chest, and when my five minutes were up, she asked the therapist, "My turn?"

"You're supposed to paraphrase first," Michael said. "Look at him when you speak."

She looked at me, her words tinged with sarcasm. "You said you feel like you disappoint me, and that's why you hold back, so I won't have anything to criticize."

"With empathy," Michael told her.

She tried to say the same thing with feeling, but her voice still sounded resigned. "Is it my turn now?"

He nodded.

She took a deep breath and began. "You say you're afraid of letting me down, but I feel like that's just your excuse for keeping everything locked inside you." Her shoulders sank, and she shook her head. "I can't talk to you about us without you feeling criticized. So, what am I supposed to do? Hold it in and get angrier? I feel alone all the time."

"What do you think she wants from you?" Michael asked.

My chest felt like ice thawing, too thin to walk across. I shook my head.

Tears rolled down my wife's cheeks. "Do you even want this to work? You have to know what *you* want."

I loved my kids, and I wanted to love my wife. But I didn't know how to talk about the murky depths where dreams and hopes waged daily war with my self-doubt. Year after year, I'd relinquished that tiny headlamp of self-knowledge that blazed a path into my own inner darkness. Marriage was a petri dish of slow-growing habits, and over time, I'd learned to resist her strong emotions, cloudbursts of demands I didn't know how to fill.

"See, you're doing it right now." She looked at me as she spoke. "Distance has always been your default, John. Don't like yourself? Disappear. Disappointed? Disappear. Fail? Disappear."

Frankly, I was amazed how well she knew me.

Michael seemed to relate very well to her feelings, and I often pointed this out on the drive home. "He'd like to ask you out. He smiles at all your jokes."

"When did I joke?" She glanced at me. "Why are you doing this?"

After three months of therapy, we'd grown careful with each other. I told her it wasn't helping. "It's making it worse."

"It helps me," she said. "If you don't want to go, don't go."

She continued alone, and one evening, after she'd returned

from a session, I asked her what she and Michael had discussed.

"We talk about all the things you and I don't talk about."

"Like what?" I asked, handing her a dish of lasagna I'd warmed in the microwave.

"Seriously?" She took a bite and swallowed. "You stopped going. You don't get to ask."

That weekend, she was going to a conference and had made it quite clear the kids should not see the movie *White Men Can't Jump*, playing at our local theater. I'd seen it years before. "It's only R-rated because of the language. They need to be exposed to more than this bubble."

We often had this conversation, *bubble versus exposure*, and mostly she won. "They're nine and twelve," she insisted. "Let them stay kids."

It rained all weekend. I was tired of playing Go Fish. Tired of her rules too. The kids kept telling me, "Mom will get mad if you leave the dishes piled in the sink." "Mom will get mad if you let us eat granola bars for breakfast." "Mom will get mad if we don't take showers after we swim. Our skin gets rashes."

I took the kids to the movie and afterwards to Ben & Jerry's. "So, you liked the movie?" I asked, watching their heads nod as they licked their double scoops. "You know you should never lie to your mother. But not telling is not the same as lying. All you have to say is that we went to the mall for ice cream and walked around. Not a lie, right? Are we on the same page?" We high-fived each other, sticky hands sealing the deal.

My wife immediately grew suspicious when my son blurted, "We *just* got ice cream."

"What else did you do?"

I saw her watching them. Katie resembled me, brown eyes, soft cheeks, a pensive brow. But my son, Lucas, looked just like his mother, same gray eyes, staring at me now, begging me to tell the truth.

She turned her furious gaze on me. "You took them to the movie, didn't you?"

"They loved it." I looked at them. "You loved it, right?"

They nodded, but they weren't smiling. They sat at the table, watching as their mother turned her fury on me.

"You told them to lie to me?"

"No, I told them not to lie. But I also told them they didn't have to mention it. That's all I said."

"This is what you call being a good parent?" Right in front of them, she told me, "I can't do this anymore. I've tried. We've both tried. You should leave. You can go stay with your brother."

"They're my children too."

"To be a father, you have to actually be an adult." Her gray eyes did not blink. "Don't make this hard for them."

The kids sat frozen at the table.

"Please," she said. "Please go."

"Or what?"

"Or I will."

The kids jumped up, clinging to her legs, crying and telling her not to leave. "Mommy, you can't."

No one was clinging to my legs. No one was telling me to stay. I took it as a vote against me, a vote for her rules. My children would grow up to live their lives according to her expectations. They would never break free. And maybe years from now, they would remember this moment and say, I should have hugged Dad's legs. This is what I was thinking as I marched up the stairs and packed my bags.

A month into my freedom, I caved. I found an apartment and made rules for myself, rules that filled me with shame—ashamed how close they were to my wife's rules: no alcohol before five, no television before eight p.m., healthy meals.

Each night when I called my son and daughter, they sounded tired, unwilling to share their lives over the phone.

"How'd school go today, Lucas?"

"Okay."

"Did you pass your math test?"

"Think so."

"That's great." I paused, listening to him sigh. "Okay, I'll be at your swim meet Thursday. Is your sister there?"

"Hi, Daddy."

"Hey, Katie-pie, how was your day?"

"Good."

"What was good about it?"

"Just was."

After hanging up, the silence grew sharp, jabbing my ribcage like spurs. I told myself we were all adjusting. But without my son and daughter arriving home at four, without reading my daughter to sleep at night, helping my son finish his homework, my days felt like water; I could reach deep, touch bottom, and not grip anything solid.

The air was damp and smelled of wet leaves. Three carved pumpkins sat on the porch, waiting to be lit. *Not four,* I thought, like all the years before.

I stood in the doorway. MPR was on the radio in the kitchen, and no one heard me come in. Elizabeth was at the stove, sautéing pumpkin seeds in oil, scooping them onto paper towels, sprinkling them with salt. She never wasted anything. She was a good cook. Tweed skirt and wool sweater; she hadn't changed from work, except for slippers on her feet and hair pinned back, away from her face.

"Lucas," she said, to stop him kicking his foot against the table leg. The kitchen was soft yellow at the end of the day, windows decorated with cardboard cutouts of witches and ghosts. She scooped grilled cheese sandwiches onto plates.

All of it familiar in a way I missed.

"Daddy!" My daughter looked up, waved her wand. "I made it myself," her fingernails painted orange for Halloween.

"Hungry?" Elizabeth asked.

"No, but thanks. I ate already."

We were polite now, and that made me sad.

"I'm old enough to go alone." Lucas pulled apart his sandwich. Cheese hung like a trapeze.

"But your sister isn't," his mother told him. "And your father wants to go with you."

I felt a wave of exhaustion pass through me.

"You should get going." Elizabeth poured cider into a thermos for me, tightening the lid. "It's almost dark."

My son put on his astronaut helmet, my daughter her crown. I told them they had to wear coats, but they refused. "Mommy made us put on long underwear."

Outside, the street was filled with families, flashlights pointed at sidewalks, kids shouting after one another. I held my daughter's hand when we crossed the street, then let her run after her brother. Her dress was too long and kept tripping her, so I tied the skirt in a knot above her knee. I nodded hello to other parents, watched our children hurry up the steps together.

By the time we returned, bags heavy with candy, my wife had showered and was standing in her pajamas and flannel bathrobe, hands in her pockets. She smelled like lavender, her face shiny with cream. "Take some of the candy home with you."

The kids sat at the kitchen table, sorting bounty. "You like coconut, don't you, Dad?" Giving me the worst of the lot.

"I should go." But I didn't move. I stood beside her in the hallway, warming my hands over the radiator. I wanted to believe there was still the possibility of going back and trying harder, trying to make things right.

My wife's eyes blinked. She always looked prettier when she was sad, her face softer, less defended. "Thanks for taking them." She opened the door, letting the cool air rush between us.

DISAPPEARANCES

Nearing the end of my father's sabbatical year in Florence, my mother convinced him to rent a house in the mountains. She slid the Holiday Homes brochure on top of his computer: "This one has a Ping-Pong table and a waterfall."

It was June, 1994, and I had just turned eleven.

Northern Italy had been deluged by months of rain, causing mudslides and avalanches. But until we arrived in the mountains, soldiers waving our car around roadblocks, my mother hadn't realized that the house we'd rented was at the epicenter of destruction.

She stared at the small cement house—mountain rising steeply behind, waterfall roaring thirty feet away—and told me, "Leah, you're not to go near the waterfall unless we're out here." Across the valley, half a mountain had been amputated by heavy rains, trees washed down the slope, houses buried in mud. The waterfall's constant roar was loud, but not loud enough to block the sound of controlled explosions set off to prevent further landslides. In the distance, chainsaws whined as soldiers cleared fallen trees.

Each morning, I followed my parents up the mountain, a daily trek for gelato at the bar near the summit. Wooden crosses dotted the path along the road, some with small bouquets of plastic flowers. Outside the bar, we sat on the wall overlooking the valley and licked ice cream cones. Bees hovered above violet blossoms. The world smelled of sour, trapped water.

One morning, a week after we'd arrived in the mountains,

my father's cell phone rang, and he fumbled to open it. He'd only recently bought a cell phone, presumably to talk to his editor in New York while we were on vacation. He flipped open the phone, then closed it, shaking his head, telling us he'd been cut off.

"Who was it?" my mother asked.

"My editor."

She stared at him from behind dark glasses. "But she just called a half-hour ago."

My father looked past us toward the road, a worried gaze, something different in his eyes, something that hadn't been there before. "Wait here." He told us he was going to the village church where reception might be better above the trees.

He didn't come back.

We had moved to Florence the previous August, renting an apartment on the first floor of an old villa. Entering through a red wooden door, we faced the kitchen with table and chairs and wood burning stove, the only heat source for the three-bedroom apartment. My parents did not fully register the small size of the icebox, the oven that had to be lit with matches, the steep hill they would have to climb carrying bags of groceries and heavy water bottles. Nor had the reality of heating with wood set in—my mother's asthma was triggered by smoke.

What charmed them was the eccentric landlord, Giancarlo, a ceramic artist who owned the villa and lived in the grander quarters above us. Right away, he insisted on giving us a tour of the garden, drawing our attention to the posted sign: *Renters*

Are Not Allowed In The Garden Without Permission. He led us through the labyrinth of olive and lemon trees, bougainvillea full of pink blossoms. Tiered stone paths opened onto patios, each containing a diorama: foot-high ceramic figures portraying scenes of a family—mother, father, and son—in a hospital room, dining room, kitchen, bedroom, and finally a train station, where the son stood alone without his parents.

"My mother was American, my father Italian." Giancarlo spoke in a halting voice. "They resided here in Florence."

"Here in this villa?" my mother asked.

"No, no, over there," he stammered, pointing toward the hill known for its large palazzos. "They disappeared when I was seven." He kept his gaze averted when he spoke. "It was during the war, and I was sent to a boarding school in England. That's when I began to draw. It was an escape, you see, from the cruelty of other boys." He explained he'd bought the farmhouse in 1974 so that he could open a ceramics school.

"We depended on the kiln." He nodded at the brick structure at the back of the garden. "Ten years ago, the city shut us down because of new pollution laws." He stopped to pick dead leaves off the tree. "All my art was purchased." He glanced at the ceramic figures nearby. "Except for what you see here."

My father seemed amused by Giancarlo, who invited us inside his quarters to see his new masterpiece, a large thick sketchbook of architectural ink drawings through the perspective of ants—Egyptian tombs, French bridges, English cathedrals, drawings of ants in the process of construction.

"He's either brilliant or crazy," my father said later, unpacking his suitcase.

"Maybe his parents sent him to England for safety," my mother said. "Maybe he's Jewish."

"Or maybe they were fascists caught by the partigiani."

Later, when my mother came to kiss me good night, I stared out my bedroom window at the dioramas lit with strung bulbs and thought about Giancarlo's parents. "Could you disappear?" I asked my mother.

"Of course not." She closed the curtains and kissed my forehead. "That was during the war, a long time ago."

Once he came to trust us, Giancarlo granted us permission to use the garden, stipulating that children had to be accompanied by an adult. My mother took to gently mocking him. "You may use the bathroom with permission." "You may heat the stove with permission." "You may lie awake, freezing at night, with permission." By then the temperatures had cooled, and my parents understood why the farmhouse had been vacant for two years and was rented at such a low price.

*

The morning my father disappeared, my mother and I waited half an hour at the café. My mother seemed more irritated than worried. "Perhaps he went into the woods to pee and got lost." After searching the deserted village and finding no sign of him at the church, we walked up and down the steep road twice, a two-mile zigzag stretch, our voices echoing, "Roooo-bert!" "Dad-deeee!"

DISAPPEARANCES

My mother stopped to stare at the river crashing down the mountain. "He hates nature. He loathes hiking. Where would he have gone?" She flagged down a truck ferrying soldiers, alerting them to be on the lookout for an American man. "Forty-eight. Gray hair. He speaks Italian."

The driver grinned. "É un uomo, Signora."

I knew enough Italian to translate: He's a man, Signora. But I didn't understand his meaning until my mother responded with anger. "He's American, not Italian."

The soldiers in back laughed.

We returned to the house to wait. Local roads were blocked by the mudslide, and the only way to reach the nearest town was over the mountain, a hazardous three-hour trip by car. Our rented Renault sat in the graveled parking space next to the house. My mother was alternatingly angry and forlorn, not yet really fearful. Every few minutes she would stand on the marble Ping-Pong table that had drawn us here in the first place and yell up the mountain, "Roooo-bert," her voice echoing across the valley, "Rooo-bert . . . ooobert . . . bert."

*

People disappear in many ways. Months before our trip to the mountains, I had disappeared into a friendship. Aria BelCastello. Tall, thin, huge eyes that watched you. Watched me. Watched all the girls, all eight of us in the fifth-grade class at the American International School of Florence. She assigned us numbers, one through ten. She herself was an eight, a self-assigned eight, and no one else in the class received a higher number. I was an eight, too, and so was Cristina, which is why we ate lunch together, the three of us eights sitting on the low wall, our backs to the other girls, all fives. Aria's mother, Signora BelCastello, was a ten—the only ten on Aria's list. A former top model in Milan, Aria's mother was from New Orleans. She'd met Aria's father when she was seventeen during fashion week in Milan, Aria explained, nodding at the new English teacher from London. "Eight face, five legs."

I would quickly learn that Aria's mother was not the only model-mother at the school. Apparently, many wealthy Florentine men went to fashion week to meet their future wives. The parking lot was full of them on Thursday afternoons when they walked across the yard from the headmaster's house. "It's a support group for mixed marriages," Aria said, rolling her blue eyes. "Mixed meaning Italian husbands, foreign wives. Tomaso's mother is Canadian." She nodded at the striking woman walking next to her mother. "She and my mother started the group."

Every afternoon the mothers of the permanent students gathered together on one side of the parking lot where they spoke in Italian. "They aren't very friendly," my mother said to my father at the end of the first week. "They make no effort to welcome new parents." On the other side of the parking lot were the Filipina nannies and just beyond them, men in dark suits leaning against the wall smoking—professional drivers hired by parents to pick up their children each afternoon. Those first days, waiting for the final bell to ring, my mother stood alone with her back to the parking lot, staring at the olive groves stretching across hills as far as the eye could see.

DISAPPEARANCES

My school occupied an old villa on the highest hill: white walls, terracotta floors, hallways that opened to the center courtyard with its fountain and garden. In the morning the hallways smelled of coffee, replaced mid-morning by scents of garlic, potatoes, fish, roasted tomatoes. Women in hairnets set tables, stirred pots. Afternoons, the wind shifted, wafting horse manure. Below the school, on the other side of the river, was a stately white stable with a jumping field. The riders, dressed in jodhpurs and riding helmets, lifted themselves off saddles as their horses took the jumps.

After school, all the model-mothers gathered around Aria's mom. She drove a red Audi convertible, often arriving with the top down and a silk scarf around her head. She was tall and thin and always wore gloves, even when the temperature was warm.

"Did you talk to her?" I would ask my mother. I wanted her to be friends with Aria's mom. I wanted her to stand in that group.

On certain days, Aria's nanny came to pick her up. She didn't sit with the Filipina nannies dressed in pastel-colored sweat suits. The BelCastellos's nanny wore blazers, had smooth blonde hair, lipstick, sunglasses. She told my mother she was a retired physicist from Harvard with a son in medical school. She wanted to travel, so she decided to nanny for the BelCastellos.

"She uses nanny as a verb," my mother told my father. "*I nanny for the BelCastellos.* She invited me to come and see her villa on Viale Mazzini."

"Why don't you go?" my father asked.

She lowered her voice. "Am I the nanny's friend now?"

My father held out his wine glass for a refill. "Nanny me. Besides, her son's in medical school."

"So, she says."

Two days later, my mother went to the nanny's villa for lunch.

"How was it?" my father asked.

"She had salads sent over from the main kitchen, and we drank wine on her balcony."

"Sounds nice."

"She has a maid. The nanny has a maid." My mother lowered her voice. "Apparently *he's* a Gucci, Signor BelCastello."

By mid-October the weather had cooled. Each afternoon, my mother walked the countryside around my school: white gravel roads, tiered hillsides, gnarled grapevines. Arriving sweaty and cheerful, she stood alone at the side of the parking lot. The beautiful model-moms stood twenty feet away, decked out in jewelry and scarves, ironed jeans. When the temperatures fell, they wore fur coats.

Aria smiled at my mother standing alone in baggy jeans and shapeless sweaters, her hair in a frizzy braid. "Your mother always wears tennis shoes." I was afraid Aria would start assigning numbers to mothers. Standing in the distance, my mother looked very plain. She belonged more on the nanny side than the model-mom side, and I felt guilty for thinking that.

Only three of us in the fourth-grade class—Kelly, John, and I—were short term, meaning one or two semesters at the school. John Houser's family had come the previous spring, so his father could do research with a pharmaceutical firm. But the family had been in a terrible car accident right after they'd arrived, and John carried photos of the smashed Mercedes in his backpack pocket, showing them to anyone who would look. He'd been on brain rest all summer and still wasn't allowed to play during recess. Whenever he got excited, he twirled his hand in the air and whooped "Still alive!" right in the middle of class.

"Poor you." Aria stroked his curly hair like he was her pet. I wondered if she wasn't also making fun of him because sometimes he leaned too close, and she had to push him away. "Maybe too alive."

Kelly and I should have been friends because our situations were similar, academic parents here on research grants.

"Why don't you invite Kelly over this weekend?" my mother urged one day after meeting Kelly's mom in the parking lot.

"She's a whiner." This was the truth, according to Aria. "She never wants to do anything. She always says her stomach hurts."

I had liked Kelly when I first met her. She had a halo of dark curls, thick black eyelashes. She wore leggings and turtlenecks in bright, mismatched colors, reminding me of my cousins in Minnesota. Right away, she asked if I would like to take riding lessons with her. She nodded toward the window that overlooked the stable. "My mother is going there today to ask about lessons."

"I love horses," I told her.

But the next day she reported back. "My mother found out you have to have your own horse to take lessons."

I was actually relieved, because Aria had pulled me aside that morning during recess. "Do you like her?"

I shrugged.

"She's so mousy, the way she slumps. Five, max." Aria imitated

Kelly hunched over at her desk, arms folded across her stomach. She batted her eyelashes, asking in a whiny voice the way Kelly spoke, "Are you going to sit outside at lunch?"

My mother would have been horrified at how much I wanted Aria to like me, how readily I agreed with her, laughing and turning my back.

Kelly brought novels to read during lunch. She seemed well prepared for rejection, and I told myself that meant she had been rejected before. Probably because she had always been a whiner, a mousy-mouse. This was how I talked to myself, with Aria's voice inside my head.

Sometimes, when Aria and I laughed, Kelly's face turned red and she excused herself to go to the bathroom, where she stayed until the teacher sent me to get her—assuming, since we were both new and daughters of academics, we must be friends.

"Kelly?" I entered the narrow bathroom with wooden stalls. "Mrs. Cantucci wants you to come back."

"I can't," she whimpered from behind the door. "I feel too sick. I might vomit."

The bathroom smelled of disinfectant, and I could see her blue tennis shoes under the door, heels raised so only the toes touched. Snacks were being handed out in the room. "What should I tell Mrs. Cantucci?"

"Tell her to call my mom to come get me."

In Florence, my father spent his days translating Gramsci's works into English. At lunch he took a break, walked down the hill to his favorite porchetteria where he stood in the sun and ate pork on a bun. My mother, a journalist for a small neighborhood newspaper in Minneapolis, had taken the year off. She took Italian lessons in the morning at Dante Alighieri. After lunch, she drove and parked in the school parking lot with Margot, an artist she'd met in her conversation class. They hiked the roads and paths around the school, then waited together in the parking lot. I was relieved my mother no longer stood alone.

"Is that your aunt?" Aria nodded at Margot standing next to my mother.

Margot could have been my mother's older sister, her hair a coppery tint, two shades darker than my mother's. Margot was taller, too, with freckled cheeks and fiery green eyes. Recently diagnosed with rheumatoid arthritis, she had left her husband and teenage children in London to study art in Florence. "My philosophy is to live the rest of my life for myself," she would say, raising her swollen hands, fingernails crusted with paint. "Forty-four is not too old to start over."

She painted huge pomegranates, eight-by-ten canvasses glistening red seeds spilling from torn skins. Margot's own parents had been "in service" to a wealthy family—her mother a cook, father a gardener. She despised what she called "the bloody gentry" and often teased me about my school. As my mother backed the car out of the parking space and I waved at Aria standing beside her mom, Margot smirked. "Be glad you don't have a mother like that. Takes a lot of maintenance. The way people look, means something."

"Don't." My mother glared at Margot. "She likes her school."

"You wouldn't wear a fur coat, would you?" Margot asked me.

I shook my head.

"I used to stick gum in fur coats," she told me. "I'd ride the bus in London and if a woman had a fur collar, I'd sit behind her, chew a wad, and stick it deep when the driver hit the brakes."

"If you don't behave," my mother warned her. "I won't bring you anymore."

"Cheeky cow," she laughed.

We ate earlier than Italians, and Margot often lingered until she was asked to stay. "I grew up in a farmhouse like this," she said, when she first saw where we were living. "Stone floors do wonders for your joints."

My father found Margot amusing. "What does your husband do for a living?"

"He's a solicitor."

My father's eyebrows lifted. "That should make your divorce interesting."

"He thinks I'll come back when my joints flare. He thinks I won't be able to paint, and I'll come crawling back, beg him to have our old life back."

"Will you?"

"We're completely different people." She tore off a piece of bread and soaked up olive oil from her plate. "I keep telling him it's over, but he doesn't want to believe me. I can't do my art and stay married to him. We live in different worlds."

"Your kids?" my father asked.

"They're invited to visit." She nodded. "They understand."

"Don't you miss them?" I asked.

"Honestly? They seem to be doing fine without me." She breathed in, her voice unfettered. "They have their own lives to live, and so do I."

"Doesn't sound like a clean break." My father refilled her wineglass.

Margot glanced at my mother. "He's a clever one."

My mother smiled and, alluding to the Guggenheim grant paying for our year abroad, said, "Hard part is getting his head through the door every night."

As my parents laughed, she glanced between them with a wicked smile. "What a tragic loss, to be happily married whilst living in Italy."

Aria told me every day, "I am going to marry Fernando."

I wanted to marry him too, but I wouldn't have said so, not to Aria. I could sense where danger lurked.

After lunch, Aria and I sat on the wall, kicking our feet and yelling "Bravo!" each time Fernando scored a goal on the grassy field below.

Aria leaned close and whispered, "His parents had to pay back taxes or leave Brazil after the new president was elected." She nodded, delighting in her superior knowledge of the world. "His mother kisses him on the lips. Isn't that weird? That's how Brazilian moms kiss their sons."

Aria told me many secrets, secrets that shocked me even though I pretended not to be shocked. She told me she wasn't allowed to travel with her mother to the United States because her father was afraid her mother wouldn't come back. "If I stay here, he knows she'll return."

She also told me that her last nanny was fired because she lied for her mother. "The new one reports to my father."

Maybe all children feel this way—malleable, victims of context. The closer I grew to Aria, the more distant I felt from my parents. Certain friends are like that. They fill you up with a world you don't belong to, a world that seems bigger, more exciting than your own.

She told me things I couldn't repeat: "Tomaso's mother is in love with the headmaster, but they can't do anything about it because his wife has MS." And she told me rumors that would make my mother worry if she knew Aria was filling my head with them: "If my mother weren't beautiful, she'd still be white trash. She grew up above a bowling alley."

"She dresses like a movie star," I said. "She even wears gloves when she picks you up at school."

"Don't be stupid." Aria gave me a sour look, as if she shouldn't have to spell everything out for me. She raised her wrist and drew her other hand across it. "It happened before I was born. She doesn't want the scars to show."

I felt older with Aria, but I also felt I was becoming someone else, someone my parents wouldn't like. I could laugh at almost anything now.

*

The week before my father disappeared, ravens cawed from power lines. The days seemed endless—hours noosed by isolation, parachute clouds moving slowly overhead—until five o'clock, when my father stopped writing, and placing his papers in a folder, sent me to get the bottle of prosecco chilling in the river.

My parents called it the *Ping-Pong-aperitivo-hour.* I played my mother first while my father sipped prosecco and cheered me on. "Great serve, Leah." Then my parents exchanged places, and I played him. I always lost, but they made me feel a worthy opponent. When it was time for them to play each other, the games took on an intense level of competition as my parents positioned themselves three feet back from the table, the distance allowing them to return balls with spin. They hit the ball hard, each determined to win, their banter back and forth an attempt to distract each other.

"We should call the Stevenses," my father said, slamming his serve. "They're in Genoa for the summer."

"I'm sick of hearing about fascism." My mother returned the ball. "He pontificates."

My father hit a shallow shot. "He knows more about fascism in Italy than any other American scholar."

"He's boring." My mother spun her return.

"That's because you're not an intellectual." My father lobbed the ball high, so she would have to look into the sun. He loved to goad her with this topic, asserting that journalists were not true intellectuals.

My mother moved back, waiting to see if the ball would land on the table, and when it missed, she caught it. "My point. I'm not taking the bait."

"Leah, stop helping your mother win." My father winked at me, stepping back from the table to serve. "Two out of three?"

My mother nodded and crouched, readying herself for my father's hard serve. "Remember last time they invited us?" She paused to hit the ball. "They served eel in cream sauce."

My father spun his shot. "Tasted prehistoric."

"You had worm breath." My mother slammed back. "I had to sleep turned away."

Laughing, my father hit the ball too hard, losing the match. He kissed my mother's cheek and congratulated her, promising he'd win the next round. By the time dinner was laid on the Ping-Pong table, chairs pulled alongside, pasta and salad tossed, they'd emptied the bottle of prosecco and opened a bottle of pinot grigio. The tensions that had built during the weeks before our trip seemed to find a momentary reprieve during the Ping-Pong-aperitivo-hour.

*

Six months before my father disappeared, temperatures fell and the villa turned cold. To buy firewood, we drove to a small compound on the other side of Florence where a group of men sat playing cards under a canopy. One of them rose and beckoned us to drive the car over a steel square set into the ground, a vehicle scale. He pointed to a pile of chopped wood, indicating it was up to us to load it. When we had shoved as much wood as we possibly could into our rented Renault, the car was weighed again. We paid for it by the kilo. As we drove away, the men resumed their card game and my father waved. "Tough job."

We stoked the wood burning stove day and night to keep the

house warm, but the smoke triggered my mother's asthma, forcing her to take inhalers twice a day. When that didn't help, the local doctor prescribed prednisone, and though it helped my mother breathe, it also made her agitated, hungry, simultaneously weepy and furious. She and my father argued every night. She wanted to leave Florence. She wanted to know why we had come to Italy in the first place if all he was going to do was work. Couldn't we move someplace else for the spring?

"We can't just take Leah out of school mid-year," my father told her. "Besides, we signed a lease."

"We can break the lease."

"Why don't you take a trip?" he suggested. "Someplace the air is clean. And when you come back, it'll be spring, and we won't have to burn wood anymore."

My mother found a cooking school in Sardinia, and she convinced Margot to go with her. They would spend February and part of March learning to make handmade pastas and sauces. She showed us the brochure, a photo showing noodles hanging in the sun like laundry. "If we stay six weeks, we get a certificate of completion, issued by the government."

After my mother left for Sardinia, my father became *Roberto.* Every afternoon, when he picked me up at school, the model-moms congregated around him like he was a rare species of husband. They laughed at his Italian. They became his teachers. They taught him where to shop: the best book and wine sellers, the best markets for leather briefcases, the best cashmere sweaters. They talked him into getting new eyeglass frames and went with him to help him choose. They planned parent field trips to villages nearby, places my mother had wanted to visit, places my father had promised to go to with her when his book was finished. Sometimes, my father and the model-moms were late coming to pick us up after their field trips. One afternoon, Aria and I exited the school to find her mother and my father standing alone at the edge of the parking lot. "Your father's a ten," she told me. "Tens need other tens."

I felt a terrible ache each night when my mother called and my father didn't mention his outings, as if my silence regarding his budding friendships with the model-moms somehow made me complicit. Instead, we'd listened to my mother describe what she'd prepared that day: "Orecchiette with pistachio pesto and fresh peas. I'll make it for you when I get home." She and Margot were supposed to share a room to cut down on the cost of the school, but right away they had begun bickering. By the end of the first week, Margot had left. "She didn't even say goodbye," my mother confided over the phone. "She just disappeared and left me to pay the entire cost of room and board."

My father told her not to worry. "If it helps your asthma, we can afford it. Stay until the end."

*

The day before my father disappeared on the mountain, my mother and I went swimming upriver from the bridge. We dangled our feet, and then our legs, finally submerging ourselves up to our necks in the frigid water, paddling a few times from one side to the other.

We heard yelling and looked up to see soldiers gathered on the bridge, waving to us. "Just ignore them," my mother said.

Then an ambulance arrived with flashing lights, and one soldier began walking down the bank toward us. The river was loud, and only when he was twenty feet away could we understand what he was yelling, "Una bomba, una bomba. Attenzione!" He jabbed his finger toward the bottom of the swimming hole, pointing at a shiny object we'd thought was a stone. He pointed up the mountain, hands sweeping downward, "Bombe degli partigiani!" implying it had washed down with mud and debris. He reached out to help us from the water, and we hurriedly wrapped towels around our bodies while soldiers applauded on the bridge. "Molte bombe," he cautioned, telling us to stay on the road until the woods had been cleared.

When we came running up the hill, my father was standing on the patio, talking into his phone.

"Didn't you hear the sirens?" My mother shivered, her arms covered with goose bumps. "We were swimming over a mine left by partigiani!"

He snapped his phone closed and nodded at the road, newly opened for the first time in weeks, convoys of trucks passing by with debris, horns honking in celebration. "This is fun. Watching people unearth their lives."

My mother stared at his phone, her voice trembling. "I thought we were here to unearth ours." Then she turned and walked inside.

*

The second week in March, my mother arrived home from her cooking school, her clothes tight, her cheeks round. "I know I've gained weight, but I'll lose it." She hugged me in her soft arms. "I missed you so much." She kissed my father. "You look handsome. You got new glasses."

He winked at me to go get her gifts. "Remember that ceramics village, the place you wanted to go to?" I handed her the candleholders he'd picked out. "Parent field trip," he explained.

"You went without me? All those times I asked you to go, and then you went without me?" My mother set the candleholders back in the box and stared at my father, his blue cashmere sweater and ironed jeans, Italian haircut and stylish new glasses. "Why didn't you wait until I got back?"

From that day on, my mother insisted on picking me up at school each afternoon, once again standing alone at the edge of the parking lot. One of those afternoons, nearing the end of the school year, I handed her the invitation I'd received, printed with a map—Aria's birthday celebration, a guided tour of the Gucci factory in Prato. "They do it every year," I told her.

When Kelly's mom arrived and saw the invitation, she asked to speak to my mother privately. Returning to the car, my mother spoke abruptly, "Get in, Leah." She was silent on the ride home, and only when my father joined us at the kitchen table did she confront me. "Is it true, Aria assigns numbers to you girls?"

I stared at my hands. "It's a joke."

"I can tolerate anything but cruelty," my mother fumed. "I

don't think you should go on this field trip, not when Aria has been so mean to her classmates."

"But the whole class is going," I protested.

My father defended the field trip, surprising us both. "Luxury goods are the backbone of Italy's economy. Artisan trades. She'll learn something."

My mother relented. "Only if you call Kelly and tell her you'd like her to go with you." She opened the school directory, dialed the number, and handed me the receiver. "All she needs is a little encouragement, one friend to stick up for her."

When Kelly came on the phone I said, "We were wondering if you want to ride with us?"

"Yes." Kelly didn't hesitate. "Have you already gotten her a gift?"

"A CD, Madonna's greatest hits." I watched my mother smile as she left the room.

"I love Madonna," Kelly said. "Do you have any ideas about what I could give her?"

"Not a book."

"She doesn't like books?"

"Nobody likes books like you do."

Her breaths sounded like hiccups before she hung up.

Two days later, we sat in the boardroom at the Gucci factory. Lights dimmed as a movie screen slid down the wall. We watched old black-and-white video clips of workers smiling and waving at the camera, holding up shoes, sitting at workbenches, leaning over sewing machines. These were followed by photos of princesses, actresses, wives of presidents wearing Gucci dresses, coats, scarves. *The End.* We swiveled our chairs toward glass windows overlooking the modern factory floor: men and women in white coats and protective glasses sitting at stations under bright lights, some sewing at machines, others by hand. Our guide explained how the materials were processed in China but assembled in Italy. She passed around swaths of animal skin—crocodile, alligator, cowhide from Texas.

We followed her to a small museum where mannequins were dressed in the Gucci fashions of each era. Kelly reached for my wrist, pulling me close and nodding at a purse in the mannequin's hand. "That's an elephant ear." Kelly cupped her hands over my ear. "Elephant feet are like stethoscopes. They can feel the earth hundreds of miles away. Their trunks are able to smell and feel at the same time. Their memories are better than ours. They're disappearing."

Aria saw us looking at the elephant ear. "It's old," she said, pulling me away and glaring at Kelly. "Can't you read the date?"

I was Aria's chosen friend, and that night I slept over at her villa. I sensed her bad mood and didn't know why. "You like Madonna, don't you?"

"I thanked you twice already."

After she put on her nightie, she knelt on the floor and clasped her hands. I was surprised that she prayed. Opening her eyes, she told me, "You shouldn't watch people when they pray." When she finished, she lay down next to me on the narrow bed, our arms touching. "Today wasn't that fun. Kelly ruined it." She stared at the ceiling. "You like Fernando, I can tell."

"No, I don't."

She turned on her side and studied me. "We can both like him. Just like our mothers both like your father."

I turned on my side, facing away, my throat aching. I missed being younger, who I used to be, and I blamed my parents for bringing me here, for making me change.

When I woke the next morning, Aria was already awake, putting polish on her toenails with her new pedicure set, a gift from Kelly. When I sat up, she kept applying her second coat. "You should get ready to go."

*

Three days passed with no sign of my father.

Twice a day my mother called the property manager, a British man who spoke perfect Italian. He lived down the road and had alerted the police. Each day he checked local hospitals.

I thought of telling my mother what Aria had said that night in her room. Silence hovered between us, gnawed inside me. So much had disappeared, and my body ached all around it.

On the fourth morning, the phone rang. My mother picked it up, and when she heard my father's voice, her eyes filled with tears. Then she fell silent, listening to him on the other end, her smile fading. Before she hung up, she said "Come home," as if she were granting permission.

Late morning, we heard a car on the bridge, and a few minutes later saw my father walking up the hill.

"Where were you?" I ran to him, anger trickling into my voice.

"I took the wrong path and ended up on the other side of the mountain." He hugged me tightly. "Roads were blocked, and I couldn't get back."

All that afternoon, my parents talked behind a closed door, their voices hushed. I started wondering how things would break apart, which edges would fall away, never fit again. I thought about whom I loved more, my mother or father, as if the world demanded preferences. When they reappeared before dinner, eyes red and faces puffy, I knew they had both been crying.

Late that night, my mother lay down beside me on the bed. The waterfall was loud, but not loud enough. I sensed her chest rising and falling, and I heard a gasp, then several more gasps, muffled into the pillow. I knew my father had spent the last few days with Aria's mother, and I wanted my mother to lift the burden of knowing from me and help me understand. I whispered, "Do you believe him?"

She hugged me close. "Your father knows nothing about nature. All roads look the same to him."

It was a new kind of loneliness, the truth dividing, and only part of it was mine.

The following day, we packed the car. Before we left, we stood together by the river and said goodbye to the waterfall—a ritual we'd always performed at the end of family trips, saying goodbye to places we'd visited. My father had his arm around my mother, and I stood between them. "We're lucky," my mother said, nodding across the valley at houses being torn down. "At least we can go home."

THE DOCTOR'S WIFE

Two days until Sami returns, his third trip home.

Driving to school, Liz thinks of all the things she has to do before he arrives—grocery store, bank, dry cleaners. Traffic at a standstill along Hennepin Avenue, she stares through the windshield, raindrops collecting between sweeps of the wipers, back and forth, distinct then blurred. The thing about love, she thinks, is that it is often hard to feel, like air or shadows. You can reach into it, be part of it, and still not know. Most of the time, she wants to be a different kind of person, the kind who doesn't constantly think about what she can and cannot give to her marriage.

Months before, Sami told her. "It's what I've trained for, Liz. I'll be based in Paris, short trips into Syria. They're paying me twice what I'm making now, so you and Nadi could come and live in Paris for a year. You could finish your dissertation."

She admired her husband, but she wasn't sure admiration was good for marriage. "If I did that, the school would lose my position. The district is downsizing."

It wasn't the first time he'd been approached by medical aid groups, but this time he'd be going to Syria, his father's birthplace. An emergency medicine doctor, Sami was fluent in French and Arabic, a rare skill set. He'd spent the summer before Nadi was born at the Weizmann Institute in Israel where Arab and Jewish doctors trained in cross-cultural simulations.

"They want a twelve-month commitment. If I take the position," he explained, "I'll be training medics in rotating surgical rooms."

At the window, she watched the elm shed brown leaves. "Basements targeted by Russian bombs. I read the newspapers."

He gently gripped her shoulders, turned her around and pulled her close. "I won't take the job if you don't want me to."

His neck smelled of the eucalyptus soap her mother put in their Christmas stockings. "What about Nadi?" she asked. Their daughter had just turned four.

"We can Skype every night, and I'll have three visits home, two weeks each time."

That night, Liz didn't sleep. Sami's body was hot, and she untangled herself, moved apart, just enough to feel alone. Outside the window, the moon was bright, wind rustling trees, voices loud from Stevens Park where drunks gathered after dark. Further away, sirens on the highway, a steady rumble of traffic.

Marriage was full of these kinds of tests, full of decisions that moved through her like muscular winds. She wondered if his wanting to go meant he loved medicine more than her. Maybe, she thought, she should love something *that* much. I love Nadi that much, she thought. I could never go to Syria.

She looked across the bed at her husband's silhouette: straight nose, deep-set eyes. Even in the dark, she could see his long eyelashes, dark fans brushing cheek bones. The world needed him, she thought, and who was she to stand in the world's way? Her breath caught like a warped door that had to be pulled open.

The next morning, she told him, "Do what you have to do.

We'll make it work."

*

A former cloak closet, her classroom has no windows. Twenty-eight brass hooks line the wall. Radiator pipes snake across the ceiling. "Coolest room in the whole school," she tells her students when they complain about the heat pouring off pipes. She points to the couch where they can read, nodding at the row of hooks where they hang their drawings. "Pop-up gallery. We're cutting edge." The room is so small it often gets noisy, and that's when she passes the story stick.

"This silence is . . ."

"This silence is tired," Lena says, taking hold of the stick.

"Tired like what?" Liz asks, reminding her to use one of the five senses.

"Tired like hard old licorice." Lena chews to show her. A big girl, clothes too tight, she covers herself with a book when she laughs, hiding her chest where the buttons come apart.

Liz smiles and passes the stick to Abdullah. She repeats, "This silence is . . ."

"This silence is staring out windows." Tall and thin, with a long face and cautious eyes, Abdullah never speaks above a whisper.

The story stick makes its way around the room.

"This silence is smelling my sister's hair."

"This silence is sweating inside the bus."

"This silence is listening to my cat purr."

By the time each student has spoken, the room is quiet. Liz

gives them pieces of yarn to weave through the corners of their drawings. "Okay, let's get those masterpieces finished, so we can hang them today. Tomorrow you're going to write your own stories to go with them."

Feradosa draws waves, only waves, and she takes a long time to draw them, as if she is unwinding one long string from the beginning of time, and the string bobs up and down, row after row, until it fills the page.

"The ocean, right?" Liz asks.

Feradosa shakes her head. Raised in a refugee camp in Kenya, she has only recently arrived in Minnesota.

"River?" Liz asks, moving her hand horizontally like a flowing stream.

Feradosa stares at the page. She has dark eyes, brown skin, slender features. She wears a hijab, and her skin smells like sandalwood.

Liz writes *river* on a pad of paper next to her. "What's in the river?"

Feradosa leans over and continues drawing lines across the page.

Sooner or later, Liz thinks, she will draw herself. She will tell the story she needs to tell.

Late afternoon, driving home from school, Liz takes the longer route around the park so she can see the sunset. During Sami's last trip home, they had come to this park to ice skate, Sami teaching Nadi how to glide. They filled his visit with activities, as if to create memories for the months ahead, but Liz still couldn't shed the feeling they were losing each other.

At night they made love, pockets of longing breaking open. Liz cried afterward, unable to explain why.

During the day, the ground leveled in their voices. They were too polite, too careful with each other.

"Do you still feel close to me?" she asked him one night in bed.

"Of course." He turned on his side and stared into her eyes, his fingers caressing her shoulder. "We both knew this year would be hard, but it'll be over in a few months. We just have to be patient."

Maybe she was imagining the emptiness that climbed onto the kitchen table when he arrived home, making their words fit neatly like Nadi's Lego pieces, castles easily built, then taken apart, boxed up, put under the couch.

The next night, she moved around the kitchen, clearing plates, putting leftover cauliflower casserole into the refrigerator.

Sami asked Nadi, "Shall we go to a puppet play this weekend? Give Mommy some time alone?"

"I love puppets." Liz began wiping off the table, moving the sponge under his elbows. "You need to trim your eyebrows. They make you look like the devil."

Nadi laughed. But Sami, too tired to be hurt, observed her with that quiet steadiness she'd grown to resent, the way it buried what was underneath. For years, he'd studied how to read faces, bodies, emotions; how to make accurate diagnoses, trust his instincts, and most importantly, not to doubt himself. Doubt, he'd told her, was the surgeon's enemy.

"You're angry," he whispered later, when they were alone.

She shrugged, "Not angry . . . tired." She wasn't sure how to explain. She'd begun to feel their love had no center, tubes of time, nothing inside.

The next morning, he showed her a photo. "Layla was found in a collapsed building. We saved her legs." The little girl looked like Nadi, big brown eyes, long eyelashes, smooth black hair. Liz knew he was trying to explain why he was there, why this work was important to him. She stirred pancake batter until every lump disappeared. She was thinking of Nadi growing up without a father, how much he was willing to risk.

The rain has turned to snow by the time she turns in the driveway. On the couch, visible through the windows, her mother and Nadi are reading a book, their heads leaning together. Liz glances in the rearview mirror, seeing what her mother will see—frizzy brown hair badly in need of a trim, smudged blue glasses, no lipstick to brighten the impatient mouth she inherited from her father. She wonders whether she has to ask her mother to stay for dinner, when what she really wants is to plant her daughter in front of television, drink two glasses of wine, and read the newspaper, unhampered, in silence, before Sami Skypes for Nadi's nighty-night story.

"I fed Nadi already." Her mother gathers her knitting, assessing her daughter's mood. "I'm off to Lilly's for bridge. Your dinner's in the oven. Don't forget to lock the doors and windows." Her mother nods at a newspaper headline, *Crime Wave Hits Phillips Neighborhood.* She has cut the article out and left it for Liz to read, unaware that her fears about the neighborhood hurt her daughter's feelings. Liz and Sami bought this house before Nadi was born, thinking of Sami's huge medical school debts ahead, thinking themselves lucky to find the two-bedroom craftsman stucco with walnut built-ins, front porch, fenced in backyard. Full of possibilities, the realtor told them, if you don't mind all the rentals on this street. Since then, Liz has come to love this neighborhood, the Mexican bakeries on Nicollet, clapboards rented to art students at MCAD, slanted front porches, and the Waldorf School's vegetable garden with the sign drawn in crayon: *Hungry? Help Self.*

She pours a glass of merlot and is sorting mail when she hears her four-year-old daughter's words. "Father, son, and wholly goes." Nadi is sitting on the rug in the den, her Barbies laid in a row on a pillow.

"Honey, what are you doing?"

Nadi looks up, round cheeks that have not yet lost their baby fat, lips pulled tight in an uncertain smile, brown eyes searching her mother's face.

Liz smiles. "Please? Mommy wants to see."

Nadi lifts one of her Barbies, dips her hand in a glass of water, and makes the sign of the cross on the doll's forehead. "Father, son, wholly goes."

Liz sits on the couch and pulls Nadi onto her lap. "Where did you learn that?"

Nadi nestles closer. "Father Mike put water on me."

"Did Grandma take you to church today?"

Nadi nods, her brown eyes watching her mother.

Sometimes anger has no pockets of air. Liz takes a deep breath.

"Do you want to watch *Frozen* until Daddy Skypes?"

Nadi melts into the cushion, eyes glued to the screen even before her mother finds the Disney channel and hits play. Liz tops off her glass of wine and hurries upstairs to call her mother, playing bridge at Aunt Lilly's. She expects she will have to leave a message and is surprised when her mother answers on the second ring. "Is anything wrong?"

"She's baptizing her Barbies."

"What's a little water on my granddaughter's forehead if it makes me feel at peace?"

"Behind my back? Without our permission?"

"I didn't plan it. I wanted her to see the stained-glass window we gave in your father's memory. The artist finally finished it, Saint Raphael, Archangel of Healing. And since we were there, I asked Father Mike if he could do a quick baptism, just as a safety measure."

"A safety measure, Mom? Really?"

"You sound tired. Let's talk another time."

"Fine." Liz hits disconnect, and sitting on the edge of the bed, looks at the photos on the dresser, her wedding party in her parents' backyard just before her father died. A physician, her father knew the chemo wasn't working, his body slumped in a chair, bluish skin, eyes sunk deep, his whole face, once so alive and engaged, collapsed into pain. They kept moving his chair from shade to the sun, sun to the shade, bringing cups of tea and the praline cookies he'd always loved, her mother complaining, "He wouldn't let me buy him a new suit."

Hearing the Skype tone, Liz pulls on a bathrobe and calls Nadi to the kitchen table, where her father's face appears on the screen. "Hey, sweetie."

"Hi Daddy." Nadi climbs on her mother's lap, and they put their heads together.

"Can you see me?" Sami brings his face forward so the screen fills with his lips and chin, dark eyes lighting up the moment they come into view.

"Yes," Nadi giggles, used to this ritual of adjusting screens, positioning heads.

"What did you eat for dinner?" His voice lags behind lip movements.

"Baked potatoes with cheese and broccoli."

"That sounds good."

"Mmmmhmmmm."

Every night the same conversation, Liz reminding herself it is 4 a.m. there, and Sami has set his alarm so he can tell Nadi a story. Most nights, Liz has nothing new to say, and these conversations remind her of that. But tonight, she wants to tell her husband about the baptism. His black hair stands on end, eyes puffy, cheeks unshaven. The room behind him is dark, the desk lamp lighting half his face, the other half cast in shadow, making him seem vulnerable, darkness encroaching.

"Why don't you tell Nadi a story?" Liz suggests. "Then she can go get in her pajamas while I talk to you."

Sami stares at her, sensing something is up. "Okay."

Liz moves into the kitchen, glancing at the photos on the refrigerator—one of Nadi the day she was born, her dark hair and eyes already resembling Sami; another of Sami and Liz smiling on their wedding day, Sami's hand on top of hers as they cut the cake. Liz finishes the broccoli-stuffed baked potato in a few heaping bites, grateful for her mother's cooking. Listening to her husband's voice coming through the computer, she wonders if Nadi can differentiate real presence from screen time. Sami is good at inventing stories, Nadi's favorite about a girl named Monique who rides a turtle across the sea, guiding boats filled with children to safety. Tonight, a lonely octopus wraps his tendrils around the rubber boat, and Monique has to fill his eight octopus arms with objects so the lonely creature will let go. When the story is finished, children rescued, she lifts Nadi off the chair. "Let Mommy talk to Daddy for a minute, okay? Go get in your pajamas and brush your teeth."

Nadi doesn't move.

Sami laughs. "Go on, sweetie. Then come back and give Daddy a kiss, okay?"

Nadi reluctantly backs away from the screen before hurrying upstairs.

"My mother had her baptized," Liz tells him. "Without asking us."

Sami laughs from across the ocean, and his face breaks into pixels, voice blurred like a record playing at a slow speed. "Sheeeeemeeaaansweeellll."

"Are you even there?" Liz says to the zillions of squares reassembling her husband's face on the screen. "Can you hear me?"

"She . . . means . . . well," he repeats slowly, spacing words, her mother's baptism meaning nothing in his larger world of war and death. Liz wishes her heart were filled with bigger truths. She'd like to believe there's enough inside her to hold it all, his world and her own, but the longer he's away, the more she feels she is holding onto an idea of marriage, thin as a paper bag, and no matter how sturdy her grip underneath, the bottom is giving way.

Nadi arrives at her side, exhaling puffs of breath into her face to show she has brushed her teeth. "Grandma bought me these. Can you see them, Daddy?" She presses the sleeve of her new pajamas close to the computer camera. "Horses."

"Give Daddy a kiss," Liz says, watching her daughter throw kisses toward the screen.

"Love you, Daddy."

Sami catches them and pats them all over his face, arms, chest, stomach. "Love you more."

Then Sami looks at her. "Day after tomorrow, I'll be home. I love you, Liz."

All she manages is, "Stay safe," sounding just like her mother telling her to lock her doors. When the screen goes dark, she thinks of pressing the phone icon, calling him back, *Love you too*, a safety measure in case something happens.

Liz snuggles beside Nadi on the couch, "Fifteen minutes before bed," resting her feet on the pillow next to five baptized dolls. She sips wine, watching the clock, listening to Nadi sing along with Anna's solos, her voice full of passion. Right before the time's up, she rinses her glass, sends a text, *Love you too.*

Later, after Nadi is tucked in, Liz crawls into bed and reaches for Sami's pillow. She doesn't wash his pillowcase when he's gone, and now she breathes in his scent, a briny sweetness of hospitals and his own skin, distinct as fresh snow. She wonders if she should've taken time off from teaching, spent the year together in Paris. But that would've been a different anger, the one her mother chose, always accommodating her father's needs before her own.

"Patients come first," her mother reminded them each time her father responded to an unexpected emergency—ski trips when the loud speaker asked for a doctor on Devil's Run, flights when physicians were asked to identify themselves, parents' weekend when a counselor dislocated a shoulder waterskiing, and her father used an anchor to yank it back in place. Her mother never seemed to mind when he was called to an emergency during holidays or family trips. She accepted her role as doctor's wife, in charge of the family, every bit as important to saving lives.

And she was.

Only later, after Liz and her brother left for college, did her mother's anger surface. Liz remembers when her parents visited her in Florence during her junior year abroad. That first night out, sitting in a restaurant Liz had booked months in advance, a small place known only to Italians, Liz was excited to navigate this world for her parents, to show off her new life. She began ordering wine and appetizers, "Vino rosso della casa, funghi ripien—"

"—I think that man has a pulmonary embolism," her father interrupted, nodding at the table next to them.

"Don't do this now," her mother told him.

But her father continued to watch the man sitting five feet away, surrounded by his family. Gray curls combed behind his ears, arched nose, he looked like many older Italian men, except his left foot was in a cast, the leg above so swollen it looked as if it might burst the seams of his pants.

"Look at the swelling," her father said. "He must've just had foot surgery."

Her mother ignored him and stared at the menu, asking Liz, "What do you recommend?"

Her father kept watching the man. "See the vein protruding on his neck? I'm sure it's an embolism." He turned to Liz. "You need to go over there and tell him he should see a doctor immediately."

Liz looked at the huge Italian family enjoying their meal. "I don't think so, Dad. I don't think you do that here."

Her mother shook her head at him. "She can't just march over there and interrupt their meal."

"Of course she can. Otherwise, he could die." Her father shifted his gaze to Liz. "Your Italian is fluent, isn't it?"

The Italians were laughing loudly when she approached, "Sono Americana." She explained her father was a doctor and was very worried about the man at the end of the table. "Un medico molto preoccupato a causa di sintomi." Liz didn't know the words for bulging veins, swollen ankles, breathlessness, but she pointed to the top of his cast where the pant leg was tight, and then she touched her chest and took deep breaths. "Dovete visitare vostro medico subito."

The family glanced at her father, then the son scowled and waved her away. "Americani," he hissed, making circles in the air with his hand. "Conoscono tutto."

Laughter rose behind her as she returned to the table.

"Didn't you explain?" her father asked.

"It's not like that here." Liz took a sip of wine. "You don't just go over and interrupt a family meal."

"Listen to your daughter," her mother told him. "She *lives* here."

"They don't worry like we do," Liz told him.

"They'll worry when he collapses," her father said. "The first clot is dangerous, the second kills."

Her mother tried to change the topic. "What's our plan for tomorrow?"

"Boboli Gardens and the Pitti Palace," Liz said. "I've already got the tickets so we don't have to wait in line."

After dinner, her father continued scanning the bill to make sure they hadn't been overcharged. Liz could see he liked Italy a little less now. Glancing at the family as they stood to leave, he persisted, "Maybe I should go talk to him—"

"—Enough!" Liz's mother snapped, her eyes furious. "Just drop it."

Her father had already been diagnosed with inoperable cancer when Liz met Sami on a flight back from San Francisco. A striking man in jeans and sports coat, Sami tucked a *JAMA* and a *New York Times* into the seat pocket in front of him. Liz nodded at the medical journal. "My father is a physician too."

Sami explained he was finishing his fellowship at Mayo. His parents had been doctors, his mother French, father Syrian, an émigré to France during the fifties. They'd moved to Ann Arbor before Sami was born. Two weeks before he'd graduated from medical school, his parents were driving home from the airport and were rear-ended by a truck. The driver was drunk. They died instantly.

A week after they met, Liz sat in the auditorium, watching him introduce simulation medicine to a new crop of medical students. He spoke about the importance of understanding patients in the larger context of their lives. "Say you have a Muslim woman whose head is covered with a hijab but you believe she is suffering from head trauma? What is the culturally sensitive approach? What if her husband refuses to let you touch her?" He paused, scanning the faces of students who looked too young to be doctors.

That night in bed, she asked, "Is it difficult to switch gears?"

"Sometimes." He ran his fingers through her hair.

She stared at his dark eyes, sweet smile. He laughed when she gently mocked his serious approach to life. He rarely drank, had never smoked pot, and he'd never swum naked in a lake. She also wasn't used to a man asking in bed, *Tell me what you like.* One of the things she liked was no conversation while they made love. Afterward, they took out their phones to check their calendars, discussing when they could see each other next. "Next weekend?" he asked.

"That's MEA. Parent-teacher conferences. How about the weekend after?"

"I'm on call."

They married eight months later. Their lives overlapped enough, but not too much. That was important to Liz, enough independence to decipher her own life.

They spent their honeymoon in a cabin on Gull Lake. One evening as the sun was setting over the lake and Sami was in the shower, she hid his clothes in the woods, refusing to give them back unless he smoked pot and swam naked. "I want you to know that side of me."

"I know it already." But he reached for the little pipe stuffed with pot. It made him cough and hardly affected him. He had that kind of clarity. The mosquitoes were bad, so she grabbed his hand and they leapt off the dock. Naked, treading water, they wrapped their legs around each other. His skin formed goose bumps and his teeth clattered. He stayed close to her, staring into the murky depths, jerking his feet away from the underwater fronds. He stayed long enough for her to realize she couldn't force him to love what she loved. "Go on," she kissed his eyelids. "Your clothes are behind the woodpile. I'll come in soon."

Nadi was named after his mother, Nadine. After she was born, Sami often rocked her to sleep at night, singing the lullabies his mother had sung to him. Sometimes, listening from across the hallway, Liz felt his grief, how much he missed his parents, how much he wished they could have known their granddaughter. Liz also knew his going back to Paris and Syria was his way of honoring them, keeping the past alive.

The next afternoon, twenty-four hours before Sami arrives home, Liz sits beside Abdullah in the classroom, reading the picture book *Where I Live,* with homes from around the world. He frowns at a picture of an igloo. "No windows."

When the phone rings, Liz hands him paper, tells him to draw his own house, then lifts the cell from her purse tucked beneath the desk.

"I know you're still mad at me," her mother says on the other end. "But I need to know if you're coming Easter?"

"I have a student here," Liz replies, her voice clipped. "I'll talk to you later."

After Liz disconnects, the phone starts vibrating and she puts it in a drawer. Abdullah stares at her, his eyebrows furrowed. He looks a little afraid.

"That was my mother," Liz explains. "She wants me to do something I don't want to do. Does that ever happen to you?"

He shakes his head, his long face serious.

"Really? You always want to do what your parents tell you to do?"

He nods.

"Well, you are clearly a much nicer person than I am."

Abdullah hands her his picture, a house with a window in the middle, sharp red lines like flames rising around the house. In the window is a face looking out. "Is this you?" Liz asks.

Leaning toward her, he speaks softly, "My brother, Ibrahim."

Liz weaves a piece of yarn through two holes and hangs it over one of the hooks. "You are telling an important story, and you have to keep telling it."

After school, Liz meets Selby at the Uptown Y. Best friends since graduate school, they swim for thirty minutes, and afterward, sit in the sauna and talk.

Selby wipes her face with the towel. "Isn't Sami back soon?"

"Tomorrow. I know I should be glad." She shrugs, releasing a long sigh. "But it feels like one more adjustment. Just when Nadi and I figure out our rhythm, just when I've got things under control, he comes home for two weeks, and it's all undone. Honestly?" Her throat catches, her eyes filling with tears. "I don't know if I love him anymore. If I did, wouldn't I be excited to have him home?"

"Not necessarily. You're married to Saint Sami and that entails a lot of work."

Liz laughs, but laughter does nothing to break up the sadness. "Thing is, I'm fine alone. In some ways it's easier. I don't have to put down the toilet seat or listen to him snore."

"Maybe I'll move in with you," Selby smiles. "He'd be lost without you, Lizzie. You know that, don't you? Not many men would get up at four a.m. for nighty-night Skypes. He'll be home for good soon. Now might not be the best time to make any decisions."

When Liz arrives home, her mother is combing Nadi's wet hair. She has made spinach pie, Liz's favorite, washed and folded the basket of dirty laundry, and filled the refrigerator with olives, cheese, and herring—Sami's favorite foods. On the counter is a set of new knives, handles displayed in a new wooden knife block.

"Yours were so dull I couldn't cut cheese," her mother says.

"It's huge." Liz pushes the block against the counter wall, so it takes up less space. "But thank you."

Her mother lingers. "What else can I do to help you?"

"Nothing. You do *way* too much as it is." Liz's tone implying both gratitude and a lingering anger over the baptism.

"Are you taking tomorrow off to meet his plane?" her mother

asks.

"I can't." Liz sorts through mail, most of it junk. "I've used up all my vacation days during his previous visits."

"I'll pick him up." Her mother drapes her apron over a chair. "After all those flights, someone should be there to meet him."

Liz lifts her mother's coat off the coat rack, holding it while her mother sticks her arms through sleeves. Unexpectedly, her mother turns and embraces her in a tight hug. "I am so proud of you. You are the strongest woman I know." Her words catch Liz by surprise, as if dropped from a great height.

"What's a happy day for you?" Liz asks her students.

"McDonald's."

"Cartoons."

"Going to the mall."

She scans their smiling faces. She doesn't want her students to feel the world decides for them. She wants them to know they have choices and can determine their own lives. She tells them to close their eyes. "Feel big. Feel very big." She watches their heads lift, chests expand; she sees them getting bigger. "Now draw yourselves big. Draw yourselves so big you don't even fit on the page. Write a story about yourself as a superhero. What's your special power?"

When the last bell rings, she checks her phone, listens to her mother's voice message. "Sami's plane was early, and we're home. He's taking a nap, and Nadi and I are making dinner."

Liz's brain feels like a beehive, tasks she should have done before today so she would have more time with her husband. She puts a stack of spelling tests into her satchel. Better to leave now to avoid rush hour, she thinks.

But instead she goes to the teacher's lounge where the bathroom has a door that locks. She has learned the art of crying silently. Outside the door, smells of microwave popcorn, chatter about last night's Lynx game. She holds toilet paper over her nose and mouth, muffling sounds, letting the tears fall. She underestimated anger. She thought of it as a stone that could be dug around, lifted, held up, See how heavy it is? She didn't realize anger was like water, a slow drip, turning the ceiling black, the floor soft, walls and beams moist. She didn't realize it would seep through her, cover everything.

She goes back to the room, gathers her keys and purse, glancing at her students' drawings hanging from the hooks. Feradosa's picture is at the end, teal blue waves, and in the right upper corner, a girl swimming with her head above water.

Half an hour later, she turns in the driveway and already the door opens, Sami's arms circling her. Inside he opens his suitcase full of dirty clothes wrapped around gifts, dolls for Nadi, scarves and perfume for her. Another hug, so close she smells airplane sweat.

A shower first. They have done this enough times to establish rules. But really, the rules are just lines she cannot cross, not yet. The rooms in the house are small, but she only feels the smallness right after he comes home, a sense of invasion, dirty laundry sorted into lights and darks, toothpaste kit spilling across the bathroom counter, wet shoes and boots piled by the back door, socks drying on the radiator, pockets emptied onto the dresser—wristwatch, wallet, coins, receipts, lip balm.

She wonders what it will take to get past this anger. Breathing space, she thinks, for the world to realign. A negotiated closeness, not assumed closeness.

"Dinner's ready." Her mother pulls the lasagna from the oven. "I have to get going."

Sami helps her with her coat, and Liz's mother turns and gives him a hug. "We're so glad you're back safely." Leaning over the couch, she squeezes Liz's shoulder. "I hope you can relax tonight."

After her mother leaves, the three of them sit at the table like other families, Nadi talking about her dolls, which ones are sad.

"Why are they sad?" Sami asks.

"Everyone is sad sometimes," Nadi explains. "You know that."

"Are you sad sometimes?" Sami asks.

Nadi nods. "But not tonight, Daddy, because you're home."

Liz listens to Nadi's words, thinking she should be the one saying them.

Outside, neighbors' outdoor lights go on and off. Rain falls, a curtain of sound. Every marriage can hear only what lands. So little lands on water—a leaf, a bug, a swimmer's slap. Liz hears the leaky downspout, rain drumming on the rain barrel, one more thing she meant to fix.

After dinner, Sami reads to Nadi in bed. Liz washes two pears, cutting away bruises, fruit flies hovering near sweet skins, faint sounds of thunder in the distance. He has taught her to eat fruit for dessert.

Later, they sit on the bed against pillows, eating pears. He tells

Liz, "We had less than two minutes to vacate the building, to get the patients out."

"Must've been terrifying." But her voice is distant like static, and she knows he can hear it, her resistance, her unwillingness to feel what he felt, that she is blaming him for something.

They are tuned to that quiet where their separate lives reside, eyes and fingers surfing each other for one clear channel. So many *somewhere elses*. So many roads and skies to look past. Round hours in different bodies, different climates, all transmitted, absorbed.

"It's too dangerous now," he tells her. "We'll lead the medics by satellite."

"From Paris?"

"I'll do it from here." He reaches for her, pulling her toward him, but she remains on her back.

You chose the world. She is full of dim revolts, archeological depths. It will take weeks for him to unearth the pearled rock, flint shards, soft soil. Sometimes she thinks he knows her better than she knows herself, how she needs to keep things separate, how closeness can feel like a loss, how he will have to travel through many kinds of silences to find her.

His hand rests on her stomach. "You couldn't have called in sick?"

"You couldn't have married a woman in Paris?"

He smiles, a tired smile. More than fatigue. He has seen so much, and this is child's play, this resentment. She can read his mind.

"Twenty-six hours, three layovers, the Frankfurt airport's always a zoo." His voice is hoarse, a stick dragged over gravel. "I'm so glad to be home." He pulls her closer, her legs entwined in his, all the distances folded into one. "Do you know how much I love you?"

She cannot help wondering who love is for, who it serves.

Only then does she notice his hands are shaking, and the shaking enters her body. She is shaking, too, their bodies shaking together, trembling shivers, tiny earthquakes cracking through to the surface. Beneath the sweet smell of aftershave and soap, she smells fear, like coins and wet leather.

GRACE'S MASK

Three weeks into the school year, Nina watched her daughter on top of the jungle gym making orangutan sounds—"*eeenh, eeenh*"—kicking her feet at two boys trying to climb to the top.

"You're hogging it," Pete, Grace's classmate, yelled from the lower rung. "You have to give us a turn."

But Nina's daughter exerted more kicks, and Grace's granite eyes lifted, staring across the treetops.

"She loves it up there, doesn't she?" Heather, Pete's mother, approached Nina. "My son wouldn't mind a turn."

"We're leaving anyway." Nina smiled, a stinging smile. Heather was PTA president, with close ties to the principal and teachers. It wouldn't serve Grace's interests to alienate the school's most powerful parent. Nina waved, signaling Grace it was time to leave.

Walking to the car, Nina carried Grace's backpack. As they passed through the playground gates, Grace leaned over to gather two handfuls of fallen leaves on the ground, kissed them, then dropped them at her mother's feet. "That's how orangutans greet strangers."

All her life Nina had heard the term *a mother's intuition* and her own intuition began ringing alarms the first week of school when Grace's teacher sent home a note:

> *For this year's class project, fourth graders have adopted a Sumatran orangutan named Lucy. Students will have the opportunity to Skype weekly*

with a biologist filming Lucy in her natural habitat, allowing students to see how scientists work on the ground to protect critically endangered species. Questions? Email me: Sarabethridesbikes@lakes.com.

Nina had doubts about Sarabethridesbikes, doubts about anyone with bicycles tattooed all over her neck, arms, and legs. But Nina kept her doubts in check, having insisted to her husband four years ago this was the right school for Grace. Sarabethridesbikes wore skinny jeans rolled up at the bottom, socks with faces of cats, black lace-up tennis shoes. Her hair rose like a wheat field above her round face, long earrings swinging when she played the guitar, her brassy voice carrying through open windows to parents standing outside the school.

At home, Nina ignored Grace's mask, the mask her daughter had made in art class the first week of fourth grade. Each afternoon, her daughter donned the mask as soon as they walked in the back door. Maybe it was Grace's red hair, but the mask gave her daughter an uncanny resemblance to an orangutan—Grace's red curls falling around the mask, gray eyes peeking through eyeholes, papier-mâché puckered mouth. "*Eeenh, eeenh.*" Grace walked on all fours through the kitchen, swinging her torso between her arms, launching herself onto the couch. At first, Nina and Ben had laughed. At first, they believed their daughter was doing it to make them laugh.

But Nina stopped laughing when Grace's charade showed no signs of ending, and instead her daughter began insisting on the same diet orangutans ate—grapes and almonds and seeds she pushed through the mouth hole of her mask.

"We're going to Skype with Mathew again tomorrow," Grace told her mother. "He lives in the rainforest and sleeps in a hammock that zips."

Nina unpacked her daughter's lunchbox. "Any homework for tomorrow?"

"Spelling test," Grace nodded, taking the sheet from her backpack and reading the paragraph aloud. "Lucy lives in a *national* park in Sumatra. Before she sleeps, she makes a *nest* in six *minutes* high up in the trees. Then she makes a *pillow* out of *leaves.* When it rains, Lucy makes an *umbrella* out of *branches.* Orangutans are the largest tree-living *primates* in the world. They depend on tropical forests for their *survival.* Sadly, their *habitat* is being destroyed by the palm oil industry."

Nina listened, her chest heavy with apprehension. The school's holistic approach to education meant themes were woven through the curriculum for the entire school year—Lucy would be with her daughter during spelling, English, geography, history, and science for the next nine months.

"I know the words already," Grace said, kneeling on the stool, taking jars and packages from the cupboard, reading labels and setting aside cereal boxes, potato chips, granola bars. "Mom," she moaned, her finger stabbing the list of ingredients on the packages. "These have palm oil. I have to make a list of everything I found at home that uses palm oil."

"I won't buy these brands anymore, but we don't waste food, remember?" Nina put the boxes and bags back on the shelf. "Do you like your teacher?"

"*Eeenh, eeenh.*" Grace nodded. "She plays her guitar when we take our seats in the morning and when we leave in the afternoon. Beginnings and endings are important."

"Is that what your teacher says?"

Grace bobbed her head and began to sing, her voice high, shoulders swaying as she sang three rounds. "It starts with us, starts with you and me, every change we make, begins with we."

After dinner, Nina walked upstairs and found her husband and daughter reading together on Grace's bed, one of several books Grace had checked out of the school library on primate behavior.

"Time to brush your teeth," Nina said from the doorway.

Ben grunted and chased Grace through a canopy of trees, down the hallway to the bathroom where her daughter had to take off her mask to brush her teeth. Ben brushed his teeth, too, brushing the way an orangutan father might, his gums bared. Ben was the fun parent, Nina thought. He had no problem pretending he was an orangutan father. "*Eeeenh, eeeeeenh.*" He chased Grace back to her bedroom, where she launched herself onto the bed, reaching her arms around her mother's neck, offering puckered lips, an orangutan kiss.

Nina set the mask on the bedside table and waited for Grace to push the quilt into a nest, blankets and sheets hollowed in the middle, her head on the pillow with leaf designs. Together, they sent Buddhist prayers to grandparents, far-away cousins, and Lucy, somewhere in the treetops of Leuser Gunang National Park. "May Lucy be healthy, happy, safe, and free of suffering," Grace repeated after her mother.

Outside, rain cascaded against windows, a steady, hard rain. Grace pointed to the stereo next to her bed, wanting her mother to play rainforest sounds, and when Nina said, "What about just listening to real rain?" Grace shook her head, hissing and grunting, "*eeeenh, eeeeenh.*"

"Can we talk?" Nina whispered to her husband, already in bed with lights off when she climbed in next to him. "Grace has stopped playing with the other girls. She sits on top of the jungle-gym and pretends she's Lucy."

"Don't you think it's a phase?" He turned to face her, resting his arm on her stomach. "She loves to pretend."

Nina reached over and stroked the gray hair above his forehead. "You need a haircut." Nudging him to stay awake, she whispered, "I looked up orangutans on Wikipedia. A thousand lose their lives each year." She paused, and when he didn't respond, nudged his arm again. "Are you listening?"

"Yes," he mumbled, his voice fading into sleep.

"I have a bad feeling about Lucy."

"Let's talk about it tomorrow." He removed his arm, turned over, and tugged the quilt toward his side of the bed.

Nina had regrets. She chose Lakes Environmental Charter School for reasons she was not proud of. It was a small, pretty red-brick building, a former firehouse, situated next to a large park, surrounded by gardens and nestled among mansions, cafes, bookstores. The parking lot was filled with Teslas and hybrids and bikes. Nina thought her daughter would be safe among people who cared about the environment. She liked the school's mission statement: Our goal is to nurture future citizens of the world.

"I don't like charter schools," Ben told her when they first visited the school. Both his parents had been public school teachers in New York City. "Most charters are too specialized, and they drain funding for public education. Better to be exposed to everything."

"They're teaching children how to make a difference," Nina said.

"They're kids," Ben responded. "Is it their responsibility to make a difference?"

Nina refused to look at him during the rest of the tour. She didn't want his strong opinions to influence her own judgment, so she walked behind, noticing he was the oldest father on the tour, approaching sixty, tall and thin with gray hair and dark eyes. Still handsome, despite his age, still playing seniors basketball at the Y two nights a week, enjoying the banter among men with whom he had nothing else in common. He pulled her aside after the tour. "It's a little precious, don't you think? Building rain-barrels? Growing roof gardens?"

But Nina's eyes were already glistening with the beauty of it: bee and butterfly gardens, hallway displays of art made from trash, the sixth-graders' science projects focused on reusing plastic waste. She leaned close, "Don't be so cynical."

Nina had dragged him to five different schools in Minneapolis. To her, choosing the right school seemed like a huge deal—seven years of their daughter's life, seven hours a day, five days a week. She had only one child, and she recognized her own need to perfect her daughter's experience, to make it as fulfilling as possible. Nina wasn't optimistic about the planet's future, and if she were completely honest with herself, she wasn't entirely convinced there would even be a habitable world for Grace in thirty years. The least she could do, Nina thought, was give her daughter a happy childhood.

Ben preferred Jefferson, the neighborhood school that offered kindergarten through eighth grade. The massive four-story building stood seven blocks away, surrounded by chain-link fences and busy streets. "Easy to drop her off on my way to work."

"You're thinking of yourself, not her." Nina stared at the cement playground, basketball and foursquare courts, the small square of sand with swings and jungle gym for younger kids.

"Actually, I was thinking of you," Ben said. "You aren't going to want to wait for the bus through winter. This way I could drop her off."

Jefferson's classes had an average of thirty-four students. The school hallways smelled of Cheetos and mildew. Nina and Ben sat in on two classes, math and science, and Nina found it difficult to concentrate with all the noise. Children with special needs sat at the back, aides whispering to them. Other children snickered while the teacher drew on the board. In the hallway, the students seemed huge, like teenagers already. They ate candy between classes. They slammed lockers, kicking them when they wouldn't close. Girls in upper grades wore matching hairstyles, straight blonde waterfalls of hair or black locks swirling around their faces. They wore make-up and bras and tight t-shirts with glittery words like *princess* and *respect.* The boys had shoes that lit up in the hallways.

"I like it," Ben said. "Has a good vibe."

"Eight hundred students." Nina shook her head. "She'll be lost here."

"She's a smart kid. She'll figure it out." Ben put his arm around her shoulder. "You worry too much."

Nina chafed, feeling criticized rather than supported. Ben's philosophy could be summed up: you do your best and the rest is luck. Nina had found his philosophy freeing before they had Grace, but now she resented it, feeling alone in her worry over choosing the right school.

Nina was thirty-nine when she had Grace. She'd been an art and environmental science double major at college, and then a marketing assistant at a non-profit that promoted community gardens. Nina had waited so long to have a baby that she didn't want to work once Grace was born. Ben's salary in marketing at Sleep Number, the luxury bed company, could sustain them for a few years, until they needed to start saving for Grace's college tuition.

After they married, they'd pooled their money and bought an ugly two-story house, the only house they could afford in the neighborhood they preferred. She tried to make the house feel artsy, and if not artsy, then at least homey, decorating rooms with art and quilts and pillows and pottery she found at estate sales.

Still, she didn't think she could ever love this house because of its aluminum siding, especially after last year's hailstorm left golf ball-sized dents that caught the late afternoon sun. The insurance had paid out ten thousand dollars, but Nina used it to install solar panels on the roof. The state was offering tax breaks, and she couldn't bear to have the siding torn off and dumped in a landfill.

"Saving energy is more important than aesthetics," she insisted.

"Not necessarily," Ben said. "Not for resale value."

"I'm trying to align our actions with our beliefs." She meant the vegan diet she insisted upon. If Ben wanted salmon or the occasional brat, he had to cook outside on the right side of the grill. Nina made sure his animal flesh did not cross the line and, after he ate meat, refused his kisses. "Not until you brush your teeth."

"How's Grace doing this year?" Heather approached Nina on Friday afternoon. "What do you think of Sarabeth?"

"Grace likes her," Nina told her.

"She's teaching them to meditate on the sounds of the rainforest," Heather remarked, her tone verging on sarcasm. "But," she shrugged, "if she can teach my son to sit still and focus, she can teach whatever she wants." She leaned close. "Checking labels for palm oil?"

Nina smiled, her eyes on Heather's large teeth, like piano keys.

"I hope you're coming back to PTA." Heather handed her the agenda for the next meeting. "I know you took a beating last year, but we need rabble-rousers like you."

"Absolutely," Nina said, even though she had no intention of returning. She still hadn't recovered from the humiliation of last year's meeting when Heather announced that Mr. Lewis, Tamika's father, had graciously offered to make his Burger King franchise the official school sponsor. "Mr. Lewis is offering to pay for the school's weekend trip to the environmental center," she'd explained.

Nina raised her hand to speak. "I appreciate Mr. Lewis's offer, but we're an environmental school. Should we really be partnering with fast food chains?"

"We offer veggie burgers," Mr. Lewis said. "We fry in vegetable oil. We've pledged to go cage-free with our eggs by 2025."

"I don't mean to be contentious," Nina explained. "But Oxford University just published the largest study ever done on climate change, and they concluded that changing our diet away from meat and poultry and even fish would have the most significant impact on climate change, more than cars or fracking."

Carmen Henry, mother of three students at the school, stood up. "Some of our students never get into nature, except for this trip." She glanced at Nina. "I'm not telling you that *you* need to eat at Burger King. But I have no problem taking the money and sponsorship from one of our local businesses. And I wish to thank Mr. Lewis."

Applause broke out, the vote unanimous except for Nina's nay vote.

She came home that night in tears and told Ben what had happened. "Burger King!" she said, describing how humiliated she'd felt when the vote was taken. "No one stuck up for me. No one took my side."

"Who cares what they think?" Ben hugged her. "You try so

hard, Neenie," his nickname for her. "I wish you could just relax and enjoy life more."

When the school bell rang, and Grace came hurrying through the doors, Nina noticed her daughter's furrowed brow. "What's wrong, honey?"

"When we Skyped with Matt," Grace hugged her mother, "we could hear men sawing trees in the valley. Lucy heard them too." Grace clenched her teeth and sucked in air. "*Schliss, schliss.* Matt said that's her distress sound."

As they walked to the car, Grace asked, "What would you do if you knew people were coming to kill us?"

"I would find a way to save you," Nina said.

"Will Lucy find a way?"

"I'm sure she will."

At home, Grace wore her mask as she stirred applesauce into the batter for banana muffins, her favorite breakfast. Across the kitchen island, Nina assembled an enchilada bean casserole. "You're turning nine next week," Nina said. "Any idea of what you want for a present?"

"Before we buy things, we're supposed to ask ourselves if we *need* or *want* something." Grace swung her legs. "*Need* is different than *want.* And sometimes we think we want something because other people have it or we see it on TV."

"Is that what your teacher says?"

Grace nodded. "I don't *want* anything. *Schliss, schliss.*"

"Honey," Nina stroked her daughter's bangs away from her

mask. "It's okay to *want* some things at your age."

"I know," Grace said. "But I don't want a party or presents." She pushed the tin across the counter so her mother could put it in the oven. "Unless—" she lifted the mask momentarily, exposing freckled nose and cheeks—"we could send money to the people who protect Lucy? Could that be my present?"

Nina wondered if Grace's altruism was a new kind of perfectionism, aimed at moral virtue. Perfectionism ran in Nina's family, a family that supposedly arrived on the Mayflower only to waste their pedigree with each successive generation. Perfectionism crippled Nina and her siblings; none were high achievers. They always needed time to recover from themselves, from the disappointment of never living up to what their parents thought they would be—doctors or lawyers, or, at the very least, *married* to doctors or lawyers.

"You've always wanted a party before." Nina stuck the tin in the oven. "Is this about need and want again?"

"I don't like parties." Grace shook her head, really shook it, the way orangutan Lucy shook her head when flies hovered near her face.

Nina said, "You're a kid. You need to have fun. Everything has a good side and a bad side. Even presents. The world is full of wonderful things."

A week later, Nina organized a surprise party, believing her daughter would be glad to see a few girls from her class waiting for her at the park—and, too, because Nina wanted Grace to be invited to other girls' parties. She called the mothers and asked for small donations for Lucy in lieu of presents. She arrived at the park early to secure a picnic table on the hill, unpacking veggie brats, veggie chips, coleslaw, watermelon, potato salad, and cake. She made sure none of the foods had palm oil. At six o'clock there would be a concert by The Primitives. The park was packed with families. Children ran up and down the hill, chasing each other through a sea of blankets, coolers, picnic baskets.

Grace arrived in her father's car, and, seeing her classmates, stayed inside. Only when her father opened the passenger door did Grace climb out, arms folded across her chest like armor. The girls ran down the hill, making a show of their friendship. "Happy Birthday, *Graaaaaace*." They hugged her and led her back to the table, where their cards were stacked beside the cake. "Your mom said no presents," they explained.

"Instead of presents," Nina told her, "I asked for donations for Lucy."

After Grace opened each card and read it, she said, "I thank you, and Lucy thanks you." When she had finished opening the cards, she stacked them neatly in her mother's purse, glancing at the helium balloons her mother had attached to the legs of the table. "You shouldn't buy balloons, Mom. They pop and shred and then birds eat them and die."

"We're not going to let them pop." Nina smiled, sensing a meltdown. "Go have fun with your friends while your father grills the brats."

Grace's eyes filled with tears. She leaned close and whispered, "They don't like me."

"Honey, of course they do."

Grace shook her head, staring past her mother toward the lake—sailboats tacked in the wind, scent of French fries and walleye burgers drifted up from the concession stand and, while the band set up on stage, loudspeakers played piped-in music. Her friends were kicking a soccer ball back and forth at the bottom of the hill.

"Sweetie," Nina whispered, "you used to have fun. Last summer you had fun."

"No," Grace shook her head. "I was pretending." She buried her head against her mother's chest.

"Grace," the girls called out. "What's wrong?" They looked at her with exaggerated concern. "Come join us."

Nina lifted her gaze and saw what her daughter saw, the way the girls looked at each other after they called to her, suppressing laughter, as if she were an object of their kindness, someone they had talked about being nice to before they came to the party. All this, Nina could read in their eyes, the way they sought approval from each other and when Grace began walking toward them, locked eyes in confirmation of her weirdness.

Ben brought over a platter of grilled veggie brats. "Don't coddle her," he whispered in Nina's ear. "She has to learn to make an effort."

During the meal, Nina made conversation, asking the girls about their soccer team and summer camps and what they liked most about their school. She was surprised to learn two of the girls didn't like their teacher.

Brittany said, "She plays favorites, especially certain boys."

"She was an activist before she was a teacher." Kaylandra nodded. "My mom thinks she's in way over her head."

"What kind of activist?" Nina asked.

Kaylandra shook her head. "I'm not sure, but she's been arrested. She told my mom."

"I like her," Grace said definitively. "Lucy likes her too."

"How could Lucy like her?" Brittany asked. "She doesn't know her."

"Lucy is our relative," Grace said. "She has ninety-seven percent the same DNA as us. She's like our great, great, great, great, great, great, great, thousand-more-greats, grandmother."

"Do you even know what DNA is?" Brittany asked her.

"It's our gene-map," Grace explained. "Our genetic information. It's what makes us who we are."

The other girls looked at each other and burst out laughing.

After the meal, while her classmates ran down the hill to dance, Grace stayed to help her mother clean up, scraping watermelon rinds, leftover brat, and tomato slices into the compost bag. When she was done, she stared at her friends dancing in front of the stage. "Do I have to go down there?"

"Go on," Ben told her, irritated by Grace's clinginess. "Fifteen minutes."

Nina watched Grace walk slowly down the hill.

Ben emptied ice from the cooler. Looking up, he caught Nina's gaze, "Next year I think we might skip the party."

"You've had enough beer."

He gulped the rest before putting the empty bottle in the recycling bag. "I know you're trying to protect her—"

"—I'm not protecting her. I just want her to have friends."

"She has to make her own friends, and if she doesn't, she's going to be lonely, and there's nothing we can do about that."

Nina's eyes filled with tears.

"I never had a party," he wrapped his arm around her shoulders. "I turned out okay, didn't I?"

Nina could've said something mean, but she didn't. She could have mentioned his parents were alcoholics and his two older daughters by his first wife were filled with anger toward him. But she didn't want him to go silent on the way home in front of Grace who would interpret his silence as her fault.

When they delivered the kids to their homes early, calling first to explain that Grace didn't feel well, Brittany's mother said, "Too much for her?"

This comment infuriated Nina, and later in the kitchen, after Grace had gone upstairs, she admitted to her husband, "We shouldn't have had the party. My mistake." Nina sat on the stool, watching him wipe out the cooler. "Go ahead. Say what you're thinking—"

"I know you mean well." Ben tossed the rag in the sink. He looked at Nina as he spoke in a soft, careful voice. "You're a great mother, Nina, but you love her so much, sometimes you suffocate her. She absorbs your fears."

Nina's mouth fell open in disbelief. "Suffocate her?"

"I think she puts on the mask to put distance between you and her. She can't handle how much you try to control her life."

"I just want her to be happy—"

"—Happy? You think *that* school will make her happy?

Watching a critically endangered orangutan mother try to survive will make her happy?" He shook his head. "I think you expect Grace to transcend your own hopelessness. Why can't she just be a kid? Why does *she* need to save the world?"

After he went upstairs, Nina sat alone in the kitchen. His words felt like a wound, a breathless gap in her chest. Part of what he said was true, but she couldn't help who she was and what she knew. Instead of seeing the dense orange sunset out the kitchen window, she saw smoke blowing south from Canadian wildfires. Instead of her neighbors' perfect lawns and manicured gardens, she saw butterflies and bees lost to chemical summers. From morning to night, Nina saw choices, measured solutions, a truce with an unfathomable future. How, in such a world, could any parent teach truth and hope at the same time?

On Halloween, Grace donned her Lucy mask and red leotard. She was Lucy for the whole day, walking on all fours, grunting and hissing, and all the kids laughed because no one could make her break out of character.

The boys tried. One boy was dressed as a pirate, and he tore down Lucy's trees and vines with his plastic sword. Another, some kind of super hero, joined the pirate, and together they invaded Lucy's mountain. *We're coming to get you.* But Grace was Lucy, defending her species and the last territory left to them. She began swinging herself at them, kicking and clawing, until both boys were in tears, screaming at Grace to stop.

All this Nina learned from the principal over the phone. "We need you to come right now," the principal told her.

Nina found Grace in the principal's office, crouching next to the chairs with the mask still on her face. Seeing her mother, Grace swung herself across the office and wrapped her arms around her mother's knees. Nina pulled her up to a standing position. "Grace, stop it now." Nina lifted off the mask. "You cannot hit other students."

Grace reached for the mask and held it in front of her face. "They were tearing down my trees."

"Please, Grace, you need to stop this game you're playing. You frighten other students. You're frightening me."

"*Schliss, schliss.*" Grace glared at her mother with a stubborn defiance Nina had never before witnessed in her daughter. Motherhood was made up of an infinite number of unwanted separations, but this one felt different. Nina looked into Grace's eyes and could not find her, the daughter she had known. Something had folded up inside her daughter. Nina couldn't untangle it, couldn't reach her.

That night, Nina asked Ben, "Do you think this is because of the mice?"

"No," he said, scowling.

The mice had arrived in August, leaving little black pellet turds all over the kitchen. For two weeks, Nina tried to get rid of them using live traps and sonar repellents. She spent a whole day putting all dry food in glass containers. But each morning, the traps were empty, and Nina cleaned up trails of pellets on counters, baseboards, windowsills.

Grace reminded her mother, "Mice have feelings too."

But the sonar repellants apparently sent the mice upstairs through radiator holes, and they entered the bedrooms and closets. Nina got up to use the toilet one night and a mouse scurried right past her foot. She screamed, and Ben came running, furious that she'd wakened him because of a mouse. "Mice won't hurt you."

She crawled into bed next to him. "Do whatever you have to do, and I'll look the other way. Just don't let Grace find out."

The following Saturday, when Grace was eating waffles, Nina heard the trap snap, and a second later, the mouse scurried out from underneath the radiator, dragging the trap on its tail, zigzagging drops of blood across the linoleum floor and trying to free itself. Grace ran after it, and when the trap caught on the stove bottom, she courageously lifted the trap, even as the mouse hung by its tail, clawing air, eyes blinking in terror. Grace released the mouse outside. When she came back inside, tears streamed down her cheeks. "You lied. You said animals are our equals. You said we don't kill in our house."

"Enough, Grace." Ben stood in the doorway. Hearing screams, he'd come running, shaving cream still on his cheeks. "I set them. Your mother didn't know. If they come back, I'll set the traps again. When you grow up, you can live with mice if you want to."

That was two months ago.

Two days after Halloween, Nina and Ben attended a mandatory visit with the school psychologist to discuss their daughter's aggressive behavior. The psychologist introduced herself as Mary and sat across from them with a notepad.

"Has there been any kind of stress or loss in the family?"

"Not really." Nina glanced at Ben, "Except about her school—"

"—You chose the school," Ben interrupted Nina, addressing the psychologist. "My wife lives out of fear. She chose the school because it's in a good neighborhood and now it's backfiring."

"That was part of it," Nina admits. "But who doesn't want their child to be in a space that's beautiful?"

"I didn't care about that," Ben said. "I wanted her to be close to home."

He shook his head. "I question the teacher's judgment—adopting an endangered orangutan as the class project. Grace worries about Lucy."

"Lucy's the orangutan?" the psychologist asked.

"Yes," Ben said, his impatient tone implying the psychologist should get up to speed.

Nina nodded. "Our daughter loves animals."

"Honestly," Ben sat back, crossing his arms. "I don't think it's that big a deal. My older daughter used to pretend she was a horse, and she trampled the neighbor's garden. Kids go through phases."

"She's getting teased." Nina reminded him. "Then she hits."

The therapist glanced between them. "What about a rule that she can be an orangutan at home and at school she has to be Grace?"

"Won't that just enable her?" Ben asked.

"We all take on roles in public," the psychologist explained. "It might be a way for her to work through it. And if you want, I can give you the name of a good child psychiatrist."

Walking toward the car, Ben said, "No psychiatrist. No drugs. We're not going to pathologize her. She's a great kid." He unlocked the car.

Climbing in the passenger seat, Nina noticed the pile of empty plastic water bottles on the floor of the backseat. "Why don't you use the reusable bottles from home?"

Ben turned on the engine. "I keep forgetting to take them."

She stared through the passenger window at overflowing trash bins in the park. If she couldn't get her own husband to stop using plastic, what hope was there? "Every bottle counts."

As he backed out fast, turning onto the street, Nina heard him mutter under his breath, "Might have to get a mask too."

That evening, after Ben left for the Y, Nina called her sister in San Francisco. Eight years older, Tamara was a Buddhist psychologist married to Joseph, a mystery author.

Tamara answered. "What's up?"

Nina explained how every day after school Grace put on the mask and pretended she was an orangutan. "Her arms have biceps the size of oranges. She hunches her back and walks her hands on the floor, swinging her torso forward between her arms—"

"—OCD-ish?" Tamara interrupted, "Or is it really just a form of play? Grace has always been imaginative."

"She's not playing," Nina told her.

"Hold on." Tamara said. "I'm googling orangutans."

"Have you been drinking?" Nina asked, checking her watch,

seeing it was only three in the afternoon in California.

"Wine with lunch, no worries." Her voice lifted, "Oh, they're so cute," then sank, "Oh no! Poachers kidnap the babies and sell them as pets." Then she moaned. "Their habitat is disappearing. They're going extinct."

"I know."

"I'll call a colleague who specializes in children with non-diagnosable disorders." Tamara told her. "I'll get back to you as soon as I talk to him."

And hour later, Tamara called back, "She's a *therianthrope*."

"What's that?" Nina kept her voice lowered in the kitchen.

"Someone who identifies as an earthly animal. Trans-species. Born into the wrong body. It's a real thing. I talked to my colleague. Some therapists believe it's caused through reincarnation or misplaced souls."

"Do you believe that?" Nina asked.

"Don't worry, therianthropy is in no way related to sexual contact with animals. Unless she's a furry." Her sister laughed.

"What's a furry?"

"People who get their sexual kicks dressing up as animals. They go to fur-dom conferences and pet each other."

Nina tightened inside, like a column holding up sky. Tamara was one of those people who prided herself on being open to everything.

"Maybe you should respect Grace's identification with nonhuman species." Tamara shifted into her soothing therapist's voice. "Maybe we limit ourselves when we identify strictly as humans."

As her sister talked, Nina googled *children who act like animals*, and read:

> *Earls and Lalumeire (2009) describe species dysphoria as 'the sense of being in the wrong (species)body . . . a desire to be an animal.' A term also used is 'transspecies,' described by Phaedra and Isaac Bonewits as 'people who believe themselves to be part animal, or animal souls incarnated in human bodies.'*

Her sister said, "Remember those caves we visited as kids, animals with human heads? This isn't a new idea. I heard a story about polar bears and grizzlies breeding because it will be the only way they can survive on the planet. Maybe spiritually Grace is way ahead of us."

"What do you think we should do?" Nina asked, impatient to end their phone call.

"My colleague thinks you should pretend you're orangutans too. Grace might miss her parents. And it might help her process feelings."

For a few days the strategy worked. Nina pretended to be an orangutan mother. For a whole weekend, she crouched down, arms alongside knees, lunging after her daughter, speaking orangutanese. "*Eeenh, eeeeh, schlisss, schlisss.*" She made a tart from fruit and nuts. She picked up leaves outside, kissed them, and dropped them at her daughter's feet. Sunday morning, Grace lifted her fingernails toward Nina's mouth. "Orangutan mothers bite off their children's fingernails, so they don't get too long."

Nina nodded. "I did that when you were a baby."

Grace put her thumbnail near her mother's mouth. "Show me."

Nina couldn't believe she was biting off her daughter's fingernails.

Monday afternoon the division between Lucy-at-home and Grace-at-school broke down during recess when Grace pushed Pete, Heather's son, off the top rung, resulting in an eight-foot fall and a deep cut on his cheek requiring stitches.

A conference was called between parents, and the principal explained that Grace would be expelled if she initiated one more incident threatening another child's safety. "That includes knocking kids off the playground equipment."

"I'm so sorry," Nina explained to Heather in the hallway after the meeting. "We'll pay all the bills. And Grace will apologize."

"No need. Our insurance covers it," Heather said abruptly, glancing down the hallway where Grace was sitting on a bench, reading a book. "Have you thought about getting help? Maybe medication?"

Shame pumped blood into Nina's cheeks. "She's going through something. Ever since she first saw Lucy, she's been obsessed with her."

"Well," Heather said, "as we both know, not every school is right for every child."

"Heather meant it as a threat," Nina said, recounting her conversation to Ben that evening before calling Grace to dinner. "She thinks she runs the school."

When they sat down at the table, Ben told Grace, "Please take off the mask, Grace. We're going to have some new rules. You're not wearing the mask to meals—"

"*Schliss, schliss.*" Grace refused.

"I said, *take it off*. I'm not playing anymore. You hurt a classmate today." His voice was loud and firm, and Nina thought it was also harsh, not at all fatherly.

"*Schliss, schliss.*" Grace sucked air through her teeth, the orangutan distress signal, then spoke from behind her mask. "He started it. He held onto my foot."

Ben stared at Grace, his tone brusque. "I asked you nicely to take it off, and I meant it."

"Please, Grace," Nina intervened. "Your father's very upset about what happened with Pete at school."

"I don't need you to tell her how I feel." Ben's voice rose, unleashing his fury on Nina. "I'm tired of how you walk on eggshells around her, letting her control our lives." He turned his gaze to Grace. "I'm going to ask you for the last time. Please take it off, *now*."

Grace took off her mask and set it beside her plate. Tears ran down her cheeks, and she refused to eat her dinner. When her father had finished, he lifted her plate and carried it into the kitchen, telling Nina, "*Not eating* was her choice. Don't you dare sneak her fruit and nuts. We need to be on the same page."

That night when Nina crawled into bed, Ben told her, "Children are resilient. Grace will come through this."

"Do you believe that?"

"Yes. I've been through it before with Jessie and Leah."

Nina turned on her side and faced him. Sometimes she cut him off when he talked about his older daughters; she wanted a separation between his former family and his family now. But tonight, she needed his assurance.

He reached his arm under her neck and pulled her toward him. "Jessie stole jewelry from the YWCA during her swim class."

"You never told me that."

"Because it wasn't a big deal. She returned it and apologized, and she didn't do it again. Leah went through that piercing phase, eyebrows, ears, nose, lips."

"Did you ever yell at them like you yelled at Grace tonight?"

"I didn't yell." He sighed. "Grace needs to know there are boundaries. If she feels the world is out of control, we need to let her know we're in control."

"Are we?" Lying there, Nina doubted it. Her love for her daughter felt limitless, but not in a good way. She didn't know how to draw lines between herself and Grace, and often Nina couldn't tell the difference between love and control, not when it came to protecting her daughter.

"She knows we love her," Ben whispered. "That's the bottom line."

Nina felt her chest grow lighter, as if her husband's certainty allowed her to release some of her worry, like pouring water from one pail into another to lessen the weight of both.

"Shall we bake granola bars?" Nina suggested the next afternoon. She was trying to make up for the dinner the night before.

Grace shook her head. "*Schliss, schliss*," her human appetite diminished. "Lucy likes fruit, bark, nuts."

"*Schliss*," Nina hissed, tiring of the charade. "You told me Lucy eats bird eggs."

"Only sometimes," Grace said. "Only when I'm really hungry and there's nothing else."

Grace, referring to herself as Lucy, sent a shiver through Nina. She watched her daughter reach into her backpack and pull out a list of companies that import palm oil: Colgate-Palmolive, Kraft Heinz, L'Oreal, Pepsi Cola. Her class was practicing their *public* voices by writing letters to CEOs, and Grace read her letter out loud to her mother.

"Dear Sir or Madam. We are boycotting Pepsi Cola because your company destroys vital rainforest habitat in Sumatra. As long as this practice continues, we will not purchase products sold by your company. Please protect orangutans and other critically endangered species by protecting Sumatran rainforests."

Nina hugged her. "Good job," then went into the bathroom and cried. She wondered at what age children learned to both feel and turn off feeling. She thought about the choices she'd made. Maybe the arts magnet would have been better for Grace. Or maybe her husband was right, and she would have been better off at the crowded neighborhood school.

The Wednesday before Thanksgiving break, parents were invited to the class poetry reading late afternoon. All week Grace's class had been working with a poet, Mia, to help them discover their *private* voices. Grace told her parents, "There's going to be a big surprise too."

Ben left work early and arrived in a suit and tie. Grace hugged him and led him to the chair next to her mother in the second row. Everyone was dressed up, even Sarabethridesbikes, in a red sweater, plaid skirt, leggings, and polished hiking boots. The students had glued their favorite poem on construction paper and decorated the edges, a Thanksgiving gift for their parents, the theme: gratitude. Some students wrote about pets, others grandparents, and still others wrote about their mothers and fathers. When it was Grace's turn, she stood at the microphone.

"My poem is called Lucy's Questions." Then, lowering her gaze to the poem, she repeated the title. "Lucy's Questions.

When does the faraway arrive?
When does it choose us?
When does the sky open its eyes to see the trees are gone?
When does air relax?
When does the real memory get lost?
When does love stop coloring inside lines?"

Sarabethridesbikes applauded. "I wish I'd written that poem, Grace."

"She's a poet," Nina said, clapping, proud tears rolling down her cheeks. But Ben was hardly clapping; he was watching Grace with a worried smile. Nina leaned over, "Clap. Show her you're proud." Ben joined in.

After all the students had read, Sarabethridesbikes stood at the front to quiet the room. "As you all know, we had a special surprise for parents today. We were hoping to Skype with Matt and introduce you to Lucy. But, unfortunately, we've just had some very sad news. Lucy has left the park and is now unprotected—"

"*Broooooohmmmmmm . . . broooooooohmmmm.*" Grace released two low bellows that resembled a foghorn, apparently the call orangutans send to each other across distances. The other children backed away, and some of the girls started crying, frightened of Grace.

"*Broooooohmmmmmm,*" Grace wailed, arms extended downward beside her knees.

Pete stood nearby with the boys, and he was the first to snicker.

Grace rushed toward him, gripped his arm, and bit hard above his elbow.

Heather was on her feet in two seconds, already grabbing Grace, pushing her toward her parents. "She shouldn't be here. She's a danger to other children—"

"—You're the danger," Ben said, lashing out at Heather as he took hold of Grace. "Parents like you take over a school and run it like it's your own kingdom."

He turned to Sarabethridesbikes, "Did you ever consider this project might be too much for some kids?" Heading toward the door with Grace in tow, he said to Nina, "Get her stuff. We'll meet you at home." Grace was still hunched over, trying to walk with her hands on the floor, but her father was strong, lifting her upright as they exited the room.

Heather glared at Nina, holding up her son's arm with teeth-marks. "She broke skin. We're calling the police."

Sarabethridesbikes stood between Heather and Nina. "Sit down, please. Let's try to sort this out among ourselves."

"That girl has to be expelled." Heather yelled. "Or I will personally sue the school for violating its own rules."

Parents were leaving, hurrying their children out of the room. Nina grabbed Grace's folders and notebooks, as much as she could fit into her bag. All the while, she could hear Heather gathering a posse. "You can't leave yet. You're my witness. You saw my son was assaulted."

Outside, crossing the street, Nina could hardly breathe. The wind had teeth, and a fat burst of rain drenched her before she reached the car. She got inside, her breath a hammock lacking weight, nothing to exhale, except an overwhelming sense of shame. But also—and this surprised her—a new admiration for her husband, the way Ben stood up to Heather and Sarabethridesbikes.

Sitting there, Nina felt a profound sadness, as if her priorities had been all wrong. She wished she could start over and be a different kind of mother, a different kind of wife—the kind who laughed more than she worried, the kind who trusted herself to know what her family needed.

Driving home, rain pelting the windshield, Nina tried to imagine what was next for Grace—new school, new friends—realizing, too, this was just the first of many endings for her daughter, the first of many kinds of grief.

And yet, she thought, every feeling needed a destination, a place to rest.

Entering the kitchen, she saw the mask on the counter. She pulled the scissors from the drawer, and glancing at her husband and daughter on the couch, lifted the mask. "We'll make a necklace of the pieces."

Grace turned and, seeing her, leapt off the couch. "*Schliss, schliss.*"

But love was made of muscle, as much as anything else, and Nina cut fast.

FORGIVENESS

Last year, after my wife's sister died of cancer, Sylvie started to worry about her own health. She lost thirty pounds, counting points in Weight Watchers and bicycling every day.

When I told her I was proud of her, she rolled her eyes. "You sound like my father."

"What's wrong with being proud of you?"

"I'm not doing it for you. I'm doing it for myself."

A year ago now, we had that conversation, before her trip to Italy, before it happened. Since then, nothing feels honest, no silence empty enough, no apology sincere enough. After thirty-two years of marriage, that's what anger does, keeps us deciding what to bury.

Sometimes, I almost break free and think we're fine, like falling in a dream and waking up. Today is one of those moments. I get the nomination after the first hour bell, a phone call from the superintendent, and right away my first thought is, Call Sylvie. She'll be so proud of you.

I don't call her. I don't want her to know she's my first thought. I don't want to share my happiness with her. I wait until dinner. Sunset grazes the kitchen table, rattle and howl of wind caught between storm and interior window. I stare at her sweater, frayed sleeves, hair falling free from its clip. "I got the nomination, Principal of the Year."

She turns, eyes bright and happy for me, but right away, I add, "I don't think I'm going to accept it."

Later, she leaves a glass of warm milk by the bed, nutmeg and honey settling on the bottom. She claims it will help me sleep, another home remedy, something else to demonstrate she's trying. As I drink it down, I listen to the shower go on and off, reminding myself she's a good person—she saves water.

The door opens, and she climbs into bed, wet hair falling over her shoulders, skin greased, shapeless maroon pajamas. "Principal of the Year! Such an honor to be nominated." She burrows under blankets, her foot searching for warmth along my leg. "Think of the recognition for your school." The bedroom is cold because she likes the window open; air circulation, she says, though it requires additional blankets to keep warm, a certain weight on top for her to sleep well. She wriggles her cold hand under my pajama sleeve.

I squeeze my arm down hard, harder than I need to. "You're cold."

"Proud, proud, proud," she says, the way she did years ago when the kids brought home *A*s and *B*s on report cards. She strokes my arm. "You've worked so hard, and it's a far better school for your efforts."

I don't care about the nomination, and I wonder if not caring is a way of protecting myself. I feel old, suspect of recognition and people who receive it. I might die soon. My mother died at fifty, my father at sixty-two. I imagine the intercom first hour: *We have some very sad news. Principal Jaffrey died in his sleep last night.* Students I've suspended would cheer. How many teachers would come to my funeral? Five maybe, if they could get paid leave. The lunchroom staff would get a card and sign it, sending carnations in school colors, orange and blue.

"Who else was nominated?" Sylvie asks.

"Mitch."

"Mitchell West?" Her laughter falls like running water. "He's always running his tongue over his lips. I find him creepy."

"He gets more students into college than any other high school."

"An arts magnet," she says. "They can go to Ashland Pottery Institute and say they're going to college."

"He's good at fundraising." I stretch my legs under the covers. "I'm tired. I want to retire before I'm too old to enjoy life."

"You're only fifty-three," Sylvie says. "What if Minnesota reduces pensions like Wisconsin?" She moves closer, her breath smelling of toothpaste. "Most people would be thrilled to be nominated."

Rising to take a Xanax, pills my doctor prescribes cautiously, allowing only six a month, I take one and stare at my reflection in the mirror—my father's hooded eyes, slaggy cheeks, thin *English* lips. Sylvie used to tease me, "You've got the Queen's lips."

Before her trip last summer, we always rolled toward the center of the bed and held each other. I call to Kafka, "Come on, boy," and the dog jumps on the bed between us, sinks his weight along my leg.

Sylvie reaches across the dog, finds my wrist. "If you really want to retire, then retire. Just make sure you're doing it for the right reasons."

Uncertainty is its own undoing. What I can't forgive, even now, are all the beliefs that fell away, including my own worthiness. The ceiling has opened to sky, and the sky belongs to her. I don't want sky, don't want a wide expanse revealing my own narrowness. Am I narrow?

She squeezes my wrist. "Please don't do this."

"What?" My voice, a steep drop.

"Don't let what happened between us ruin it. You deserve the award."

I wait for the Xanax to take effect, thoughts slackening like flags on windless days. I wonder why the nomination feels like a burden, something else to dread. I listen to branches break outside the window, ash trees casting off dead wood with each gust of hard wind.

Nine months ago, her first night back from Italy, I brought home takeout, calling first to ask what she wanted.

"Pad Thai, no tofu." That's what she'd asked for, and that's what they gave me, except I'd forgotten to say, *No baby corn, either.*

"Thirty-two years of marriage." She stared at the baby corn in her Pad Thai. "I've never eaten baby corn."

I glanced up, noticing the force of her voice.

We were sitting at the kitchen table, bank of windows overlooking the back yard, tithonia thick with orange blooms, birds loud, ignorant of tragedy. That time of day, as dusk began to fall earlier, the sun fell through the windows, giving the kitchen a soft light. The sky was orange above the trees. We ate in shadow, preferring the gradual ebb of natural light to brighter LED bulbs above the table.

She picked out the baby corn. Normally she ate fast. I'd always found her eating habits masculine, the way she relished food. Big German fingers that helped push food onto her fork or chopsticks, oily lips, unselfconscious appetite. That was one of the things I'd had to stop noticing, her greedy eating habits.

She barely ate, and I apologized twice for the baby corn. She stirred the noodles, looking at her plate.

"What was the theme this year?" I asked, inquiring about the Italian school where she did her research.

Sylvie took a long sip of pilsner, before she set down the bottle. "They designed all kinds of ways to study water."

An education professor at Augsburg, she took student groups every summer to spend a month in Reggio Emilia, a communist area in northern Italy known for its progressive schools. Sylvie was writing her second book on learning environments.

"They built a waterslide from the tree house," she explained, "and they analyzed puddles for organisms. Then they turned the slide into a water wheel that produced energy." She took a small bite of rice. "Then they wrote a play about the future of water and put it on for the community." Her somber tone didn't match her praise. Usually she bubbled forth.

"Was the biking hard?" I asked.

This year she'd stayed on an extra two weeks for a BiciSole bike tour through the Dolomites. She picked at her food. "Not that hard. Scenery was beautiful."

I'd just dished out my second helping of green curry with shrimp when I noticed her eyes filling with tears.

"I have something to tell you."

I sensed her reluctance and knew right away, by her silence, by the way her chin dimpled and lips tucked, something bad had happened. "Did someone do something to you?"

My worry made her flinch. "No, no, not that." She set down her chopsticks and reached across the table, held my wrist. "You and I, we're in this life together, and I know that." Her voice trembled. "So please try to listen and understand. I made a terrible mistake." She stared at the table. "I met someone."

My chest was suddenly full of wind, wind blowing hills of sand, burying whatever was there before. I breathed deeply, consciously expanding my belly, trying to absorb her meaning. I pushed aside containers of food, shrimp glistening like tree ornaments, leaving the taste of murky water in my mouth. I stood up, dumped my shrimp curry and rice in the compost bin.

That night, I walked Kafka after dinner, circling the block, stopping to look at our small bungalow on the corner, lights in upper windows where Sylvie was unpacking. Thirty years we'd lived there, raising our children in that house, Judy and Gordie, married now, with children of their own. Sylvie had pulled the curtains closed in our bedroom. I stared at the other houses on our block and wondered if our neighbors were happy, televisions flickering behind shades. My eyes kept going back to our house, shock falling through me like rain in headlights. I thought of the staircase I'd sanded while she was gone, the yard I'd mowed, the rhubarb I'd picked and had frozen in baggies so she could make rhubarb bread. So many entrances to the future, and I wanted to block them all.

Back from my walk, I fed Kafka a biscuit, then took the stairs two at a time, finding her bent over her desk sorting mail. "Show me a photo. I need to see him."

"I erased them," her voice hoarse from crying.

I stood beside her desk, shoulders casting a shadow over the papers she was organizing. "Give me your phone."

She looked away as I scrolled photos. She actually had erased them, except for one group photo at the end of the trip. I recognized Marco right away, standing beside Sylvie. His face was deeply tanned, a wide smile, sporty sunglasses resting on his shaved head.

I thought seeing the photo would make him real, would give my anger a surface to stand on. I thought proof would settle my thoughts into a single outrage. "Is he married?"

"He doesn't believe in marriage." She looked past me, at the window, as if it were easier to see me as a reflection.

"No kids?"

"No." Her voice sounded tired, and yet I could also hear a flickering underneath, a spark not yet extinguished, and it made me feel ill. "I need to know everything. I deserve to know."

All that night, and for days and weeks after, I asked questions, as if there were a way to uproot the betrayal, pull it out by the roots, shake off the dirt and boil it into some kind of wisdom. "Did he sleep naked?" "How did he touch you?" "What did you talk about?" On and on, I kept returning to the same questions, until finally she admitted, "It was his smell. From the moment we met, it overwhelmed me, almost a chemical reaction."

"What kind of smell?"

"A body smell." She shrugged, staring me in the eye. "Like animal pheromones. I can't explain it better."

"You risked us," I waved my hand at the photos of our children and grandchildren on the dresser, "you risked all of this for a smell?"

Every conversation made me angrier. "What did you tell other people on the tour? Could Judy or Gordie find out?"

"No one knew. He'd be fired from the company if they found out."

I considered reporting him. After that night, I began changing into my pajamas in the bathroom, self-conscious about moles, fleshy waist, my bald patch, the spot she used to rub at night in bed, tickling my exposed scalp. "Neanderthal," she'd say, and smoothing my overgrown eyebrows, "Wolfie." Rubbing more, "Turtle," all the nicknames she had for me.

Months have passed, almost a year. We are separate, and I grieve the separateness, shadows living in the same house, shedding all but the necessary—fold, rinse, when will you be home?

She says something like, "Think we should hire Zanelli's again? They didn't come after the last big snow."

And I think how easy it is to disappoint her. "They've cleared our driveway for years. Zanelli's a nice guy."

We bought Roku, needing a way to spend time together.

She'll say, "How about a comedy, something light?" and I'll say, "I'm in the mood for a thriller," and she'll say, "I'm tired of watching women die," and I'll say, "Men die too. In fact, men die sooner." She'll insist, "In the last three shows, women have been murdered."

She's right. I can't argue.

And then she'll gather her knitting and say, "You go ahead. I don't care about watching."

And again, I feel abandoned, and again say, "When did you start wanting something else?"

At the beginning, she'd sit back down. She owed me that. "I don't want to fight anymore."

"You thought you could get away with it." I make her say it.

"I thought I could have a separate experience without hurting you." Tears roll down her cheeks. "But when I got home, I couldn't lie to you."

"You can cheat on me, but not lie?"

"Lying would've been worse, between us forever."

Part of me understands, but understanding fuels a different anger—she has taken control of deciding what to tell me.

Saturday morning, I wake thinking of the nomination. I have the weekend to decide. Monday, the nominations will be sent to the committee. I suspect I am the compromise candidate, no one's first choice, no one disliking me enough to argue against me either, the only reason I might actually win.

I smell bacon. One would think breaking a spouse's trust would somehow modify a couple's routine, but not in our case. We still have a big breakfast on Saturdays, dividing sections of the *Times*. She takes the main section, and I wade through the sports.

Sylvie has been up since six, has already taken Kafka around the lake for a walk. The fan is loud above the burners, and Kafka is standing behind her, nose lifted toward bacon draining on a paper towel.

"Before you decide about the nomination, you should talk to someone." Sylvie cracks an egg. "I don't want you to make a mistake you'll regret." For years she's been encouraging me to make friends, going so far as to list possible candidates.

"I talk to you." I sip coffee and drizzle honey on toast, listening for what's behind her silence, wooden spoon tapping the bowl, slippers sliding across the wood floor, sighs full of measured air.

"Yes, but you're angry at me." She hands me a wet napkin to clean honey off the table, then nods at my fingers. She hates when I leave honey marks on the newspaper and the pages stick. "Maybe you should call Alex." Alex is a former teacher who's become a Buddhist monk. "He'd be a good listener."

I take a bite of toast, remembering when I was the more powerful one in the relationship, how power had come from knowing what I wanted—marriage, two children, principal of an urban high school. Whereas it took her years to know what she wanted, whether to get pregnant, how many kids, whether to finish her PhD, apply for tenure track positions. She used to tell me *not knowing* had nothing to do with strength. "It actually takes strength not to know," she said. "*Not deciding* is different."

After she spoons eggs onto two plates, she hands me one. I sprinkle salt and pepper.

"That much salt?" She sits across from me, gives me a meaningful glance. "We all need someone to confide in. It's not good to hold everything inside."

"Do women count?"

"Sure."

FORGIVENESS

"Michaela?"

"Kafka's dogwalker? You're going to tell her about your deepest fears?"

"I like her. We have good conversations."

"I know you do, but she's twenty-five. That's a little desperate."

"Is it?" I finish off my third piece of bacon. Add more salt to my eggs. Drizzle honey all over the toast without wiping my fingers.

There is a life in which my anger wins. Instinctive. More habit than I want.

Our daughter Judy knocks, pushes open the door, hands full with baby and diaper bag. "Do you have time to look at the stroller wheel, Dad?" She kicks off her shoes. "Front right wheel makes a terrible squeaking noise."

Sylvie takes the diaper bag from her arms. "Your father wants to retire early."

"Really?" Judy hands me the baby. "Since when?"

I smell Kafka under the table, gassy in old age. Or it's the baby, resting on my lap. Judy looks like Sylvie, except she's grown rounder during her pregnancy. She has her mother's straight nose, dark eyes, frizzy brown hair pulled back behind her ears. "Nine-month check-in yesterday." Judy beams at the baby drinking from her sippy cup. "Her head circumference measured in the eightieth percentile."

"Takes after your father," Sylvie smiles. "He's been nominated for Principal of the Year."

"Dad, congratulations." Judy high-fives me, then leans over and takes the baby from my lap, kissing her cheeks. "Hear that, sweetie? Your grandfather's the best principal in the whole state."

"I'd rather retire." Standing, I zip my fleece vest, give my daughter a hug, kiss Emily on her forehead, and, glancing at Sylvie's scowl, head to the garage to see about the baby's stroller.

I like fixing things, taking things apart, putting them back together, an antidote for all the things that can't be fixed.

Unresolved anger will bury you, I tell my students. They smile back at me, eyes like asphalt under puddles. Sometimes I feel like a container, and the world is loose seeds shaking inside me. Someone has to take responsibility. Someone has to be the steady force sitting behind a desk when parents come to discuss their sons' and daughters' behavior. "Your daughter was texting and when the teacher asked for her phone, she stuck it down her shirt." Or, "Your son pushed a girl's face into the drinking fountain and she chipped a tooth. We do not tolerate this kind of behavior." I watch parents regard sons and daughters with a mixture of shock, recognition, and helplessness. Their shock is real when I describe posts originating on their son's or daughter's social media page: a photo of Jimmy Tan's webbed feet in the boys' shower—paddles of flesh with toenails—titled *duck boy*; another post showing Mr. Sachs, the physics teacher, picking his nose at a red light; the post showing Mrs. Beltro, our beloved drama teacher, with her chemo wig askew during a fire drill.

As I unscrew the wheel, I listen to Sylvie play patty-cake with the baby in the kitchen.

We haven't made love, not since it happened.

Twice she asked if we could "do our taxes," the phrase we used when the kids were young and we'd lock the bedroom door and didn't want to be disturbed.

"Today would be a good day to do our taxes," she whispered one morning as I sat at the table reading the newspaper. Snow fell outside the window, and the kitchen was warm and smelled like toast.

But her kisses had changed, no longer pecks, but water drawn from a well.

She learned that from him, I thought, unwilling to live as a comparison in her mind. Her breath grazed the back of my neck. Instead of hugging her, I kept reading the newspaper.

Another afternoon, she got into bed next to me while I was trying to nap. She cupped my body from behind. Leaves rustled, and geese squawked overhead. Her hair smelled like oranges. I pretended to be asleep, and eventually we did nap until thunder woke us. "This is nice," she said, pressing her cheek to my shoulder blade. "I miss you."

I rose from the bed and left her there. My heart was full of old machinery, pistons and chains that refused to move. Mostly it was fear, that my body would make her miss him more.

Sylvie pushes the door opener button, and sunlight pours into the garage. "Judy's coming back later to get the stroller." She's dressed in leggings and fitted jacket, carrying a helmet under her arm. "Get a bike," she says, urging me to exercise. "Come with me."

"Hurts my back."

She pushes off, shoulders lowered over handlebars, wisps of

brown hair floating behind her helmet.

Since last summer, she's evolved into a set of distances. She gave away her high heels. Lattes, instead of black coffee. Fingernails trimmed low, unpainted. Buttermilk pancakes weekdays, which I don't mind, but she's always been so careful about carbs. Bicycling hundreds of miles every week, not like before, just on weekends, but every day to and from work with bike lights and fluorescent jacket. Turmeric tea she drinks all day long. I smell it in cups even after she's rinsed them. "Aids digestion and inflammation," she tells me. "Helps my muscles after bicycling. You should try it."

Sunday afternoon, Sylvie suggests we visit an art gallery. I know what she's doing, reviving our old ritual, all those winter afternoons during college when we'd go to gallery openings, drink free wine, and decide what we'd buy when we had money to spend on art. She's heard about an opening at Intermedia Arts, an exhibit composed of books on pedestals with nothing inside the covers, just blank pages. Visitors can write anything they want on the blank pages, and whatever they write is immediately projected onto a screen, a screen running continually, *twenty-four-seven*, hence the title of the exhibit.

The gallery is small, and apparently about to close. A sign says, *Moving! Pushed out by gentrification! Art never dies! It moves to the suburbs!* Inside, the room is packed with young people, many with wet hair, escaping the sporadic showers outside. I stare at illuminated walls. The movement of words gives me a headache. The crowd is young, girls with nose rings and pink hair, boys in tight jeans and fitted jackets. The room smells of pizza from Galactica across the street. Instead of music, the sound system plays a heartbeat, and when it speeds up, the words fall faster, and when it slows, the words slow. I find it pretentious, words pouring down walls, words about saving wolves and organic apples and snowshoeing in winter and the tooth fairy.

I whisper to Sylvie, "This isn't art."

She frowns at me. "You're always angry at students for being on their phones. Well, here's a young artist trying to show what's happening to language."

"Young people make me feel old."

"Old people make me feel young." She moves to the pedestal next to us and begins writing. *I would do anything to go back in time and not make the same mistake.*

People reading turn and watch us. I lean over Sylvie's shoulder. "Stop it. Stop doing this right now."

She keeps writing. *You deserve the nomination, and you deserve to be Principal of the Year.*

I close the book, close it hard, slamming her hand inside it.

"Ouch." She lifts her hand and stares at me. "I'll come back another time without you." She heads to the coat rack, pulls on her coat, fishing in her pocket for car keys.

"I didn't mean to hurt your hand." I walk fast to catch up. "Don't overreact."

Opening the heavy glass door, she glares at me. "You've become a very negative person." She lets go of the door and keeps walking ahead until she reaches the car.

Sitting in the driver's seat, she doesn't turn on the engine. Her hands grip the steering wheel. "If you want to do this, you can."

"What am *I* doing?"

She stares straight ahead. "If you want to hate me, you can. And if you want to love me, you can. Either way can take on momentum. But just so you know? There's a moment when it stops being my fault, when what happened before isn't as big as what what's happening now." She looks at me, shaking her head, tears welling in her eyes. "I don't know what you need to get past this, or if we even can get past it."

All these months, I've kept it buried deep, like an animal frozen to death in its own burrow. "I don't want you to go back to Italy."

She stares at me. "We've got ten students signed up. I need to finish this book to become a full professor." Her hands drop to her lap and she looks through windows beginning to fog. "At some point, Liam, you need to decide if you can trust me. Otherwise, what are we doing?"

Sunday nights the train passes through south Minneapolis, crossing the Cedar Lake Bridge. The horn wakes me, summoning me from sleep. I lie in the dark thinking of my father, how he never forgave my mother for her illness, complaining about her walker, its squeaky wheels, or worse, her cane tapping, heavy arrhythmic footsteps as she moved up or down the stairs. So many interruptions, he told us, he had no choice but to renovate the garage into a studio where he did his engineering drawings, ate his turkey on rye, drank Scotch, and slept on a daybed, leaving us, his sons, to care for our mother after the aides went home. My older brother Teddy and I made excuses for our father: "He's finishing a project that's overdue." "He's behind again." But our mother refused to make us complicit in our father's neglect.

"Your father has never been able to handle disappointment," she'd say.

I miss my mother now, miss my chance to love her. But I also recognize I only felt this way after she died, when she stopped needing me. By the time I started high school, my mother had lost control of her bodily functions. Her fine angles had drawn sharp edges. Her eyes pulsed with vigilance, each movement demanding effort, as if her whole focus became strategic, how to get to the bathroom and back. Even then, sixteen years old, I felt my love for my mother had run out, and I didn't know how to make it come back.

Monday morning, I can't find my car keys. Searching the top drawer of Sylvie's desk for her spare set, I find her second cell phone, T Mobile, clamshell phone. My body stiffens, every molecule recoiling from the surface of my skin. I press the large green icon, but the screen remains dead. I dig through the drawer, looking for a charger, but I can't find it. I think of taking it to Luke, the technology teacher at my school, to see if he can download whatever is there, love letters, texts, photos. I try calling Sylvie on our landline, anger surging through me, and I'm immediately put through to her voice mail. I hang up. I leave the cell on top of her desk so she'll know I've found it. I grab her keys. I think about changing locks. Or packing my bag. Or taking Kafka and never letting her see him again. I need to walk.

Ten minutes later I'm at the dog park. Next to me sits a young woman, black hair curtaining her face, eyes hidden behind dark glasses, scrolling on her phone while her dog does its duty ten feet away. "Excuse me," I nod at the dog crouched behind the tree. "Isn't that your dog?"

She glances at me through dark lenses before returning her gaze to her phone, making no move to pick up her dog's poop. She is scrolling some site quickly, maybe Tinder or Snapchat, thumb moving with that repetitive slide I often see among students in the hallway.

"Pollutes the lakes, phosphates go into the water table," I tell her.

"Seriously?" Without raising her gaze, she mutters, "You need to chill."

Caught off guard by the strength of her voice, the authority of a woman so young, speaking to me, a fifty-three-year-old man, in such a hostile tone, I am taken aback. I stand and walk behind the tree, pick up the dog poop in one of my eco-bags, then place it on the seat next to her. "How hard is that?"

She sticks her phone in her purse and stands, walking away from the bench quickly, leaving her dog's poop bag behind. "Freak."

I pick it up and walk after her, the bag swinging slightly at my hip. "Excuse me!"

She glances behind, calling to her dog, "Cheerio, come boy."

But Cheerio is sniffing Kafka, and I catch her dog by the collar, tossing the poop bag to the ground near her feet. "Pick up the poop and throw it away like a decent person does."

FORGIVENESS

The dog park encompasses two acres of field and woods, people sitting on benches and standing in groups. The young woman shouts, "Could someone please help me get my dog away from this guy?"

Two men start walking toward us as I hold Cheerio's collar. "All I'm asking is for her to pick up her dog poop," I call to the men. "Then she can have her dog."

The young woman, sensing protection in the men approaching, yells at me, "Who do you think you are, God of the dog park?"

Cheerio, hearing his master's shriek, wiggles free and runs to her. The girl laughs, "Come on boy," and leaves through the double chain-link gate, tugging Cheerio's leash. "Asshole." She gives me the finger over the roof of her car.

I pick up the bag, throw it in the bin, and, sensing people watching me, feel both ashamed and justified, confused because of the anger roiling inside me. I face the two men, throw up my arms, as if to claim my own innocence.

"Oh my God, have you seen what was posted?" Jan, my secretary, shows me the link on her phone, *High School Principal on Poop Crusade,* the YouTube video showing me chasing the girl, holding up a poop bag, screaming at her to put down her phone and take responsibility. "What were you thinking?" Jan whispers.

I don't remember yelling so loudly, but here I am, captured online, hundreds of students commenting:

God of the dog park needs a muzzle.

Mr. J. loves picking up shit.

Hurray for Cheerio!

Leave Mr. Jaffrey alone. He's a good guy.

Six-hundred *likes* and counting. I head back into my office, Jan calling after me. "Sylvie wants you to call her office right away. She saw the video. She's called twice already."

"Tell her I have appointments."

The hallway buzzes with students replaying the video. I don't leave my office, not until I need my afternoon Diet Coke to stay awake. I go to the infirmary where I keep it in the refrigerator. The nurse comes Tuesdays and Thursdays and it is Monday, so I'm surprised to see a girl lying on the cot, reading a book. "Excuse me? Are you supposed to be here?"

Her short brown hair is shaved along one side, skin pocked, eyes caked with makeup. She turns her head toward me and smiles. "Are you going to chase me away too?"

I breathe deeply, nodding at her book. "That for a class?"

"Humanities." She lifts the book, *Crime and Punishment,* so I can see the cover. "Have you read Dostoevsky?"

Her pronunciation is good which surprises me. "Always meant to. Am I missing out?"

"Raskolnikov kills a prostitute to see if he can get away with it."

"And does he?"

"I'm not finished yet." She takes a bag of Doritos, squeezes it so that they break into smaller pieces, then tears open the bag, lifting it to offer me some.

"No thanks." I sit down on the cot across from her, Coke in hand, not sure if I should leave. "Something up with your classes?"

"No."

"Family?"

"Can't I just stay here during lunch? I'm not bothering anyone."

"Mind if I listen?" I lie down on the second cot, thinking of the rule about leaving a door open, and instead I tell her, "Wake me if you hear footsteps," and then I say, "There was a Chinese King who had all the doors removed so he could hear his enemies approaching." And then I add, "I've reached that stage."

She laughs. "You're funny."

Eyes closed, I nod. "Very few students realize that."

She begins reading aloud. I remember when Sylvie used to read to me in bed, and now, listening to the girl, my hands cover my heart. Beyond her voice I hear basketballs dribbled in the gym, a coach's whistle. The team is playing Minnetonka Friday night, and already the whole school is gearing up.

When I wake, the girl is gone, my phone is ringing. I'm expecting the call from the superintendent, and right away I say, "Yes, I'm sure. It's time."

"Sylvie? Sylveeee!" I call her name, glancing out the kitchen window. She's on the bench, sitting in her yellow slicker under a steady rain.

I want to forgive her. I'm tired of myself, as if I were born in a tight skin meant to hold everything intact, but instead it is holding me away from life, away from her.

I put on my slicker and rubber boots and join her on the bench. "Any reason in particular you're out here in the rain?"

"Rain is good for crying."

Geese fly over. Kafka sniffs the base of the bench. Congregations of darker clouds move stoically across the sky, thunder rolling in the distance.

I feel a sneeze coming on and dig into my pocket for a Kleenex, fingers going through a hole. I've been meaning to ask her to thread a needle. I sneeze twice, trying to hold it.

She hands me a Kleenex. "Don't hold it. You'll collapse a lung."

Her voice is so tender, so familiar, a nail pushed back into its hole after the picture is removed. "I didn't hide it from you," she tells me. "It's an Italian phone I got from the school. I left the charger in Italy. I thought I could use it when I go back. I didn't tell you because I didn't think it was important."

What's lost stays lost, but I don't tell her that.

"We can't go on like this." She digs into her pocket for another Kleenex and wipes her eyes. "If you want me to find my own apartment, I will."

There's no immortality in anger, no satisfaction.

The rain is loud, a curtain of sound.

"I could go with you this summer, now that I'm retiring."

She takes my hand, holds it tight on her lap. The reach hurts my shoulder but I stay quiet, listening to the rain in its multitude of landings: flowerpots, rain barrel, the long wooden fence.

THIS DISTANCE WE CALL LOVE

Some endings borrow everything—toothpaste, socks, dreams. Some endings are birds in winter, eating their body weight in seed every day. Some endings are frozen lakes you walk across, never reaching the other side.

Other endings live in your fingertips, objects you can touch—spaceship, periscope, clay mask. *Dad, come see what I made.* His voice falls through you.

At first, that's the hardest part, everything reminding you. Freckles or a dimpled smile, ears that stick out, a boy smell, sweat and flannel.

Anything flannel.

You live through it all again. A wound you don't want to heal. You get tired. Pure fatigue. Your mind's a thicket and thoughts won't climb through, his absence cut from winter ice, blue-veined, water pockets underneath, your body no longer tethered to the future. Time unwound, unwinding, wrapped around days and meanings that made you feel whole.

Never again.

Without him, our life together appeared to stop. Marriage is all about demands and expectations, and maybe that was what we had left to lose, the right to need each other. Grief is a taut song, pulling north and south, crescendo climb, edges multiplying beyond ourselves. Not stoic tears, blinked and swallowed, but muscles of water.

My wife started going there after the funeral.

"Why Texas, middle of nowhere," I asked that first time, "when there's a yoga studio on every corner here?"

"It isn't Core Power. We meditate. Sit in silence. More like therapy."

"What if it's a cult?"

"Oldest Hindu ashram in the United States?" Her calm voice that didn't seem like her real voice. I didn't trust that voice.

She flew from Minneapolis four times a year, staying three weeks each time to study this particular lineage of yoga and meditation with this particular teacher. She arrived home a little softer, a little less angry.

"Maybe I should come with you next time." I'd been afraid to ask, afraid she might say no.

"Why? The flights are expensive, and you don't meditate." She was folding laundry, making neat piles, his and hers, opposite sides of the bed. "Let me think about it. Some things can't be shared."

That pissed me off. We'd been through the worst. I didn't get how she could grow up in Minnesota, full of Protestant and Catholic grief, and want a whole different philosophy to lead her forward. She bought a prayer shawl and special beads, sat in the sunroom with the doors closed, chanting first, then sitting silent, a meditation app ringing bells every five minutes.

To me it felt desperate.

After the funeral, she never once spoke his name. I wanted to yell at her, *Just say his name.*

"Let me miss him my way," she told me.

The next day, I came home late from the university. Thursdays, I taught a graduate seminar in the education department,

Childhood in the Age of Social Media. That afternoon, I'd talked about neurological impacts of screen time on children. Flashing through the PowerPoint, I summarized recent studies. "More than two hours of cumulative screen time, and that means television, computer, iPad, and cell phone use combined, studies show children are much more prone to depression and anxiety." I paused to let them study the graphs and take notes before I continued. "We know screen use changes neuronal connections, but we need more research on type of screen use, Snapchat versus researching penguin migration." I looked up and smiled when a few of them laughed. "But the newer studies are conclusive. Brain changes are relative to the amount of screen use, and the impact is not only physiological but also psychological."

Many of my students were parents, their hands shooting up with the same question. "How do we control it? Even if we don't buy our kids phones, their friends have them."

"We do our best," I told them, words that couldn't land because my best hadn't been enough. They knew it. My son's accident had been in all the papers.

The room turned quiet.

I shuffled notes. "Two generations of digital natives and, as you've seen, impacts in higher suicide rates, social isolation, mood disorders, obesity, and screen addictions."

Two hours later, I turned into the driveway, rain illuminated in streetlights, huge puddle at the bottom of the hill. "Capecod," the realtor told us when we bought the house. We didn't know architecture. It was our first home. We wanted to stay in the city. Louise was pregnant, and we both had debts from graduate school.

Two bedrooms, two baths, fenced-in backyard, the selling point—its location near Burrough, where Louise taught. The realtor, Janice, was the parent of one of Louise's students. "The family before you only moved out because they outgrew the house," she told us, adding, "They stayed in this neighborhood because of the schools."

After the funeral, Louise took a leave of absence from teaching.

"Everything I love enlarges my grief."

"Me?" I asked.

She nodded. "I'm not sure we can stay in this house. It's full of echoes, just more and more of ourselves."

The grief therapist said time would help.

The kitchen light was yellow this time of day, and I could see Louise inside the window, stirring a pot at the stove. She stood with her back to the window, white curls leaning into the steam. She had just turned forty-nine, but she looked like an old woman, the angle of her head, narrow shoulders.

When I stepped inside, she held out the ladle for me to taste. "More coconut milk?"

I tasted. "Maybe more salt."

"You can come." She salted the soup and kept stirring. "But I don't want you to criticize. And no jokes." She gave me a stern glance. "I don't want you to make fun of people." She turned down the heat to simmer. "You won't get it at first. No one does. But if you're open, you can sometimes get beyond yourself."

"Do you think I need to get beyond myself?" I stopped reading the newspaper headlines and looked at her. "What does that even mean?"

"I know this sounds *woo-woo*." She turned back to the stove. "But sometimes when I meditate, I feel my awareness expand until it's all connected, and it's not about how long he was here or why he was taken from us." Her eyes grew watery and she wiped them with her sleeve. "For a few seconds, at least, I feel free."

"Free of what?" my voice rising. "Of me? His death?" I felt she'd got it all wrong.

She turned to rinse the spoon in the sink.

I looked out the window, not sure why I felt so enraged. Streetlights made the rain look like a curtain, like the sky wasn't far away. I have always been skeptical of people devoted to spiritual matters, but I was trying not to doubt everything I didn't understand.

"Silence can be difficult, and we're silent the whole time," she said, as if to discourage me from coming with her. "I just want you to know what to expect."

"Even at meals?"

She nodded. "Except to ask questions at the end of lectures." Setting two steaming bowls of soup on the table, she glanced at the window, rain coming down harder now. "That's good. The trees need it."

Waiting for the sunrise, air dense with cedar and pine, I close my eyes and listen. The earth is dry, and the wind rattles the dryness. Wild grass glistens frost, canopy of mist above the pond. Across the road sits a horse farm, two dark silhouettes standing still near the fence. On the opposite hill stands the temple, phallic thrust of gold against a blue sky, pink, red, and green geometric designs painted above the white base. The rest of the place is a dump, a clean dump with good drainage, two big dining halls with linoleum floors, eight large cement dormitories, four beds to a room for the big Hindu festivals I'd been told take place during the summer.

I thought my coming here would bring us closer. But when you stop talking about what hurts, everything else becomes unnecessary.

Six a.m., the first bell rings.

First warning, I think. Below the hill, flashlights bob in darkness as people leave their rooms, shawls and blankets wrapped around shoulders. Mornings are cold if you're not climbing hills.

Inside the main hall is a table with stacked mugs and a large pot of chai, steeped in cardamom, cloves, and cinnamon. People stand in line to ladle tea into their thermoses. There's bad coffee from a percolator, and that line's short. I prefer not to wait.

Some of the women are beautiful, even in the morning, sleepy and soft in sweaters, scarves, and fleece. My wife is still beautiful, and seeing her sit upright on her bolster near the front, my heart lifts, the way it lifted many years ago on the Carleton campus. Still the same blue eyes and sharp chin, same shapely legs. Her body has thickened around the middle, a relief since she lost so much weight after the funeral. I sit behind so I can watch her chant, straight posture and loose curls, a white halo when the sun pours through the window.

I find myself missing her even though she's only fifteen feet in front of me to the left. At night, lying in twin beds, she sticks to the rules, facing away from me, yellow plugs planted in each ear in case I try to talk to her.

From the back row where I sit, the teacher remains a blur, a tall, thin blur, only the color of his shirt and jeans and pale face coming through. My eyes have gotten worse, and I need a new prescription, but it's better this way, easier to listen. He's got a beard. I can tell that. He has a deep, sonorous voice that carries through a small microphone clipped to his collar. Someone is taping him. There are several helpers, lesser yoga teachers, who get there early to turn on the heat and sound systems, light candles, bring him cups of tea and coconut water. His eyes are closed, and he sings the chants in a voice that sounds Indian, even though he's Jewish from Brooklyn, his father an accountant.

I wonder how often he has sex, if he's cheated on his wife. Louise never used the word *guru*. She referred to him as *my teacher*.

Once, when she was packing to leave for a retreat, I lifted my foot to the edge of the bed. "You can wash my feet if you want," I said, trying to be funny.

She got up from the table and left the room. Later, I apologized. I stood in our bedroom door, nodding at the suitcase. "Just seems like you're always packing and unpacking."

To fall for him, you'd be falling for someone tuned to the universe, and that would be a different kind of loneliness. A few younger women rise at five a.m. and put their notebooks and blankets in the first row so they get an unobstructed view. Most of us wander in just before the first bell and squeeze between two other people, propped on bolsters or zafus, a few like me in chairs at the back. If I were at home, I'd be watching Arsenal beat Manchester. Instead, I am trying to read Sanskrit on the handout, humming along. "Om, namoh, namoh, namaha."

Afterward, we eat breakfast in silence—high-definition chewing and swallowing and sips of miso soup, porridge with raisins and almonds, bananas and muesli, coughs and clearing of the throat, spoons and forks clinking. I eat my oatmeal, then go back to the room to shave. From the window, I can see Louise walking the maze, eyes cast down.

Sometimes when it rains, peacocks stand for hours on the staircase leading to the second-floor rooms, tail feathers hovering like diving boards above the ground, a study in asymmetrical balance. Only rarely do they splay their feathers upright, blue, green, gold, maroon orbs. A woman dressed in a sari, with a dot on her forehead, watched me pick up a tail feather. "Do you know the meaning?" She smiled, nodding at the circle of gold in the feather. "Eyes of knowledge," her voice lilting, "will bring you good fortune."

I don't know what good fortune means anymore, but I nodded, fingering the feather, barbs soft as my son's bangs.

Gravel gives underfoot as I turn toward the hill. I know less now than I did before the accident. That's what grief does, softens everything—opinions, beliefs, theories, hopes. Memory is inexhaustible, and what rises to the surface is transparent, spilled water running over the edge.

The nurse, Gillian, twenty-five and just off work, was reading a text from her boyfriend. Confused about where to park, which end of the lake, she glanced down, her jeep hitting Patrick sideways, throwing him against the streetlight. Twenty-eight miles per hour, but accelerating into a turn, all eighty-five pounds of my son hitting the steel pole head-on. His helmet split open. I didn't know that helmets age. I'd given him my old one.

Our neighbor, Tara, was walking her dog, and she called me. "You have to come, Seamus. There's been an accident involving your son. Thirty-Sixth Street intersection."

I hung up and started running. The ambulance and police car were already there. They had him on a gurney. His best friend, Joey, had been riding behind him. Joey was sitting in the back seat of a police car, waiting for his parents. I climbed into the ambulance, ignoring the EMT guys, planting my hand on Patrick's ankle over his sock. "I'm not leaving." Louise came quickly to the hospital. We weren't prepared for all those dark islands of blood inside his brain. We cried, holding hands, staring through glass.

After the funeral, family and friends reached out.

"Do you mind going to my sister's for Christmas?" she asked.

"If you want to."

All her sisters had children. We never said it out loud, but I felt it, how unfair it was. We pretended it didn't make it worse, even to each other we pretended. Afterward, after wine and Yorkshire pudding and roast beef, after watching Patrick's cousins unwrap gifts, after singing carols around the piano, we climbed into the car and drove home in silence. At a stoplight, I reached out and took her mittened hand.

"We never have to do that again," I told her.

"It's slippery. Use both hands." She pulled back. She was quiet for a moment, and then she said, "I'd rather be with them than just the two of us."

"Are you angry at *me*?"

She waited until the car was parked, engine turned off. "Big knowledgeable professor," she said in the car that first Christmas Eve. "How much would a new helmet have cost you?"

We slept in different rooms that night, wakened Christmas morning to opposite ends of a cold house. She came downstairs and handed me her gift. "I'm sorry. I didn't mean it."

I fingered the ribbed collar, a blue sweater she'd knit herself, his favorite color. I knew she'd bought the yarn before he died.

I handed her a box with fancy wrapping. Inside was a sweater I'd bought, black-and-white Norwegian design that zipped up the front. "Looks warm," she said, putting it back in the box. "I'll try it on later."

From that day on we formed a habit of not saying things that might hurt each other.

"Downward-facing dog won't save you, no matter how long you can hold the position." The teacher smiles. "If you want to know your future, look at your thoughts."

I hear my wife's particular laugh, piano scales up and down. She hasn't laughed at my jokes for a long time.

"Notice the patterns," the teacher says. "The way your thoughts return again and again to the same place. Your thoughts govern your heart and your behavior. If you want to change your experience of the world, begin with thoughts."

Memory tills my chest.

Last summer, she insisted on giving away his belongings. Other kids can use them, she said. She stood in the garage and nodded at the bike, toboggan, fishing rods hanging on hooks. "Do you want those?"

"I might fish this summer."

She lifted a box of fishing tackle, huge glistening orbs attached to hooks. "Musky?"

"You can give those away, but keep the flies." I opened a wooden box with my father's initials engraved on top, hand-tied flies I'd hoped to leave to my son.

I closed the box and set it back on the shelf. "I've been thinking about your birthday. Just a few friends and family to wish you well? Champagne and cake?"

She lifted two skeins of tangled fishing line and tossed them in the trash. "Please don't do this."

"Do what? What am I doing? It's your fiftieth," I said. "Maybe we should go someplace new—Hawaii? Costa Rica?"

Her eyebrows furrowed. "I don't like beaches."

"How about a puppy?"

Climbing the ladder, she handed down the toboggan, sled, skis, and poles. "That's the last thing I want."

"I grew up with poodles," I told her. "Hypoallergenic and smart. Great dogs."

She came down, grabbed my hands, squeezing my fingers in her fists. "*Listen. Please.* You always do this."

"Do what?"

"Push things when it's clear I don't want you to."

I began sweeping out the corners of the garage. I hadn't yet committed to the ashram, hadn't yet booked my flight. "Okay, then. Let's go to the ashram for your birthday. I'll come along."

"You don't have to do that."

I stopped sweeping and stared at her. "If you're going to be in Texas on your birthday, I'm going to be in Texas on your birthday."

"We'll be in silence," she reminded me.

"If that's what you want."

Her face softened and, nodding, she leaned down to hold the dustpan while I swept.

The teacher seems to look right at me. "Even before we're born, some of the arrows have already been fired."

Is he talking about Patrick's arrow? I wonder.

The bell rings. We're back in silence. My body aches from sitting. I'm supposed to feel the energetic current running along my spine, breathing up and down *the central channel.*

He leads us in a chakra meditation. "Just gently place your attention and wait until you feel an energy." So many places feel dead, except for the dull throbbing either side of my sacrum. He moves up from the pelvic floor to the heart center, behind the sternum. I rest my attention at each point, but I cannot find a place to put down this sadness. I reach into his absence, my eyes digging out sky. Each lightness is sad, should be heavier. Edges come loose easily. I could slide off them, how far down they go, the bannister of an old staircase. It is the falling I cannot stand, echoes off every surface, and still nothing lands.

That's when I feel the light pour into me, soft yellow light the color of his hair pouring through the crown of my head and filling my chest. *Patrick's light*, I think, and I know this was what my wife meant when she talked about feeling connected. My heart feels so full, and afterward, after the bell rings, I wait for Louise. No law says we can't talk, but she's made it clear she observes the rules. I walk alongside her, keeping my voice to a whisper.

"I know we're not supposed to talk, but I need to tell you something. I felt a light pour into me, and I think it was Patrick."

For a moment she says nothing, her green eyes drained of light, two dry stones. "I knew you would do this." Her mouth flinches. "I knew you'd make it about you. I think I should get my own room. I think it's better if we don't share our experiences."

"I can't tell you what I feel?"

"That's why we have journals." Her voice is angry. "Write it down."

"You're the only one who loved him as much as I did." My voice throbs with our shared sadness.

"I know." Her voice softens, almost pleading. "But we both have to do this our own way. I'm trying to let go of anger."

"Anger at me or the world?" I lift my arms to hug her, but she steps back.

"It's harder with you here. Because I know you need me."

She walks back inside to the front desk, where they assign rooms. Then she comes back to our room and packs her things. "I'll be in the next building, room sixteen."

I listen to her rolling wheels scrape pavement, her voice urging peacocks away from the steps. "Move over, please."

From that morning on, I open the door to find peacock

droppings next to my shoes. My son would've laughed, would've said it's a sign of something. He and his friend Joey used to pretend the purple morning glories were portals into another world. Weeding behind the fence, Louise and I smiled, listening to our son and his friend speak gibberish into the blossoms, their own secret code. Later, they told us they'd gone into the future and come back.

On the morning of her birthday, I leave a small bag at her door, gifts from the ashram store—shawl, small bottle of lavender essential oil, CD of healing chants, and my peacock feather.

She's staying on one more week, but I'll leave the next morning.

That night I hear a knock on the door. My bags are packed for the early-morning shuttle, and she steps past them, pulls me next to her on the bed. We're sitting side by side, her hand clasping mine.

"Last night I had the strangest dream." Her eyes are red and swollen from crying, and her voice trembles as she speaks. "In the dream I have a tail, a small flap of skin at my tailbone that I have to keep tucked into my underwear so other people won't see it. I keep my tail a secret from everyone, including you. But in the dream, I'm terrified you'll discover it."

I look down at our entwined fingers.

"One day when we're hugging, you *do* discover it," she continues. "You're shocked that I've kept my tail hidden all these years. You insist on examining it and I'm ashamed, but I let you touch it, and you tell me I have to have it surgically removed because it is still growing and it will get larger as I get older and will eventually kill me. But I refuse because I know I wouldn't be the same person without my tail." Tears roll down her cheeks.

I put my arms around her. "I love you with or without your tail. You can have tails all over your body, and I will still love you."

She releases my hug, leans back, and looks at me with the saddest eyes. "But it's not about your love, is it?"

Maybe it's human nature to measure our lives by what is missing.

Every year on the anniversary of Patrick's death, Gillian writes us a letter on good stationery. It always says the same thing, how a day doesn't go by when she's not thinking of Patrick and of us. I don't hate her. She gives lectures at schools on the danger of texting and driving. She shows photos of Patrick. Louise went to hear her once, and when she got home, her voice was hoarse from crying. "Her life has been destroyed too. I forgive her. She's trying to prevent other families from having to go through this."

We sprinkled Patrick's ashes on a plot above the lake, and there's a small marker with his name: *Patrick Setterlund-Davis, 2001–2011*. Frost coats the gravestones in the morning. I walk there often, wild turkeys grazing in the middle of the city. Sitting beside his grave, I look through binoculars, watching ducks and loons migrate. It's good to focus on where things go to survive.

I don't know what it takes to feel alive again, instinct or imagination.

Jenny, the woman at the humane society, has eleven dogs up for adoption. I walk past cages. "Any non-shedders?"

"This pup's a poodle mix, five months old, family just brought her in. She pees when she's anxious."

"So do I."

She grins and opens the cage. "Every time the doorbell rings?"

The yellow, curly-haired pup starts to lift her leg, and I scoop her up in my arms, letting her squirm while I stroke behind her ears. "What's her name?"

"They called her Peanut."

I rub under her chin until her eyelids close. "You're not a Peanut, are you?" I pause, staring at her regal nose. "Queenie." I smile. "Much more dignified."

Jenny watches me. "You need to be realistic for it to work. She's a handful. Take a week and see how it goes. You can bring her back if she's too much."

First, I let her sniff the kitchen and den. While she's exploring, I set up the crate and bed, give her toys—a stuffed monkey that squeaks, a plastic ball. After she's lapped water from her new bowl, I carry her into the front hall and set her down next to my shoes.

I step outside and ring the doorbell, then quickly reach inside and scoop her up before she has time to lift her leg. I move outside and set her down on the grass to pee, rewarding her with treats. "Good girl."

Some patterns are harder to break.

That night I send Louise an email with photo of Queenie. *You don't have to love her. I'll do all the work.*

The world asks for everything, asks us to watch light-years speeding toward us, asks us to turn suffering into compassion, asks us to risk knowing what we cannot change.

Our life together has become a thin layer on top of what came before.

I can't pretend silence is closeness.

Life doesn't wait. Our hearts aren't smart.

Grief carries you everywhere you don't want to go—speechless soil, blind windows, all the years ahead without him. What survives is what I have left to give—Queenie's nose buried in my armpit, heat pouring off her silky coat, her heart beating, beating, beating, into my open hand.

UNDER THE STARS

I didn't want to choose sides.

Eleven months together. Right away the house had energy, female and strong, but also broken and mending. We'd become a family, coming home to each other from jobs—Dorothea and Carolyn designing fabrics at the studio up the mountain, Libby coaching youth swim teams at the Y. I was in charge of squirrels at the wildlife rehab center.

"Our very own squirrel nurse." Libby pointed me toward the bathroom. "Wash your hands, Gillian. Squirrels carry diseases."

Then a week ago, Libby's underwear and bras went missing. It felt creepy, Libby's underwear and bras stolen from the dry-rack in the bathroom, but not our jewelry or money or computers.

Two nights later, I heard footsteps hurrying up the back stairs, Libby's frantic voice calling to me, "Gillian? Gillian!"

I opened the back door.

"Somebody was peeking in my window." Libby stood on the outside landing, hugging herself inside her rain jacket, bare legs tucked in Ugg boots. "He ran toward the alley."

Part of me didn't believe her. Since Dorothea and Carolyn had been staying nights at the studio, working late to finish their first print order, Libby often found reasons to come upstairs. I grabbed my flashlight. I was the youngest at twenty-eight, but also the one with the most to hide. Nothing scared me anymore.

Descending the outside stairs, Libs held my jacket from behind, looking over my shoulder. Searching for footprints, I pointed the flashlight toward the ground. That area along the back of the house was walked on all the time, hardened dirt and dead grass.

"He ran toward the alley," she said.

We crossed the backyard, and I knocked on the door of the renovated garage where Gabe and Abby lived with three-year-old Miguel and baby Julia. Gabe and Abby managed the duplex in exchange for free rent in the garage, a deal they made years ago with the owners in California. They'd turned the garage into a modest home, solar panels on the roof, second floor loft they built themselves, flowerpots by the front door.

Gabe answered with the baby in the crook of his arm, Miguel playing on the floor behind him, a bottle warming in the pan on the hot plate. He looked at me and smiled. "Sorry, but Abby's at a meeting."

"Someone was outside my window peeking in." Libby scanned the room, her gaze landing on his shoes behind the door.

"Sure it wasn't the cat?" Gabe asked.

"I heard footsteps." Libby stood with arms crossed. "Someone ran in this direction."

He nodded across the backyard toward Libby's bedroom window on the first floor. "I've seen the cat on your windowsill." The refrigerator hummed behind him. Gabe was stocky and muscular, an unusual mix of dark and light—bronze skin, blue eyes, sweeps of blond curls. "Argentinian grandparents," Abby told us when we first moved in. "They moved to Arizona after they were forced to sell the ranch. It's a winery now, better for money laundering."

I squatted. "Hola," holding my arms out for Miguel, peeking at me from behind the couch. "Do I get a hug?" Twice a week I babysat for Abby and Gabe. Miguel smiled slowly and hugged me, then disappeared behind his father's legs.

Gabe jiggled the baby to calm her. "I'll check the locks after the baby goes to sleep."

Libby followed me up the back stairs and into my apartment. "It's *him*," she whispered. "It's Gabe."

"No way," I shook my head. "He's devoted to those kids."

"All he had to do was run across the yard." She glanced at the couch. "Can I sleep up here?"

The following evening, we gathered in the backyard, our Friday night ritual. Carolyn and Dorothea wiped off the plastic chairs, and I arranged them in a circle to catch the last of the sun, the empty chair for Abby who would come after work. It was a large yard, stretching between garage and duplex, two raised vegetable gardens at the back near the alley. The ants were busy. It hadn't rained in three weeks, unusual for late April in Fort Collins.

"Gabe has access." Libby stirred the pitcher, glancing across the backyard toward the garage. "When he changed our locks, he told us he kept the spare key."

"Abby's one of us," I balked. "You're talking about her husband."

Libby poured the juleps, passing cups. "Just the way he pretends not to see us. We're ten feet away, and he acts like we're not there, like he's ashamed." Since her wedding had been canceled, Libby had a generalized distrust of men, but especially Gabe, who often took off his shirt to work in the yard. "Something's wrong with a man who walks around half naked in front of his kids while his wife supports the family."

"You have to stop sprinkling flour in front of the door, Libs." Carolyn lifted her shoe to show the white on the toe. "I track it all over."

"It's to get his footprints," Libby laughed. "I saw it on *Law and Order*."

Beautiful Libs, with dark hair and long legs, and Carolyn, a husky blonde, best friends since college. Now in their early thirties, they'd moved here a year ago from Illinois, Libby fleeing the humiliation of a canceled wedding, Carolyn grieving her mother's recent death.

Carolyn leaned forward, as if confiding Libby's secret. "She keeps a hammer in the shower."

"Well, you're never here anymore." Libby's tone was sharpened by the first julep. "Woman of few words needs the most julep." She poured the remainder into my cup, casting a wicked smile at Carolyn, "*She* was here last night when I needed her."

Once, maybe twice in a lifetime, you end up where you need to be.

Eleven months ago, I moved to Fort Collins. One-twelve Laurel Avenue. Old gray clapboard on a street of student-infested clapboards, four blocks from campus. The rental sign said *Women Only.* I called the number on the sign, said I was out front in my car. Abby appeared in t-shirt and shorts, Miguel clutching her hand, two-week-old Julia squirming in her arms. Abby's brown braid hung to her waist, breasts spilling milk, dark blue stains where she was leaking. "This isn't a great time," she said, "but no time is great right now." She led me inside the duplex. "Three women are interested, and they're looking for a fourth."

Two days later, we signed the lease, Libby inviting us all to a cocktail party late afternoon in the backyard. The duplex was cheap, fourteen-hundred split four ways, identical two-bedroom apartments up and down, linoleum floors and counters, front porches, shared backyard. There were two entrances to the upstairs apartment, front and back, one inside the downstairs front porch, and another at the top of the back outside staircase.

Dorothea and I would share one of the apartments. The eldest at forty-eight and recently divorced, she'd arrived in Fort Collins three months before the rest of us, hired to run a print studio fourteen miles up the canyon. "First day I arrived, the owners handed me a list of applicants and told me to hire an assistant," she explained. "I called the first person on the list—"

"—You saved me." Carolyn smiled at Dorothea. "Two weeks after my mother died, you called and offered me the job—"

"—And you saved me." Libby leaned her head against Carolyn's shoulder. "You got me out of there so fast, my mother had to send back all the wedding gifts for me."

I couldn't be saved, but I didn't tell them that. Eight years old. He came out of a blind alley on his bike. The sun was in my eyes as I glanced at my phone to see where I should park. Then a thump, and I braked. He lay against the light-pole, his helmet split in half.

The second-floor apartment had more light, so we flipped a coin. Dorothea chose heads. She and I took the upstairs apartment. I had never lived with someone older, someone who wore a hand-stitched dress made from material she'd printed herself and white-rimmed glasses that matched her long white hair. "Conscious housing, like we did in the sixties," Dorothea insisted. "We'll vote if there are disagreements."

Carolyn said, "No parties unless we all agree, right?"

We voted no to parties.

"What about men sleeping over?" Libby asked. "If we're in relationships?"

We voted no to men sleeping over, but Libby added with a coy smile, "Lot of cowboys in this town. We might have to rethink that decision."

I felt far away from openness, far away from myself—torn between what I wanted and what I deserved. I studied the other women, how they navigated new relationships. Right away, Dorothea announced, "I don't take friends to the airports or plan birthday parties, and I don't share food. I've reached the age when independence is more important than duty."

Libby said, "I do trips to airports. I do birthday parties. I share food."

"Her nickname's *wifey*." Carolyn gave Libs a one-armed hug.

That first night, after we'd unpacked our cars, hauled computers and suitcases into bedrooms semi-furnished with beds and dressers left behind by previous tenants, Libby called us into the backyard for her special mint juleps. "Welcome home, girls."

Abby joined us. Manager of the university co-op, she offered us containers with Perfect Protein Salad, Tempeh Tarragon, two kinds of hummus. "Don't worry about the expiration dates. It's still good." Miguel came outside and climbed on Abby's lap, pulling up her t-shirt, unsnapping her nursing bra. He gripped his mother's breast in both hands and drank.

Abby rubbed Miguel's back, seemingly aware of the ensuing silence. "I'm all about strong immune systems. In some cultures, they nurse until five."

"Which cultures?" Libby asked, explaining she'd majored in early childhood education at UIUC, had worked at a daycare center in Chicago while planning her wedding.

"The Copper Eskimos and several tribes in Africa." Abby wiped Miguel's mouth with her sleeve. He kissed his mother's cheek and climbed down, running across the yard toward the neighbor's porch where the cat lived. "There's a lot of research that says breastfeeding lessens sibling rivalry." Abby snapped her bra closed, pulled her t-shirt down. "They're sharing me. It's a good lesson."

"Maybe my ex-fiancé breast fed until he was five and that's why he couldn't commit." Libby stood and went inside to get the pitcher of mint juleps.

"Libs was supposed to get married in June," Carolyn whispered to the rest of us. "Night before the rehearsal dinner, when her fiancé was already on the plane to Greece, she found his note saying he wasn't sure he loved her—"

"—He was a dick." Libby returned with the pitcher, her voice sing-songy as she passed out glasses. "I'm moving on, thanks to mint juleps and my new roomies."

"Would you mind using plastic?" Abby asked. "I let Miguel go barefoot back here." She retrieved five clean plastic peanut butter jars from inside the garage. "Here, they're yours whenever you're drinking out here."

Libby caught my gaze and rolled her eyes, pouring the heavy green concoction. "My own recipe, fresh mint, mint syrup, bourbon, blended ice." Holding up her jar, she scowled. "This is so tacky, drinking mint juleps from peanut butter jars."

Carolyn raised her glass. "To tacky-time," and we all chimed in, "To tacky- time," our Friday night ritual born.

Sitting there, my throat burning from bourbon, spreading warmth through my body, I realized I was enjoying myself. And then I asked myself if I had a right to enjoy myself. And then I remembered what my therapist told me. "You have a right to live until you die."

"We need to catch him in the act," Libby whispered the following Friday. Nine days had passed since her underwear and bras had been stolen. "Yesterday, I turned on the shower," her voice low, "and right away Gabe hooked up the hose to the faucet beneath the bathroom window, like he's watering the flowers, wink, wink." She held her glass like a nozzle and craned her neck as if looking in the window. "I'm not signing the new lease until I feel safe." She passed the spinach dip served in hollowed-out bread, carved squares around the edge for dipping.

Carolyn, Dorothea, and I took turns dipping as Libby proposed her plan. "Tomorrow, I'll go running late afternoon, and when I get back, I'll turn on the shower. I know you two won't be here." She glowered at Carolyn and Dorothea who had begun working weekends at the studio, then shifted her gaze to me. "You'll be home, won't you?"

"I'm not going to spy on Gabe," I told her.

"Wouldn't you want to know if your husband was peeping through windows at your friends?" Libby stood, her voice irate, long legs exposed beneath denim shorts, leggings underneath. "Does Abby ever talk about their marriage? I bet she married him to rebel against her parents."

"Christ, Libs," Carolyn said. "That's racist. Maybe *he* married her to rebel against *his* parents."

Libby refilled my glass. "Abby never mentions her family though, does she?"

Our conversation was interrupted as Craig, our neighbor, parked his black truck along the side of the alley, its loud engine spitting exhaust, bumper sticker visible on the back window, *Black Trucks Matter.*

"He's the racist," Libby whispered. "Not me."

"Might be Craig who took your underwear." I dipped another hunk of bread.

"Craig doesn't have a key," Libby said.

"Might not even be the same person," Dorothea added. "The Peeping Tom and underwear thief."

"I think it's the same person." Libby nodded at her corner first-floor bedroom, thick canvas curtains drawn tight. "I ran out here in less than five seconds, and he was gone. The only person it could be is Gabe. All he'd have to do is run across the yard and close the door behind him."

Dorothea stared at the garage. "Most husbands feel cheated after children are born. Mine did."

Our conversation fell silent when Abby rode up on her bike.

"Give me five minutes to say goodnight to the kids. Save me a large julep." Two minutes later, she joined us with a bag of leftover pastries from the co-op.

Libby filled Abby's jar. "So, what's Gabe been up to lately *besides* gardening?"

I glared at Libby.

Abby seemed too tired to notice. She took a long sip, almost a guzzle, then lowered her glass. "Have you signed the lease yet? If you don't sign by the fifteenth, the owner can raise the rent. That's two weeks from tomorrow." She lifted her glass, scanning our faces. "One more year at least, right? You're family now."

The following afternoon, Libby turned on the shower, and a minute later, pipes churned, the particular kind of churn that happened when Gabe cranked the outside faucet to its maximum volume. I glanced out the window toward the backyard, hoping to see him watering the vegetable garden by the alley. But he was below my window, out of view.

Libby left the shower on and came running up the front stairs, hurrying through the door. "You saw him, right? You heard him hook up the hose? He's definitely the Peeping Tom."

"I'm sure there's an explanation." I poured honey into my mug, dunked my tea bag in and out. "Want a cup of tea?"

Libby looked over my shoulder through the kitchen window. "You can't even see below."

I nodded toward the alley. "Abby just rode up."

"Well if she hadn't, he'd still be peeking in my window."

We watched Gabe cross the yard and lift the baby from the bicycle seat, talking to Abby while she unloaded groceries.

"I wish he'd put on a shirt. It's only sixty degrees." Libby frowned. "I never saw my father without a shirt, did you?"

"Didn't you ever go swimming with your father?"

"I played tennis and golf with him. Shirts were obligatory at the club."

I laughed, shaking my head at her. "You better marry *up.*"

Abby must've heard us laughing. Seeing us in the window, she took the baby's hand and waved. I waved back.

Libby's eyes settled on me. "If it's him, you can't protect her."

The first time Abby asked me to babysit, I wanted to say no. I'd avoided children since the accident, but Abby needed me—Julia's temperature had spiked, and Gabe was working at the ranch where his phone didn't get reception. Watching Abby stuff diapers and a pacifier into her purse and load the baby into the bike carrier, I thought about how much energy her life required, cloth diapers, no car, a full-time job and two kids. I held out my car keys. "Take my car."

"It's faster if I bike and cut through campus," Abby told me.

After she left, I read to Miguel, but he grew fussy and tried to undo my shirt. I took his hand and showed him how to play thumb hockey, letting him win, my big thumb pinned under his tiny thumb.

Once Miguel fell asleep, I explored the room, everything compact, built by Gabe and Abby—crib hanging from the ceiling, walls painted burnt red to match the Native American rugs, sunlight pouring through the skylight. On shelves were photos, one of Abby and Gabe on their wedding day—Abby smiling in a simple white dress, hair braided with flowers, her jawline and figure twenty pounds thinner; Gabe beside her, black slacks and white shirt, bolo tie with a turquoise stone, polished cowboy boots. Horses stood inside a corral in the background, bougainvillea alongside a white trailer home, platters of food on a picnic table.

When Abby came home, she put Julia in the crib, pushed it gently into a swinging motion, then reached into the refrigerator for two Coronas, handing one to me. "Strep throat. I hate giving babies antibiotics." Miguel was asleep so she spoke in a whisper. "Gabe's going back to school part-time. Accounting." She drank several gulps of beer, nodding at me to sit.

"You've made it so cozy in here," I told her, glancing around the room. "How long have you lived here?"

"I moved here from San Francisco fourteen years ago for college. I wanted to be a vet." Her shoulders rose and fell, shrugging off that dream. "The animal science department's year-end party was watching the prize stud inseminate the prize mare. That's when I applied to do my internship at Circle Y, a horse-rescue ranch."

"Is that how you met Gabe?" I asked.

Abby nodded. "He moved here from Tucson. His dad ran a ranch." She tucked wisps of brown hair behind her ears. "Don't tell the others, but we're hoping to buy the Circle Y if we can save enough money." She had muscled arms and legs, tanned from biking to and from her job at the co-op, clear blue eyes that watched her son sleep as she spoke. "If I didn't have to work for health insurance," Abby confided. "I'd go back to school too."

"What would you study?" I asked.

"Pediatric neuroscience."

I was disappointed. I wanted Abby to pursue a dream that was attainable, not something that had passed her by. I didn't feel I had a right to dreams, something my therapist had said we needed to examine.

"I studied nursing for a while," I said. "But I prefer working with animals."

I could have told her I'd quit nursing because I couldn't bear to see families with dying children. I could have told her the judge issued community service instead of prison, and I did hundreds of school visits all over Minnesota, telling high school students about the dangers of using cellphones while driving. I could've told her I enrolled in MSU's vet-tech program, that I'd grown up in a house of rescue dogs, each named for a President—Reagan, Nixon, Bush, and Clinton—our spotted pit bull from Georgia that humped everyone's legs. I could've told her the truth—since the accident I'd felt like a rescue, my instincts vigilant, sensitive, acute.

"Once Gabe starts classes, I need a babysitter two evenings a week. Feel free to say no. I can only pay eight dollars an hour."

I wondered if it would be a mistake. "Yes," I told her.

Since then, Abby and I often had a beer together after I babysat.

"I'm trying to write a children's book," she confided a few nights ago, nodding at her journal. "But who isn't?"

"What's it about?"

"Still brainstorming," she smiled, and, tucking her long hair behind her ears, glanced toward the duplex. "How are things in the manor house?"

I laughed, hoping she didn't know about Libby's suspicions, hoping they would blow over soon.

The morning after the shower incident, I woke to a loud knocking below, Gabe's angry voice calling to Libby. "Open up. I need to talk to you."

I pulled on my sweat-suit and hurried down the back steps to see Libby open the door.

"What the hell?" Gabe said, nodding at piles of sticks covering the garden alongside the house.

"I want to be able to hear the Peeping Tom." Libby nodded at her stick teepees. Apparently, she'd gotten up early and gone to the nearby park to gather sticks, dumping them under her downstairs bedroom and bathroom windows. Not just little piles, either, but two-foot-high stacks that flattened Gabe's flowers.

Gabe nodded at the flowerbeds, just beginning to bloom. "Those are perennials. You'll kill them."

"They'll come back." Libby leaned toward Gabe, her voice low. "Someone waters the garden under my window every time I take a shower—"

"—You're accusing me?" Gabe laughed, a sharp bitter laugh. "It's the water pressure. We need the water on full to reach the garden."

Libby stood tall, arms crossed. "Safety is more important than flowers."

"Don't worry." Gabe walked toward the garage, his voice full of sarcasm. "I keep a very close eye on things."

"So reassuring," Libby told us the following Friday, before Abby arrived. "He keeps a *very* close eye on things." But since then, she explained, she hadn't heard any more noises outside, not even the hose turning on when she took a shower. "He knows I know. Which doesn't make me feel any safer."

Libby passed the plate of hot spinach-stuffed mushrooms to Carolyn. "Wifey made your favorites."

Carolyn devoured one, speaking with her mouth full. "*Mmmmm.*"

Libby looked at me. "Has Abby mentioned my stick teepees?"

"Nope," I said, gazing at the sky, clouds moving in from the foothills. "She did mention the lease. She asked why we haven't signed yet."

"Did you tell her I suspect her husband?"

I stared at Libby, shaking my head.

Dorothea reached for another mushroom, glancing at Libby, "Do you consider cooking your art form?"

"It's your comfort zone, right, Libs?" Carolyn answered for Libby.

Libby frowned at Dorothea. "You always try to make me analyze myself more than I want to." Her gaze shifted to Carolyn. "And you feed into it."

For a moment, we all fell silent.

When the evening train blew its horn before crossing Main Street, I asked Libby, "When's darlin' back?"

"Not until Sunday." Libby had begun dating a train conductor who drove the north-south line, Calgary to Denver, long oil trains that took seven minutes to pass through towns along the route. Frank called every woman *darlin'*. *Good to meet you, darlin'*. So, we teased Libby. *Darlin's got nice buttocks. Darlin's got a new buzz cut. Darlin's such a gentleman.*

"Did you know it's really hard to join the railroad union?" Libby asked. "Jobs are handed down father to son. Frank says he's never met a female train conductor."

"Is he relieved or sorry?" Dorothea chewed a sprig of mint.

Libby leaned back in her chair. "Don't you think opposites complement one another in life?"

"The question you should be asking is," Dorothea said, "if you get him, is that the life you'd want?"

Libby tipped her empty cup toward Dorothea. "Should you really be giving advice?"

"There are laws of human nature," Dorothea said. "One of those laws is the need to keep growing."

"I'm growing," Libby shifted her gaze to Carolyn. "But *you* wouldn't realize it because you're never here anymore."

Carolyn sighed. "Please, Libs, let's not do this—"

"—What?" Libby's eyes widened. "Talk about how I moved here to live with you, and now I basically live alone?" She glanced at me, "Except for you, Gil. But you're upstairs."

Carolyn chafed, "We don't own each other, Libs."

Saturday morning, we were all invited to the studio up the mountain so Carolyn and Dorothea could show us their finished prints. Abby canceled early that morning, saying the baby had a fever, but I wondered if Gabe had talked her into staying home. Dorothea went ahead to prepare the blintzes. Libby woke early to prepare a frittata with corn and basil and smoked mozzarella.

"Wifey," Carolyn climbed into the car, twanging like a cowboy, "tha-yit smay-ells dee-lay-shus."

The three of us drove together in Carolyn's old Volvo, turning off County Road Six onto a rugged dirt road.

Libby sat rigid up front holding the frittata in her lap. "Slow down."

Carolyn glanced sideways, "Let me drive. I take this road every day."

"Please slow down," Libby begged. "I get car sick driving in the mountains."

Carolyn slowed. "Control freak."

Libby pressed her mitten under her nose but sneezed anyway. "God bless me."

The sun was bright, the sky blue above the frost-covered field. The studio had been built thirty years ago, when the owners were growing their business into one of the best design studios in the country—contracts with Marimekko, orders to be filled each spring. The owners still lived up the road in the large house where they'd raised their children.

The studio, once an old caretaker's cabin with kitchen and bathroom, had been expanded into one large room with banks of windows on three sides, daylight illuminating two printing machines and a pair of drafting tables. Up two steps stood the original cabin with a woodstove, daybed couch, and a table with wooden chairs. Dorothea and Carolyn had set the small table with a tablecloth they'd printed themselves, tiny wheelbarrows filled with flowers. Glasses and plates were mismatched, pottery collected by the owners over years.

Inside, looking out, I felt part of nature, part of the mountain itself. I stood at the window, watching two deer at the salt lick. "Now I know why you love it here so much."

"If it had central heat, I'd move here," Dorothea said, filling little glasses with iced vodka. We drank them fast to warm up, and right away, started talking about luck, how after her divorce, Dorothea had sent letters to forty printmakers across the country, asking if they were looking for new designers.

"Us ending up here, working together," Carolyn took a deep breath, "feels like more than luck."

The blintzes were delicious, fluffy and dense at the same time, sour cream on top. I preferred strawberry compote to salmon caviar. The vodka tasted bitter and pure, different in the morning than at night.

We ended up talking about which dreams you hold onto, work or love or children or place. Dorothea said, "There's an age when you've left home, finished school, and you're trying out careers and figuring out what's next, whether you can do what you love and make money at it, or you make money and do the thing you love on the side. I'm forty-eight, and it's the first time in my whole life I'm doing what I love *and* making money."

She spoke while pouring another round of vodka. "Here's to all of you." She touched her glass to each one of ours. "Don't waste your freedom."

"This isn't freedom," Libby said. "It's free fall. Not knowing the future." Libby drank her vodka fast, her face softer when she drank. "I'm deeper than you think," she said. "Ask the vodka."

Afterward, Dorothea brewed green tea in a pot her son had sent from Japan. The tea was loose, steeping in a strainer for seven minutes before it was poured. The round cups warmed our hands. Carolyn brought out their finished prints while Dorothea described the artistry that goes into functional design—which colors and patterns catch the eye, how the designs interact with paper, plastic, linens, and cottons.

"Animal themes for kids' rooms," Carolyn said, as she held up material printed with turtles swimming through blue water. "For sheets and pillowcases."

Dorothea lifted a second print with brightly colored umbrellas. "Shower curtains."

"Paper plates and cups." Carolyn unfurled a bicycle-themed print. "I thought of it after I saw Gabe and Abby riding off with the kids."

I clapped after each one, clapped loudly to make up for Libby's small clap, her hands barely touching, her smile pursed. Dorothea and Carolyn rolled up the prints and slid them into cardboard tubing. "I'll have UPS come tomorrow and pick up the rolls," Dorothea said. Pouring the last of the vodka into two glasses, she toasted Carolyn, "Here's to us," hugging her again, an extended embrace, almost a slow dance. "We did it."

I felt Libby's eyes staring at me, asking if I was seeing what she was seeing—all those days at work, the passion Dorothea and Carolyn shared for making prints. She wanted me to confirm or deny, but I shifted my gaze to the red cardinal pecking the suet-feeder outside the window.

Libby said how much better vodka tasted when it's been in the freezer, and Dorothea, who referred to her Russian ex-husband as *the professor*, said he kept a huge freezer in the garage full of Beluga Noble. "A melancholic man who drank all day." Vodka flushed her cheeks. "In a patriarchal society like ours, marriage is an excavation of self."

"You use the words patriarchy and melancholy a lot," Libby told her.

Dorothea nodded. "I wouldn't marry again, unless it was to a woman."

"Do you think women who marry each other are less angry?" Libby turned her chair to face Dorothea on the couch. "You don't think one woman takes on the male role?" Libby was trained as a ballet dancer and her back lengthened as she spoke, as if she were performing.

Carolyn refilled Dorothea's cup of tea, and Dorothea took a sip before speaking. "I don't think it has to happen that way."

We left soon after. Dorothea stayed at the studio so she could send the prints early the next morning. Driving home, Libby said, "Dorothea never talks about her children, does she?"

"They're in their twenties." Carolyn drove with both hands on the wheel. "Her son lives in Japan, and her daughter lives in California."

"Most mothers would mention their kids more often, even after a divorce."

Silence filled the car and lingered there.

"I love your prints." I tried to lighten the mood from the backseat. "I'll never look at sheets and pillowcases the same way."

Up front, Libby kept her gaze fixed on the passenger window, and Carolyn concentrated on the road.

Two blocks from the house, Carolyn sighed, "Can't you just be happy for me, Libs? She's brilliant. I'm lucky to be working with her."

That evening, Libby came upstairs. "Carolyn went back to the studio." She joined me on the couch where I was cutting calluses off my toes. "A pamper night? Why didn't you invite me? Do you have extra teeth whitener?" Libby tucked her feet under her buttocks. "I promise I won't stay long."

I nodded toward the kitchen. "There's wine in the fridge if you want a glass."

Libby shook her head. "Makes me more afraid. I start hearing things outside."

"I'm right above you." I kept filing my heels. "I'll save you."

"Not if you-know-who holds his hand over my mouth and you can't hear me scream." Libby massaged her toes inside her sock.

"You can sleep up here anytime."

After a moment, Libby asked, "Don't you think it's weird how Carolyn lost her mother, and now she and Dorothea are inseparable? I mean, fifteen years is a huge age difference."

I shrugged, rubbing moisturizer into my heels.

"Carolyn and I used to tell each other everything," Libby confided. "She was going to be my maid of honor. It's like she's dumped me, dumped wifey for anti-wifey."

I smiled. "Maybe she's trying not to hurt you by keeping their relationship private."

"I just don't want *her* to be hurt," Libby said. "And honestly, I know this sounds crazy but *I'm* hurt she was never attracted to me. Not that I'm into women, but she never seemed that way with me *at all*, and we lived together two years." Then, turning to look at Dorothea's drawings on the wall, "Definitely melancholic patriarchal wheelbarrows." She shook her head. "She's got the worst breath in the world. How can Carolyn stand it?"

Hearing a thud on the back landing, Libby grabbed my arm. "Someone's there."

I listened. "Just a branch falling. Happens all the time."

"Shush," Libby whispered, turning the music low.

Wood creaked outside the backdoor. I was on my feet, hurrying through the kitchen. "Who's there?" opening the door to find Gabe unscrewing the light bulb from the motion detector above the door.

"What're you doing here?" Libby edged past me. "You already changed the locks."

He lifted the bulb out of the socket. "Motion detector lightbulb is out."

"I'll throw it away," Libby said, reaching for it, a move that could only be interpreted as distrust.

But Gabe placed it in his tool bag, zipping it closed. "Needs to be disposed of properly." He turned abruptly, descending the stairs without saying goodnight.

"Thanks, Gabe," I called out, trying to keep the peace.

Libby tugged me inside and closed the door, her eyebrows hopping. "Who changes a bulb at nine o'clock on a Sunday night?"

After she returned to her apartment, I sat at the kitchen table, staring out the window at the garage—squares of yellow light visible through skylights. I hadn't expected to find Gabe outside my door, and now a crack of doubt had opened, Libby's suspicions rubbing off.

Sunday morning, Abby knocked on my door. At first, I thought she'd come to talk about Libby. But she didn't mention the stick teepees or Libby's argument with Gabe. Instead, she asked if I could go with Gabe and the kids to see the rehabilitated horses released to pasture. "My assistant manager quit, so I have to go in to work," she explained. "Gabe has to open the gates, so he can't take the kids alone. Miguel's counting on it. It's such a beautiful thing, watching the horses set free."

Driving in the Circle Y truck, I tried to make conversation. "So, you grew up on a ranch?"

"Outside of Tucson." Gabe nodded, his voice level, too level. Maybe a little angry. I couldn't tell.

"Abby says you hope to buy the Circle Y?"

He glanced at me with a frown. "We're trying to keep that quiet."

"I won't say anything." I noticed his hands gripping the wheel tightly. He looked smaller in the truck, his face lined around eyes and mouth, lines I hadn't noticed before. This close, he seemed ten years older than Abby, mid-forties at least.

We drove in silence for a few minutes, until he said, "We need the lease signed."

"I know."

"What's holding it up?"

I breathed in deep, wondering how to answer.

"It's her, isn't it?" He glanced at the kids in the rearview mirror, keeping his voice low. "You don't think we see her watching us?"

"It's because her underwear and bras went missing—"

"—I'd say it's more than that," he scoffed, his voice a tire spitting gravel. "As if I'd ever be attracted to a skinny bitch like her."

My body stiffened and I looked straight ahead. "She's not a bitch. She's afraid."

We drove the rest of the way in silence and arrived in time to see the horses stampeding along the sandy ravine toward open pasture. As Gabe opened the gate, I held the baby and stood with Miguel behind the fence. Even before the horses came running around the bend, we could feel the ground trembling and hear their thundering hooves. Tears wet my eyes at the sight of them, horses charging through the open gate, galloping toward their freedom, some kicking and throwing their heads, others rolling in mud.

"Ya Allí." Gabe waved his cowboy hat toward a tall brown horse with black mane, regal in bearing, the last to come around the bend. The horse stopped at the fence, and Gabe reached out his palm with two sugar cubes. "When we got her," he explained, stroking the horse's nose, "she was starving and could barely stand. I named her." He nodded at Miguel. "Tell Gillian what Ya Allí means in English."

"Already There." Miguel grinned as his father placed his cowboy hat on his son's head.

We drove back in silence, but it was a different silence now. All those horses had been given a second chance. I wanted to believe in second chances. Each morning I still woke to the same thought: Patrick's parents waking up without him. For two years following the accident, I saw a therapist. She helped me acknowledge that making mistakes, even tragic ones, was part of being human. I felt better after each session for an hour or two, but also separate, an existential separateness, as if I were the one who had died, banished from the normal world into a glass closet. "I can see everything," I explained to her, "but I'm no longer part of it." This was my penance, this separateness. It was her idea that I move someplace else, someplace I wouldn't be reminded all the time. "We can still do therapy over the phone," she offered, "but you deserve a second chance."

After Gabe parked the truck in the alley and lifted Julia from her car-seat, he glanced at me, his eyes worried, almost apologetic. "Their mother's got a big heart. Sometimes too big for her own good."

I didn't know what to make of his words, if I was meant to protect Abby or talk to her. Monday morning, I tested dead gophers for the plague, an epidemic spreading across the plains of eastern Colorado. The veterinarians weren't concerned about the disease spreading to humans, but they were concerned it might infect squirrels. I wore gloves and a mask, and when I left the lab midday, I washed my arms up to my armpits with chlorhexidine.

At noon, I bicycled across campus to the co-op. When I

asked for Abby at the cash register, the girl with pink hair waved me through to the back room. Hearing doors open, Abby looked up from where she was sitting on the floor, and seeing me, grew alarmed. "Are the kids okay?"

"I just came over for my lunch break."

"I can't take a break right now." Abby nodded at the boxes surrounding her. "Donated clothes for homeless teenagers. They're picking them up this afternoon. I need to sort them, make sure they're wearable." She held up a pair of blue jeans with holes worn through the seat and tossed them into the trash bin.

That's when I saw the box behind her, hand-written label: *Gently used bras and underwear.* I stared at the box from two feet away. Abby saw me looking and released a heavy sigh. "Have you seen that motel outside of town, Motel Fukhertail, parking lot's always filled with semis? Police raided it Easter morning, eleven teenage girls rescued. They needed clothing, especially bras and underwear."

I reached down and gave Abby a hug. I knew good people made mistakes. I didn't blame her for taking Libby's things. I didn't blame anyone who had a good reason to hide the truth.

The day before our lease expired, Libby poured juleps, explaining her plan to catch Gabe. "You'll tell Abby you're leaving me alone tomorrow to go hiking. In the morning, you'll leave through the front door and take positions behind the neighbor's fence. When I turn on the shower, you'll have your phones ready to film Gabe." She looked at me. "If nothing happens, I'll sign the lease."

Carolyn's voice was resigned. "Whatever you need to do, Libs."

Dorothea nodded in agreement.

Libby turned her gaze to me. "It's as much to rule him out."

I shrugged, and Libby took my shrug for *yes*.

From across the street, we could hear children's voices rising with the Star-Spangled Banner, commencing the Catholic school's Friday night fish fry. Libby put her hand across her chest. "Ever hear this song played with bagpipes? They played it at my grandfather's funeral. Not a dry eye."

"We're like old women," Carolyn said. "Look at us, huddled in our folding chairs with our plastic cups." Blankets draped our laps except for Carolyn who always wore her mother's red sweater. She lifted the sleeve to her nose. "Smells like her. I still haven't washed it."

"You're getting more like Abby," Libby said, and we all laughed, even me, because it was true. Abby didn't believe in washing things. "Clothes release microfibers into the water," she told us. Libby looked at me. "I'm laughing *with* her, not *at* her."

Hearing a clatter near the trash bins, Libby eyed the container where a squirrel scrambled out of the hole chewed through the plastic top. "I don't know how you can love squirrels," she told me. "They're very destructive."

"You'd like Willie." I reached for my phone, opening to a video of a squirrel with a huge cone around his head, tossing peanuts in the air and catching them in the funnel so he could eat them. "Doesn't he look like a renaissance juggler?" I passed the phone to Libs, but she refused it. "Dirtiest surface in the world is a phone."

"What was wrong with him?" Carolyn asked.

"He kept licking his penis until it became infected."

Dorothea laughed. "We're all guilty of something."

"What are you guilty of?" Libby asked.

"I talked myself into believing my children were better off with a drunk father than no father at all." Dorothea sighed. "Now Misha lives halfway around the world, and Tati married the first man who loved her."

"I don't feel guilty about anything," Libby said.

"You will," Dorothea told her.

"What does that mean?"

"I think what you find mysterious now will bore you later."

Libby's mouth tightened.

"I feel guilty all the time, every day," Carolyn said. "There's absolutely no reason my father shouldn't be with Joan. I think my mother would've been glad. She loved them both. He keeps sending emails asking when I'll visit. I can't even call him."

Dorothea reached out and squeezed her hand, and Libby, a little drunk, took Carolyn's other hand. "She's mine," Libby said to Dorothea, in that flippant tone she used to make a joke.

Dorothea stared at Libby, her gaze steady as a wall.

Libby laughed. "You're supposed to say, *No, she's mine.*"

Dorothea released Carolyn's hand. "Eventually," she said to Carolyn, "you might be relieved your father has someone to take care of him. I'm happy my husband met someone young. She can empty his bedpan when he goes into liver failure, and I can do my art."

"Wow," Libby said to Dorothea. "Your version of love is really selfish."

"We all have to be selfish," Dorothea said. "Otherwise, we'll never do what we're here to do."

I stared into my glass. "I feel guilty whenever I'm happy."

"Why?" Libby's voice, full of astonishment.

The evening chill came on fast, a cold stone between my shoulders, a different kind of loneliness. Sorrow was its own kind of wisdom, and I had a keen sense of endings, how little it took for the future to shift course, every life traveling at a separate velocity, spinning in its own orbit. Already I missed them, missed living together, this island of time, exhausting and expansive, all the questions coming loose, shaping emptiness.

Libby smiled. "Can't be as bad as being married to a Peeping Tom."

"Stop it, Libby," Carolyn's voice grew sharp. "Stop making other people's pain your entertainment."

"Is that what you think?" Libby stared at Carolyn, her eyes filling with tears. She walked inside, and I followed her, handing her a Kleenex.

"I'm not the one who's changed." Libby blew her nose and leaned against the counter. "What did I do to deserve that?" She smiled through tears as I reached out to offer a hug. "Have you washed your hands since Willie?"

By the time Abby arrived, the stars were bright. Libby handed Abby a julep and made a pouty face. "They're leaving me alone tomorrow to go hiking."

"Where are you going hiking?" Abby asked, scanning our

faces.

I looked up at the stars, constellations of light against an infinite darkness—five lives tipping toward wider openings, seeing ourselves in each other, who we wanted to be and who we didn't want to be.

"Actually," I said, "I'm on call for the rehab center. I can't go hiking." I felt Libby's furious gaze, but I refused to look at her.

"I want bagpipes at my funeral," Libby said. "Remember that, Gillian, if I'm murdered in my sleep."

"What are you talking about?" Abby reached for Libby's blanket and spread it over both their legs.

ACKNOWLEDGMENTS

I am deeply grateful to editors of the following journals for publishing my work and for keeping literature alive by publishing voices that are both recognized and new to the literary landscape.

Colorado Review: "Near Misses"

Narrative: "The Dog" and "This Distance We Call Love" [under the title "Distance of Closeness"] (both finalists for *Narrative*'s 2018 Winter Story Contest)

Nimrod: "Grace's Mask" (honorable mention for The 2020 Katherine Anne Porter Prize)

Ploughshares: "Almost"

Salamander: "Disappearances" (finalist for The 2020 *Salamander* Fiction Prize)

Stonecrop: "The Doctor's Wife"

The Willesden Herald (UK): "Forgiveness"

The Worcester Review: "Ice Bells"

Thank you to all the people who have encouraged and sustained me during the writing of these stories.

To Miriam Karmel, love and gratitude for walks and talks about writing and books and life. Our friendship has been invaluable to me.

To Carol Bouska, love and gratitude for teaching me so much about nature and animals and families. Your stories about working with animals have found their way into this book. Thank you for sharing your wisdom.

To Marcia O'Hagan, love and gratitude for decades of friendship and for keeping childhood memories and laughter alive.

To Dianne Heins, love and gratitude for your friendship and deep wisdom about family life.

To Gail Hartman, so much gratitude for helping me find my way back into my work.

Thank you, too, to my wonderful community of writers for your ongoing friendship, insightful writings, and constant encouragement: Annie Follett, Judith Katz, Leslie Morris, Patricia Cumbie, Carla Hagen, Alison Morse, Marcia Peck, and Julia Singer—all of you have been vital to the writing of this book. Thank you for being generous and skillful editors and for inspiring me through your own writing.

Thank you to Adrian Van Young for your early guidance in shaping several stories and pointing the way forward.

Thank you to Christine Hale and Kevin McIlvoy for giving my book a home, and a very special gratitude to Kevin for your amazing generosity in guiding me through the final edits and cheering me over the finish line.

Many thanks to Luke Hankins for your remarkable vision in founding Orison Books, and your deep commitment to Orison's authors.

To my parents, Bette and Dave Dines: I am so grateful for all your love and support and for always providing shelves of books to nurture our imaginations.

To David and Margie Dines, much gratitude for all the ways you support our family with humor and kindness.

To Hanna, Mike, and Anya: you are my hope.

Lastly, my deepest love and gratitude to my husband, Jack Zipes, for your willingness to read each story one more time, and for always encouraging me to write from my heart. You have made our life together a wonderful adventure.

ABOUT THE AUTHOR

Carol Dines is the author of three novels for young adults, *The Take-Over Friend* (Fitzroy Books, 2022), *Best Friends Tell the Best Lies* (Delacorte), and *The Queen's Soprano* (Harcourt), as well as a collection of short stories for young adults, *Talk to Me* (Delacorte). She has been awarded The Judy Blume Award as well as Minnesota and Wisconsin State Artist Fellowships. Dines's stories have appeared in *Colorado Review*, *Narrative*, *Nimrod*, *Ploughshares*, *Salamander*, and *The Worcester Review*, among other places. She lives in Minneapolis with her husband and their standard poodle.

ABOUT ORISON BOOKS

Orison Books is a 501(c)3 non-profit literary press focused on the life of the spirit from a broad and inclusive range of perspectives. We seek to publish books of exceptional poetry, fiction, and non-fiction from perspectives spanning the spectrum of spiritual and religious thought, ethnicity, gender identity, and sexual orientation.

As a non-profit literary press, Orison Books depends on the support of donors. To find out more about our mission and our books, or to make a donation, please visit www.orisonbooks.com.

For information about supporting upcoming Orison Books titles, please visit www.orisonbooks.com/donate/, or write to Luke Hankins at editor@orisonbooks.com.